# Jana's Journal

# Jana's Journal

## JEANETTE WINDLE

Kregel
Publications

*Jana's Journal*

© 2002 by Jeanette Windle

Published by Kregel Publications, a division of Kregel, Inc., P.O. Box 2607, Grand Rapids, MI 49501. For more information about Kregel Publications, visit our Web site: www.kregel.com.

The persons and events portrayed in this work are the creations of the author, and any resemblance to persons living or dead is purely coincidental.

Cover design: John M. Lucas

**Library of Congress Cataloging-in-Publication Data**
Windle, Jeanette.
    Jana's journal / by Jeanette Windle.
        p. cm.
    Summary: Seventeen-year-old Jana keeps a computer journal of her senior year at Christian high school in San Diego, California, as she faces a new set of emotions and dangers at home and school.
    [1. Interpersonal relationships—Fiction.  2. Self-esteem—Fiction.  3. Christian life—Fiction.  4. Gangs—fiction.  5. High schools—Fiction.  6. Schools—Fiction.  7. San Diego (Calif.)—Fiction.  8. Diaries—Fiction.]
    I. Title.

PZ7.W72435     Jan 2002   [Fic]—dc21   2001050858

ISBN 0-8254-4117-x

Printed in the United States of America

2  3  4  5 / 06  05  04  03

# Jana's Journal

*Part One*

## Valentine's Day, February 14th

Brian asked at the Valentine Banquet tonight if he could read my journal.

Well, it wasn't quite like that. I'd just mentioned how I've been writing down everything that's happened, and he said he sure wished he'd thought to keep a journal these last few months. So without even thinking (okay, so what's new!) I said, "You can read mine if you want." And he said he'd really like that.

So tonight I pulled it up on the screen and read it through, clear from that first entry that seems a century ago now. Somehow I don't think I'm really going to want those hypothetical grandkids of mine reading all this. I'd certainly do a lot of changing if I had it to write over. The girl I see through these pages isn't a person I'm particularly proud to claim. In fact, I must admit I considered a serious edit job before printing it off for Brian, but that seems too much like cheating.

Besides, though I'd never have thought so at the time, I'm not so sure I'd really want to change these last months because the good times wouldn't be in there without the bad. And I cringe to think of where—and who—I might be if none of this had happened. So, I guess I'll just leave it as it is—the mistakes I made. The stupid things I said. Denise and Annette and Sally. Sandy. Maria. Luis and Icepick; I still wake up shivering when those two faces invade my dreams. The triumphs that turned out to be so hollow and the failures that turned out to be anything but. The excitement and the shame and the tears and the downright heart-stopping terror. And the joy at the end as unexpected as that ending itself. The whole wild roller coaster these last months have been.

∽

SIX MONTHS EARLIER

∾

## *Wednesday, August 28th: My Birthday!!*

Aunt Jana's birthday present managed to make it on time this year.

Aunt Jana is my father's oldest sister. She's a good twenty years older, as a matter of fact, and likes to reminisce to family members about how she single-handedly raised him to be the good citizen he is today. Grandma, of course, sees things differently. Aunt Jana also happens to be a very distinguished Professor of Sociology, Ph.D., So. D., B.S., W.W.A. (Who's Who of America), A.A.A. (not the auto club, but American Association of Anthropologists), etc., ad infinitum, having earned those titles when it really meant something for a woman to reach those heights of academia. I was named after her, minus the "distinguished" and the alphabet soup. How I feel about that, I've never been quite sure. Famous—or at least well known in her field—Aunt Jana may be, but no one has ever managed to mistake her for your average, garden-variety human being. In fact, the less charitable (my mother, for one) might characterize her as downright eccentric.

Not that Aunt Jana spends a lot of time worrying about what people think. She's too busy mucking around in odd corners of the world where the locals carry machine guns and use them, digging into their present-day affairs as often as she does into their history. Last year it was early Druse settlements on the Syrian-Israeli border. (That's right, she was one of those anthropologists who made the news in that backfired terrorist attempt. The one, if you remember, where the elderly looking lady swung her purse at the terrorist leader, causing his gun to go off among his own men, killing half of them and allowing the security guards who'd been caught flat-footed to jump the others. You guessed it, that elderly woman was Aunt Jana!) The year before, she was in Kosovo writing a blistering indictment of those ethnic Albanian refugee camps.

Even though she's a little original in lifestyle, Aunt Jana is one of the kindest people I know. She has a strong belief in just allowing people to be people and has fought her way out of too many molds of her own to try to shove anyone else into one. I adore her. And she never forgets my birthday, though her gifts can take their own sweet time about getting here, depending on what part of the world she's holed up in at the time. Like the year she was down on the Amazon with some beleaguered Brazilian tribe and mailed my package sea mail. I got it for Christmas.

Her birthday presents can't be called your average, garden-variety aunt-niece gifts either. The Amazon gift was a dart gun with real poisoned darts, which Dad promptly confiscated. Then there was last year's English-Arabic dictionary—just in case I ever thought of studying that language! Not to mention the gift subscription to World Vision for one of those Kosovo orphans.

But this year's gift is at least a little more practical. It's a journal. Not one of those puffy, quilted things with a sentimental little pink heart on the cover that provoked a certain nausea even when I was still pre-adolescent. A computer program. Since my sister Julie escaped to college, I have Dad's old office computer to myself, and I guess Aunt Jana knows my typing is a lot more readable than my penmanship.

The graphics have the look of one of those old-fashioned diaries—actual script instead of print letters. Pick out the font that looks most like your own handwriting and there you are! And unlike the usual Stone Age diary, it comes complete with spell check and thesaurus. No smudges, crossed-out lines, or eraser marks. What appeals to me most, though, is the security system, guaranteed to be hacker-proof by siblings as well as parents. The set-up comes with its own paper, diary-sized, of course, with gilt edges. If you want an actual hard copy of your journal, you simply adjust your printer for paper size and run off the file. It actually looks hand-written (only neater!) and fits into this maroon leather binding that looks like it belongs in the library of some old Victorian manor, complete with gold lock and the cutest little gold key you ever saw.

I'm leaving room here to paste in the note that came with the package:

> *Dear Jana,*
>
> *A journal is a fascinating thing. It isn't just a place where you can pour out your deepest thoughts along with the happenings of your day, it is a record of where you've been and how far you've come. Jana, I've seen your talent for writing blossom over the years, and I thought you might enjoy trying your hand at keeping one. You are on the verge now of one of the most important years of your life, your senior year of high school, and I know this is an exciting time for you. Someday you—and your children and grandchildren—may enjoy leafing through these pages and reliving these months again.*
>
> *Love, Aunt Jana*

Well, I do like to write; Aunt Jana is right about that. And the clincher is that security system. My little brother, Danny, has to be the snoopiest second-grader since they were invented—and one of the most deadly on a computer. As for my mother . . . well, suffice it to say I wouldn't even consider a diary if I thought her computer skills could make it by that security password!

So, what all does a person write in a journal? I suppose if those hypothetical grandkids of mine are going to read this, I'd better put something down about myself. I was born Jana Thompson exactly seventeen years ago this morning. If this were that fiction novel I'm going to write someday, I'd add that I'm talented and gorgeous and one of the more popular students at Southwest Christian Academy, the private school I hope to be leaving behind in about nine months. But it isn't, and I'm not, and if I'm really going to pour out my deepest thoughts in here, I'd better start out being honest.

I'm sitting (obviously!) at the computer desk Julie and I shared until a year ago, and all I have to do is swivel around for an unforgiving view of myself in the full-length mirror on the closet door. Hair dark and curly and rather a mess right now because I've been trying to grow it out all summer. My face never launched a thousand ships (but then, who'd want to? If I were Helen's husband, I'd have let her rot in Troy. By all accounts, Paris deserved her!), but it does have an occasional redeeming feature. A nose that's straight and none too large. The mouth might err just a shade on the wide side, but the teeth are white *and* straight, thanks to all those years of braces and preventive dental care. And if my eyes can't make up their mind whether they're green or gold or just plain brown, the lashes themselves are satisfactorily long and dark and curly enough to make Denise Jenkins, SCA's acknowledged frontrunner in the beauty stakes, grit her teeth.

Then there's the rest!

If God has His reasons for making a seventeen-year-old girl 5'2" and about as curved as a lamppost, I wish He'd let me in on the joke! Character building, I suppose. At least that's how our pastor lumps everything rotten that ever gets dished out on the plate of life. Sally Friesen and Annette McCauley, the closest thing to best friends I have, assure me I'm cute. I assure them of the same thing. Need I say any more? Denise Jenkins, whose pressed-on, curled, and dyed state of lashes is one of the poorer kept secrets in the girls' locker room and one of my few consolations in life, loves to flutter their length down at me from her stately 5'10" and coo as she runs a not-so-subtle hand along her 36-24-34 curve line, "Jana, you're *so* slim! I *wish* I had your figure!" But then, not even Denise's most sycophantic (no, I wasn't using the thesaurus, grandkids! If you don't know what that means, look it up!) bootlicker of a hanger-on would give her credit for being sincere.

On an intellectual level I, of course, despise modern society judging a woman solely on the basis of some artificially imposed standard of outward beauty. And I *do* mean artificial! Who is Hollywood trying to kid? Does a 6-foot, 120-pound blonde with a Barbie bustline and a refugee-camp-size waist in any way typify the feminine half of this planet? Give me a break!

On a personal level and keeping it just between me and this journal, if someone offered me the chance to look—and be looked at—like Denise Jenkins, I'd give it a shot!

As for other areas, I'd have to characterize myself as about as average and garden variety as Aunt Jana is not. I *am* a pretty good writer. At least my teachers seem to agree with Aunt Jana on that. No, just a minute! If I'm going to make an honest confession of my negative attributes, what's wrong with being honest about the pitifully few good ones I can boast? The truth is, I'm a *very* good writer. In fact, Mr. B. tells me I'm the best writer he's seen come through the doors of SCA in years. I've been on the school newspaper since I was a freshman, and I made copy editor of the yearbook by the time I was a sophomore. This year I've got a good shot at being *the* editor—you know, the head honcho.

But that's about all the fame and fortune Jana Thompson can claim. I'm definitely not the cheerleader type, and if I was never the last picked on a team back in the days when that still mattered, no one ever fought a battle to get me on their side either. I'm a fair pianist. I should be after twelve years of lessons. But any singing I do is strictly in the back row of the choir.

As for academics, I get decent grades since my parents are the sort who hit the roof if you bring home a B. But I learned long ago that a 4.0 doesn't win any ribbons in a popularity contest. And if I've never dropped so low as to be plastered with the label "nerd" or "geek" or whatever the latest terminology for "totally uncool" happens to be, no one has ever signed me up for one of those popularity contests either. Average. Ordinary. One of that invisible "middle" that I guess has to make up most of any crowd and the bulge of every Bell curve. That's what I am. But who am I to complain? At least I have plenty of company.

So, am I really excited about starting school? I don't know. It seems every year's the same. You get all worked up for the first day. For once, everything's going to go just right. You waste hours trying on a dozen outfits. Practicing that new hairstyle. Fantasizing about that first walk down the hall with just the right phrase tossed nonchalantly over your shoulder. The look in quarterback Scott Mitchell's eyes as he murmurs to one of his football buddies, "Wow, have you seen what happened to Jana Thompson over the summer? . . . Yeah, the one who used to sit back in the corner. . . . No, I wouldn't have recognized her either!"

Then the first bell rings and reality clicks in. Before you've caught your breath, you've been startled into answering—correctly—Mr. Schneider's trick question about the Berlin Airlift, followed by Denise Jenkins' loud whisper that no one but a real geek would know what an airlift is! Or you've tripped over the wastebasket right in front of Scott Mitchell's desk. Or worse, he hasn't even noticed you're in the room because those incredible blue eyes of his are glued to Denise's flawless silhouette. And suddenly, it's just another school year, and your biggest concern is whether anyone— never mind Scott Mitchell—is going to invite you to the Valentine Banquet or whether you're doomed to end up one of those pitiful females whose solitary trail through life began with the trauma of being conspicuously ushered to the "no date" table at the farthest end of SCA's rented banquet hall.

Okay, so that was last year. Maybe this year will be different. But just once, I'd like to be one of those fortunate females who have only to glide down the hall, flip their hair back over their shoulders, and smile—and every male in the school promptly falls over their feet in the rush to open the classroom door! When Jana Thompson walks down the hall, she's lucky to have a member of the male persuasion offer a helping hand if she passes out at his feet!

And if that isn't enough soul-searching for one journal session, it should be. Mom's yelling from downstairs for me to turn out the light, and the last thing I need is for her to decide to come on up. It *will* be nice to see a little more of Sally and Annette and the rest of the class too, minus two or three I could do without. And anything's better than spending every day trudging between home and the grease pit of the neighborhood Taco Bell. So, yeah, I guess I'm excited to start this so-important year of my school career.

## Thursday, August 29th

So much for easing us into the routine!

The schools around here always start on the Thursday before Labor Day weekend, theoretically so they can get all that necessary orientation over with and be ready to jump right into classes with the first full week of school. It is a theory with which SCA is sadly unacquainted. I have homework in every class.

Still, it's good to see Annette and Sally—and the rest of the crowd too, give or take a couple (as per previous entry). One thing about attending a private school—at least in a city this size—is that you don't see a whole lot of your friends outside of class, much less during the summer months when everyone is scattered to the four winds on vacation or, if they are peons like Annette and Sally and myself, working summer jobs at opposite points of the metropolitan area. Speaking of which, I guess I should mention a little about where I live.

Julie and Danny and I were actually born in Thompson Falls, Montana, a pocket-sized little town right up in the Rockies that could be classified as a county seat only in a place where there are a lot more deer than people. I was in seventh grade when we moved to San Diego, California. Talk about culture shock! The reason for the move was Dad's job. He's a police officer—Sergeant Dave Thompson, formerly of Sanders County Sheriff's Department, now SDPD. San Diego is supposed to be a big step up in his career. And I guess if one goes by how many more people he gets to slap behind bars over here, it's been a wildly successful move.

At any rate, a private academy in a city the size of San Diego is a far cry from a small-town neighborhood school where you walk home with your pals and get together after school and on holidays. SCA is by no means the biggest private school in San Diego—maybe six hundred students altogether K–12th. But those students come from all over the city, some from more than an hour's commute away. So you tend to have your school life and your outside life, and unless your friends happen to live in the same neighborhood or attend the same church—Sally and Annette don't fit either category—those two lives don't meet much.

We do, of course, have a scattering of kids in my own church who attend SCA, even a couple of seniors. But neither are exactly kindred spirits. Take Amos Lowalsky. That's *the* Amos Lowalsky. His father is head deacon at our church. I've always detested the way people will write someone off as a "nerd" just because they wear glasses or prefer a good book to a rock video or have a decent brain on the end of their spine. But Amos is the one person I know who comes by the title honestly. It isn't his brain that's the problem—

he's never shown any particular signs of genius—and he doesn't even wear glasses. It's his total lack of social grace. His concept of polite conversation with a member of the opposite sex is to blurt out some personal and utterly offensive remark, then stammer and shrink into himself.

I've never forgotten his invitation to the Valentine Banquet last year, stumbling over his shoelaces as he did so and compounding that error by grabbing at my T-shirt to steady himself. When he'd recovered, he had the nerve to inform me, "I'm perfectly happy going to the banquet by myself, of course, but if you haven't found anyone to go with, you're welcome to accompany me as my date." I'd have preferred the humiliation of parading through the happy couples of SCA with a billboard announcing my solitary status, but I pride myself on the tact of my restrained refusal. "Then let me make you happy," I told him sweetly. That this was a *no* and not a *yes* took a week to sink in.

Then there's Sandy Larson.

Sandy moved up from Alabama a year ago and has this fabulous Southern accent, slow and sweet as honey—when you can get her to say anything! She's as quiet and gentle and ladylike as Melanie in *Gone With The Wind* and would seem to have stepped into the wrong period of history, as though she were meant for one of those Deep South plantations, carrying food baskets to the poor and destitute in between genteel teas and sewing parties, rather than in a southern California high school. She looks the part too with honey-blonde hair, dainty little hand motions, and a smile as honey-sweet as her accent. I like her, of course. Everyone does. But like Scarlett O'Hara and Melanie, we have absolutely *nothing* in common.

Not that Sally and Annette and I have a whole lot more. Sally is round as a doughnut, sentimental to the point of being drippy, and talks even more than I do—and I've never had any major difficulties vocalizing my opinions. At the risk of sounding egotistical, at least my opinions make sense! Sally hates school—or anything that requires a major exertion of the gray matter between her ears—and consoles herself in a bag of Reese's Peanut Butter Cups every time she flunks a test. One has only to look at her to know how often that is. She's always trying out some new diet, though I've never known her to lose more than a pound or two, and has this "love-hate" relationship about hanging around with slim-as-a-lamppost me. When I tell her I'd honestly be glad of a few extra pounds, she gives me this disbelieving stare like who could possibly be too skinny. She reminds me a little of Winnie the Pooh—as loyal and kind as a friend could be, but "of very little brain." And when she says something dumb—which always manages to be right when everyone else has fallen silent—this wave of beet red climbs up her neck, clashing *horribly* with that strawberry blonde hair of hers.

On the other hand, she has a soprano voice that brings tears to your eyes. And when it soars into the final notes of *The Star Spangled Banner* at opening assembly, it's easy to forget the extra poundage and that she's always asking you to explain your jokes—*after* she laughs.

Annette is at the other end of the spectrum, the no-nonsense sort who always knows exactly where she's going and what she's got to do to get there. While I'm still floundering with what colleges I want to apply to, she has the next ten years planned out: law school, a partnership with her uncle, district attorney by age thirty! She keeps half the committees in the school running, and she's so well organized, she has plenty of time left to make straight A's.

She really is—or could be—very attractive with a figure I'd gladly trade for, a mass of red hair, and a snub nose with five freckles she's been trying to get rid of for years, but which I think add a welcome touch of frivolity to that business like air of hers.

It's always surprised me that the guys don't pay more attention to her than they do. But then, there isn't a male student in the school who can touch her in the brains area, and that habit she has of staring down that snub nose every time they act a little less than mature, as though they were some new and particularly repulsive insectoid specimen, would unnerve the most determined of masculine admirers.

Then there's me, in the middle again. I study hard enough to make the honor roll and stay fairly busy with yearbook and piano. But I'll never be as brilliant and organized as Annette any more than I'll ever sing like Sally.

As different as we all are, it surprises me, at times, that we've stayed such good friends over the years. But it's been Annette and Sally and I since seventh grade when we were the new kids and got assigned to the same science project. By the end of the project, we'd nicknamed ourselves "The Three Musketeers" (okay, so that was corny, but what else was there? The Three Pigs? The Three Bears? The three witches out of Macbeth?), and we've been hanging around together ever since. Habit, maybe. But at least it means never having to worry about someone to sit with at lunch and a perfect threesome for chemistry experiments while other unfortunates are still standing around, wondering who's going to volunteer for their group.

Like I said, we don't see each other much outside of school hours—or even necessarily during school hours as Sally, at least, won't be in a lot of my classes this year. But ever since seventh grade, we've made a date every week or two of riding the bus home together to Annette or Sally's house (Mom isn't much on me bringing friends home), where Annette and I try to coach Sally up to a passing grade in between lots of talk and food.

And there's always lunch period. It's not, after all, as though there's a whole lot of competition for our attention.

One hears a lot these days about intellectual freedom and equality and *sameness* between men and women. You know, we're all just human beings! Forget those environmentally induced male/female differences and let's all just be *people*. Maybe that goes over in other high schools, but not at SCA. Oh, sure, if a girl is feeling exceptionally brave, she might talk her friends into plopping trays down in front of a couple of unattached males and striking up a conversation. And of course there's always a few couples staring into each other's eyes and forgetting to eat. But walk into the SCA cafeteria at any meal time and you'll find the biggest portion of the student body still huddling in their own little masculine and feminine cliques, eyeing each other across the aisles as though they were two separate species instead of one human race.

Unless you're one of the "beautiful people."

We live in a democracy, or so I've been told in every social studies class since first grade. And somewhere in all that democratic, post-civil-rights-movement code of law that exists up there in Washington, D. C., there must be some provision that allows for free seating in school lunchrooms.

Maybe. But at SCA we have one table smack in the middle of the lunchroom where no one—but *no one*—sits without a special invitation. In some ex officio manner whose origin has been clouded over by the mists of time, it has been expropriated by the "in" crowd—Denise Jenkins, Scott Mitchell, and their friends and hangers-on. And if some unwitting newcomer sets down his tray on "their" table, the indignant outcries and resulting humiliation are enough to scar the poor soul for life!

Scott and Denise and their bunch are what I mean by the "beautiful people"—at least according to Hollywood. They all come from the same part of San Diego where houses have long driveways and swimming pools. Where Annette and Sally and I brown-bag it as often as not, they all eat the hot lunch. And where most of the parents are struggling with finances and even holding two jobs just to pay the private school fees, these guys all got brand-new cars for their sixteenth birthdays and simply drip with money. Not to mention the good looks that, in some of Denise's cronies at least, are as much expensive haircuts and clothes as any real physical attributes.

Again, of course, intellectually, I despise the whole philosophy of basing popularity on nothing more than money and good looks, not to mention the ability to dive across a line on the ground with a blown-up piece of pigskin in your arms. But it'd sure be nice to try it sometime. To sit enthroned with all the other beautiful people in the middle of the cafeteria, catching the envious glances of the less fortunate as they hurry by to a vacant seat.

Fat chance, of course. But every time I slink by with my brown paper lunch sack, I experience the irresistible urge to rebel and pull up a seat right between Scott and Denise. After all, I can't imagine the lunch room monitor would go so far as to throw me out. They don't actually own the place! But I haven't gotten up the nerve yet.

Well, I'd better stop rambling and get cracking on this mountain of homework if I'm going to be in bed before midnight. In all my digressions from the day's happenings, I forgot to mention that Mr. B. called the first yearbook meeting for tomorrow. I'm doing my best to restrain my enthusiasm, but it isn't easy. I'm almost sure I'm going to be editor this year. It may not earn a position at *the* table, but the yearbook editor is definitely *someone* around SCA. Ask who the copy editor is and you'll likely be met with glazed-over eyes, but everyone knows who the editor is. Plus last year's editor graduated, and Annette, who was in charge of layout last year, has said often enough that she doesn't want to leave her crew. Of course I'm not 100 percent sure I'll be chosen, but who else does that leave?

## *Friday, August 30ᵗʰ*

The class schedule is a little less of a blur today, if no lighter on the homework. Most of my classes this year are AP (Advanced Placement, if the term no longer exists by the time you grandkids come around). AP Chemistry. AP English Literature. AP Spanish. AP Psychology. With the AP courses I took last year, I should start college with at least a half year of credit. Maybe even a full year. A big help when you have to earn your own way through. But they sure don't believe in letting you catch your breath!

Still, the classes themselves look rather interesting, and I only ended up in the wrong classroom once. Freshmen, fortunately—not too humiliating. That bunch are too lately junior high brats to worry about their snickers. Our class is shaking down too. Three more new students came in today, and a handful never returned from last year, leaving a grand total of forty-six. Of the new students, three are girls and two are guys, all too negligible to describe here.

And Brian Andrews.

It's taken me two days to figure out that Brian Andrews isn't—quite—a student here. Nor is he—quite—a faculty member. It would seem from what Sally tells me (for a girl "of very little brain" she certainly manages to be the first with any scuttlebutt!) that Brian finished his first two years of college—something in the sciences. Then his money or his scholarship or whatever ran out, and he had to drop out for a while. So he's working as a teacher's aid this year, and in the meantime, since he can get them free here, he's taking some AP courses to add to his college credit. So I've got him as a classmate in AP Spanish, English Lit, and Psychology, and as a teacher's aid in AP Chemistry. A unique situation, but at least no one is suggesting we call him *Mr. Andrews.*

Anyway, negligible though the other new additions to our class might be, Brain at least has definite possibilities. I wouldn't call him exactly good-looking. But he's a full six feet tall and has a lot more muscles than the couch potatoes who make up most of the masculine half of our class. And that smile . . . ! We could have used a lot more than three new guys around here, though, as we girls still outnumber them twenty-six to twenty. When you take into account how many are likely to invite underclasswomen to the Valentine Banquet, there's going to be a lot of senior girls left hanging.

Okay, so it sounds stupid to worry so much about a silly banquet! But since SCA doesn't have prom, the Valentine Banquet is *the* social event of the year. I didn't do too badly my first two years. In ninth grade I went with the son of one of my dad's friends. (I'm still not convinced Dad didn't arrange it.) At the time John Paul was shorter than me, and I don't remember that we said a word to each other all evening.

In tenth grade I went with a senior from my church youth group whose girlfriend had already gone off to college. No strings attached—just friends. We had a great time. But last year, the male-female ratio in the higher grades was pretty low. I had almost sunk to reconsidering Amos Lowalsky when a freshman from our church, who was too scared to invite any girls from his class, saved my reputation. A little like dating your brother, but at least it kept me from being branded for life! At any rate, you can see why, even at this early date, a partner for the Valentine Banquet is on all our minds—except for those privileged few like Denise Jenkins who never have to worry about anything so paltry as having a date.

I guess I should put something a little more concrete in here about SCA. When we first moved to San Diego, my older sister Julie and I attended one of the larger public junior highs not far from our very middle-class neighborhood. It didn't take us long— or my parents either—to find out that the public schools here weren't much like Thompson Falls. But it wasn't the gang fight that busted up the gym or the security guards in the halls or even the pushers lounging against the chain link fence just off school grounds that prompted my dad to pull us from there. It was the day I brought my seventh grade sex ed curriculum home and innocently asked my dad to explain a paragraph I didn't understand (no, grandkids, I'm not going into any details. Hopefully, by the time you come along, that will all be just a footnote in the history books). Dad is usually pretty quiet, but, boy, did he hit the roof that time!

A week later, Julie and I, Danny not being in school yet, were at Southwest Christian Academy, and we've been here ever since. It isn't the sort of place one affords on a cop's salary. But Amos Lowalsky's father isn't just head deacon at our church; he is on the school board as well. It seems SCA has a policy of granting so many scholarships a year to deserving students, and I guess a police officer serving the community counts as deserving . . . so . . . as long as we keep our grades up . . . which explains my parents' preoccupation with those Bs.

In return, Dad serves as a sort of unpaid security consultant to the school—tells them which alarm system to get, how to run a fire drill, etc. He's the one they called when someone broke into the sound equipment room last year and when the P.E. teacher found a package of marijuana in one of the football lockers. Three kids ended up expelled over that scandal, and we lost the regionals for private school football because one of them was the star half-back or full-back or one of those "backs."

That isn't the only such incident we've ever had around this school either. When I first came to SCA, I somehow assumed, this being a Christian school and all, that the students would all be saints. Don't ask me why!

But I soon found it wasn't like that at all. Oh, sure, a lot of the kids are from different churches around the city, and I guess most of them are decent enough. I'm not saying we have anything like the gangs and drugs and violence you hear about at the public schools. The discipline here is too strict for that.

But there are plenty of parents around San Diego who seem to think that SCA is the next step to a reform school and who send their kids here with the naïve expectation that rubbing shoulders with all those church kids will counteract whatever problems their kids have gotten into at the public school. As for some of the language you hear when the teachers aren't around, it would burn the ears off a street bum (excuse me, I mean a homeless person)—and it's not all from the kids who've never set foot inside a church either!

The teachers are all right, though, and a lot more what I'd call real Christians than some of the kids. Take Mr. Bradford. He's the high school English teacher and our yearbook supervisor. A lot of the teachers are too busy rushing around to take much notice of the students. (Not that I'm blaming them. The powers-that-be keep the staff on pretty full schedules here, and most of them have families of their own.) But Mr. B always has a minute to sit and talk. And even when you've done something utterly stupid, he makes you feel that just possibly there might be something about you worth salvaging. Just between myself and this journal, I'll admit that back in my early days on yearbook I—like every other girl there—had a hot and heavy crush on him. He's single and only twelve years older than I am—not too much of an age gap if one believes the romance novels I used to devour in junior high (okay, so maybe I still indulge on occasion!). I'd daydream during copy sessions that one day he'd glance up long enough to notice I was growing up. Fortunately, I did grow up enough to recover before it got embarrassing. But he's still my favorite teacher.

Speaking of Mr. B, we had our first yearbook meeting today. Just a short one to see who's interested in working this year. We had quite a turnout too. Annette, of course, and Sandy Larson, who worked on copy with me last year. The biggest part of last year's crew has either graduated or moved away, but there will be plenty of new kids to choose from—including, believe it or not, Amos Lowalsky. Now, why would *he* suddenly decide his senior year that he wants to start on the bottom rung of yearbook?

Yearbook can be a lot of work and, at SCA at any rate, it's considered an extracurricular activity so you don't get classroom credit for it. But it looks good on your college transcripts, and the *QUEST* has won awards for being one of the best yearbooks in the ACSI (Association of Christian Schools, International) so there is a certain prestige to being on staff. Besides, word has leaked out about some of the parties we throw in between work sessions. So there are always a fair number of high schoolers who sign up.

Only thirteen make the final cuts, though—four in each section plus the editor. Mr. B announced that the staff list would be posted in the next week or so. *And* that he'll be contacting certain individuals in the next few days to see who'd be willing to serve as editor and head photographer as well as copy and layout editors. When he said "editor," he glanced right down at me. I'm so excited! I have real plans for this year's *QUEST*. It's going to be the best yearbook this school's ever produced.

That settled, I'd better stop writing in this journal and get started on that satire for English Lit—seeing as I have no other plans for this lovely Friday evening. Dad's on duty, and Mom's out doing a lecture at the local chapter of Mothers Against Drunk Driving. Me—I'm babysitting Danny. To add insult to injury, as I was slogging out the door behind Denise Jenkins and her cronies this afternoon, I overheard Scott Mitchell and his buddies inviting them to head to that new video arcade over on their end of the city to get some pizza.

Still, the church is throwing a Labor Day picnic tomorrow, so I can't say my social life is a total loss. And if you were talking to me instead of reading this, the sarcasm in that last line would be evident!

## Monday, September 2nd

And so pass the last days of summer. So much for celebrating! It poured rain Saturday morning, and even though it cleared up by noon and the church decided to go ahead with the picnic, Mom said it was too late to bother. Since Dad was on duty again, that ended that!

Sunday morning we made it to church, but afterwards Dad had to head back downtown and Mom had one of her headaches so I had to stay home from my only remotely social outlet—youth group—to keep an eye on Danny. She was fine today, though, and has been out of the house all day—I'm not even sure where this time. Guess where that left me! Sometimes I feel like the kid's mother.

I mentioned that Dad's a police officer. I didn't mention Mom. Dad's income may not be much for a place like SCA, but government jobs don't make peanuts either so Mom's never had to work outside the house. On the income-tax forms, she's classified as a housewife.

But that doesn't mean Mom stays home to mend socks or bake chocolate-chip cookies. She's got to be the world's champion volunteer. It's something that's always surprised me because Mom's not really much on people. But she's great at organizing things—as long as she's the boss. She heads up the Neighborhood Watch, the Neighborhood Recycling Committee, the aforementioned local M.A.D.D. chapter, not to mention some citizens group protesting against teenage drug use. I lose track. She gives advice over the phone at a marriage crisis center (I'd like to listen to that sometime!) and even shows up at SCA once in a while to organize special functions. My sister, Julie, says Mom missed her calling as a drill sergeant.

Danny came along when I was ten and Julie was twelve. He wasn't planned, and to say that Mom was upset is putting it mildly, but still falls into the category of truth. He didn't slow her down much, though. He wasn't more than a few weeks old when she got back into the swing of things. Out every day and half the evenings. Since Dad works odd hours, Julie and I ended up with Danny.

It wasn't so bad until Julie left for college. At least we took turns. Now it seems all I do is baby-sit. Okay, so maybe my social calendar isn't exactly overbooked, but does that mean I have to spend every free hour I've got with a seven year old? And though Danny was an absolutely adorable baby, right now he's just a pest. I hardly get my books open before he's wanting me to play catch with him, or read him a story, or fix him a snack. I wouldn't mind so much if I got paid like I do when I baby-sit other people's kids. But of course I don't.

The reason Dad's been out all weekend was on the news tonight. Some big gang war down in Werewolves territory. Real Werewolves, that is. Not those slathering creatures in horror movies who get their kicks out of howling at a full moon, but one of the worst street gangs San Diego's ever had. You can see that fanged wolfhead of theirs spray-painted all over the less reputable parts of old downtown. And sometimes in the not-so-disreputable parts. I saw one painted on the back side of the mall last week. Like dogs—or wolves—marking their territory. Disgusting.

Anyway, they were at their usual—fighting, looting, smashing everything in sight. It seems some rival gang had invaded their territory, and of course they can't allow that! So half the cops of the city had to give up their weekend to try to keep the two sides from killing each other. I don't know why they bother. Personally, I think they should just cordon off the area and let the gangs shoot it out. If they kill each other off, there'll just be that many less to steal and sell drugs and prey on decent people. And maybe the SDPD would have a little more time to spend with their families, too.

And with that piece of profound advice, which no one will ever listen to, I'll get out of this and print off that Lit satire. Speaking of which, I still haven't heard from Mr. B. I was more-than-half expecting him to call over the weekend. Maybe he went out of town.

## Thursday, September 5th

Life is a rat race!

I don't know who said that, but it had to be someone famous and deeply intellectual. These AP courses seem to be designed along the theory that they're either going to prepare us for an Ivy League college or kill us in the attempt. Add yearbook to that and an hour a day of piano and the articles the hapless junior who ended up with the school newspaper because no senior would take it has talked me into contributing, and this year is going to be so busy I won't have time to brood over my social life. And now the music teacher, Miss Kitchener, has sprained her hand (falling out of bed; how dumb can you get!) so she's asked me to fill in on the piano at choir practice for the next few weeks.

Anyway, that's my excuse for neglecting this journal.

But I'm loving twelfth grade. This is definitely the best year I've ever had. I'm actually managing to say and do the right things, and I haven't put my foot in my mouth once. *And* I received my first compliment from no less a personage than Brian Andrews. Though I have to admit that was Denise Jenkins' doing.

It started yesterday. Denise Jenkins, for reasons men puzzle over but which no woman would have any difficulty explaining, has always been a lot more popular with the guys than the girls. She talks in this cooing little-girl voice that can't possibly be natural for anyone of her statuesque proportions but which she thinks adds to her image as a femme fatale (Annette, more accurately, says it makes her sound like a whining three year old). I'm not debating its effectiveness. But however saccharin she might keep that coo for the male half of the population, when she turns it on her own gender, there's generally some nasty little dig hidden underneath. And if anyone responds in kind, her eyes widen with this innocent, oh-so-hurt expression.

"What did I do wrong?" she wails. "I was just trying to be nice!"

Last year, I overheard her telling Scott Mitchell: "I just don't know why the girls are so jealous of me! I try so hard to be friendly!" She batted those fake eyelashes and managed to look heartbroken and persecuted at the same time. Scott, of course, fell for it like a brick.

Well, maybe we *are* jealous. But Sandy Larson is just as pretty in her own way, and everyone likes her!

At any rate, Denise definitely prefers male company to female. But she does keep a couple of toadies around, Gloria Williams and Lisette Costranova, who made it into Denise's inner circle by fawning all over her and hanging onto every word she says. I was washing my hands after lunch when they strolled giggling into the bathroom to touch up their makeup and admire themselves in the mirror. I was just adding a touch of lip gloss when Denise stopped ignoring my existence long enough to lean over and inform me silkily, "You know, Jana, you'll never be pretty. But you could be passably cute if you'd just do something about that hair!"

I saw red! Mainly because I know it's true. I've never claimed to be as pretty as Denise, and my hair *is* a bit of a mess right now. It's been short since kindergarten when Mom told me if I couldn't keep my hair neat it'd have to go. I still remember how I howled when she chopped off those waist-length ringlets. She used the old bowl cut, and with my hair as curly as it is, it poofed right out so that I look like a sheep dog in all my elementary school pictures. All through junior high and high school, I've kept it short and layered. But this summer I decided to grow it out. It's down to my shoulders now, but the problem with naturally curly hair is that it just doesn't curl where you want it to.

I wouldn't have quite traded a million dollars, but I'd have given up a fair share of my prized possessions right then to wipe that drooping little sneer off Denise's Tangerine Splashed lips. Instead, with half-a-dozen other girls gazing on with bright-eyed interest, I swallowed my rage and managed a cool reply. "Thank you for that insight, Denise. Maybe you have a suggestion for me?"

There wasn't much I could do then, but this morning I got up early and dug out Mom's curling iron. Due to lack of practice my curling job wasn't perfect, but I liked the effect. I was feeling pretty good when I sauntered into AP Psychology first period, so it was like a kick in the stomach when Denise took one look at me and threw up her hands with a horrified gasp loud enough to be heard across campus. "Jana, what *did* you do to your hair?"

The bell chose that moment to ring, and everyone rushed for a seat. I was so totally humiliated that instead of looking around for Annette as I usually do, I dropped into the nearest chair, desperately wishing one of the cracks in the wood floor would widen enough to allow me to slip through.

Now, since I'm being honest in this journal, I'll admit I do as much seat maneuvering as the next girl. But this time I didn't even notice that Brian Andrews had dropped into a seat next to me. Scott Mitchell has been at the top of my "Guy I'd Most Like To Get To Know" list since seventh grade when he was six inches taller than the other boys and already well aware of the effect of those melting blue eyes on the female populace of SCA. But in these last days my vote has shifted slightly toward Brian Andrews. Maybe because I like a guy to have something more in his head than football plays and Denise Jenkins' phone number.

I mean, let's face it! Scott may have a perfect profile and a build that won him a second-place finish in last year's Mr. Country Club

Teen competition, but he hates to crack a book and wouldn't know an abstract concept if it bit him. Not to mention that he's just a little too impressed with himself. He can't even take off his football helmet without immediately digging out a comb to slick back those impeccably styled gold waves!

Brian's hair is an ordinary brown and usually a little tousled because he runs his fingers through it when he's studying, and he's got the kind of look fiction writers describe as rugged rather than handsome. He's quiet too. Whether that's because he's shy or just doesn't know anyone yet, no one's quite figured out. But when he does speak up in class, it's clear that he's really been thinking.

And of course there's that smile!

Maybe it's because it comes so rarely that Brian's smile already has the girls sighing. It's a rather slow smile, but unlike Scott Mitchell's flashing and well-practiced grin, it reaches all the way into his gray eyes, crinkling the corners and lighting up that ultra-serious expression so that you wonder for just a moment if maybe he isn't as good-looking as Scott. And then decide that maybe you don't care.

Not that I've had a whole lot of experience with that smile myself. My seat maneuvering hasn't been overly successful, and though once he actually stepped back to wave me ahead of him through a door, an episode of gentlemanly courtesy so unusual in this school I almost dropped my books as well as my jaw, Brian had never given any indication he even knew my name. So it was a total shock when, as I was doing my best to pretend I was the Invisible Woman, he leaned over to say quietly, "I really like your hair like that, Jana."

Well! I've planned out a few fascinating and sophisticated speeches, just in case Brian actually did speak to me someday. But somehow none of them came out. I managed to choke out "Thank you" from between paralyzed vocal chords before a wave as fiery as my lip gloss crept up to burn my cheeks.

And that's when I got the full blaze of that smile!

That's all there was to it. Mr. Schneider called the class to order right then, and Brian didn't glance my direction again. But it put a spring into my step for the rest of the day and made it possible to ignore Denise and her cronies' snickering comments and glances.

I wonder, did Brian say that about my hair because he felt sorry for me or did he really mean it? Is it possible . . . ? No, of course not. . . . Still, hope doesn't cost anything.

There was one other happening out of the ordinary today, though of far less significance. Mr. Schneider had a visitor in AP Psychology this morning. Ms. Langdon. She's on the young side—maybe mid-twenties, definitely on the plump side, and fairly quivers with excitement when she talks, which she does at the fastest pace I've ever heard. She is finishing her Masters in psychology and will be at SCA for a month or so to do research for her thesis. What her thesis is, she didn't mention. Us?

Anyway, she administered what she called a "temperament analysis" test to the class. One of the easier tests I've ever taken, though it seemed highly irrelevant in spots. What does whether I would keep a newborn kitten dropped on my doorstep have to do with anything? Especially since in my house that's not my decision but Mom's. From what Ms. Langdon says, the test is supposed to tell you all your good points and bad points. As if I need my bad ones spelled out!

I still haven't heard from Mr. B, and he hadn't posted the *QUEST* staff list when I checked after choir. I'll check again in the morning.

*Friday, September 6th*

Still nothing on *QUEST*. I must say I'm a little surprised at the delay. I saw Mr. B call Annette up to his desk today after English Lit, but he was rushing off by the time I wandered over there. And now another weekend's closing in. I wish he wouldn't drag this out so long. I may be the only logical choice for editor, but I still can't help experiencing a certain nervous tension.

## Monday, September 9th

I can't believe it! This has got to be the worst day in a long life of unpleasant surprises that seem to lash out of a clear-blue sky every time I dare to dream that I'm finally beginning to get a handle on things. I'm so furious I could scream, and I would, too, if it wouldn't bring Mom storming up the stairs to find out why I'd disturbed her relaxation period. How *could* Mr. B humiliate me like this? There, now I'm getting the keys wet. I've got to stop crying!

The day started so perfectly. Mr. B chose my satire to read aloud to English Lit. It was a spoof on a news clipping I'd found about some 5'2" Polish assembly-line worker who was suing his company for a cool few million because they hadn't ensured a "proper respect" on the job for his "ethnic origins" and "short stature." The whole class roared as Mr. B read my admonishing letter to the company and accompanying recommendations for improving the squalid conditions of their workplaces. Piping educational broadcasts into the workplace about pint-sized heroes like Napoleon and Simon Bolivar, rewriting Polock jokes using Antartican aborigines, and group hug sessions instead of coffee breaks were only a few. Granted, such concessions might bring the too-tall, too-large, hump-nosed, flat-footed, and left-handed clamoring for their share of attention, but hey! What's the efficiency level of American industry compared with keeping everyone happy?

Mr. B's approving smile as he finished was like a pat on the back. Brian Andrews was smiling too—I checked! And on the way out of class, Brian actually paused by my desk to tell me how much he'd enjoyed my writing. Then he asked if I was looking forward to the senior class retreat next weekend. It seems he's planning on going.

Not that I'd be caught dead showing up now! Not with Mr. B as staff sponsor. The worst part is that he didn't even have the decency to tell me himself! We'd no sooner walked out of English Lit when Annette rushed over to burst out, "Did you hear? Sandy Larson's the new yearbook editor!"

The cloud I'd been floating on exploded under me like a bomb. I didn't want to believe it. But as I stood there slowly solidifying into a pillar of stone, Annette prattled on with the details loud enough for anyone within ten yards to hear. I don't care how many years we've been together; I've never felt so much like strangling anyone before!

"I've got to say I was surprised. I don't know why, but I had it in my head that he was going to ask you, Jana. But it's true, all right. I asked her myself. It just goes to show you can't count on anything, I guess. And of course I'm layout editor again. Mr. B asked me Friday. But you're not going to believe who's the new head photographer! Amos Lowalsky. They say he's some kind of photography genius. . . . And since most of last year's crew is gone . . . I didn't even know the guy could focus a camera! And I heard Mr. B asked Sharon Spinelli to be copy editor—"

That's when Annette shut up. Maybe she realized what she'd just said, or maybe my stony silence finally penetrated her babble. If I still had any hope that she had her facts screwed up, I lost it when my limbs unstiffened enough to turn around and see Sandy clutching her books in the doorway of the Lit room. She must have had at least some inkling of how much I was counting on this because her peaches-and-cream cheeks were fiery red, and she looked as guilty as though she'd stolen my SAT results. She stammered and stuttered but had to admit it was true.

She looked so miserable I couldn't vent on her the seething fury I was feeling. Besides, everyone was watching. So I thawed my frozen features into a smile that I hope didn't look as insincere as it felt and congratulated her on her new position. And it must have been adequate because the peaches-and-cream crept back into her cheeks and she lingered to chat long enough to let her own pleasure at being chosen to be editor seep through. With any luck, no one in this school—not even Annette and Sally—will ever guess what a fool I am and what stupid assumptions I was making.

But I'm furious with Mr. B! I thought he was my friend. I mean, really! Sandy Larson and Sharon Spinelli? They were both working *under* me last year. I was the one who taught them everything they know! Sandy did a decent job, I guess, but she can hardly open her mouth to get an order out. How is she supposed to be editor? And Sharon's only a junior. Okay, so I was copy editor as a sophomore. But there weren't any upperclassmen then to do the job.

And where does that leave me? Demoted back to rank-and-file? Talk about a slap in the face!

I guess it's myself I'm really furious with. Much as I want to blame Mr. B, he really is one of the nicest people I know. And I've never known him to be other than fair. So if he feels this strongly that I deserve to be demoted like this, then the problem has to lie with me, not him. Obviously, I didn't do anywhere near the kind of job I thought I was doing last year. I know he thinks I'm a good writer, so it must be that I'm no good with people. Mr. B did get after me a couple of times for being too hard on my crew. Told me I was expecting too much out of them. That's probably it right there. All the writing skills in the world aren't enough to make up for the fact that I'm a rotten leader!

So why didn't Mr. B tell me himself instead of letting me find out like this? In fact, when we finished last year, he told me I'd done a great job. Even if that was just the usual psychological drivel teachers spout to make a student feel useful, he could have given me some indication he'd found me this inadequate!

I am utterly miserable! Tomorrow is the next yearbook meeting, and the staff list will have to be up by then. With the lack of experienced personnel coming back from last year, I can't imagine Mr. B would throw me off yearbook altogether—not unless I've screwed up even worse than I think! But how can I possibly walk in there and have Sharon Spinelli ordering me around and remembering the times I made her rewrite stuff last year? Not to mention that everyone's going to know I've been demoted.

I just can't! I won't!

## Tuesday, September 10th

The world has tilted back on its axis again. Mr. B called me up this morning after English Lit and asked me if I would serve as copy editor. I guess all those rumors about Sharon Spinelli were just that—rumors. Mr. B apologized for taking so long to get around to me.

"These first days of school have been pretty hectic," he told me. "Besides, I knew I could count on you."

Well! If he had any idea what he's put me through! He did tell me he'd seriously considered making *me* editor and Sandy copy editor.

"But Sandy has done both layout and photography work on her school yearbook back in Alabama," he explained. "That gives her the most well-rounded experience on the crew. Besides, Sandy is a little too quiet and shy to handle that rowdy bunch you've got in the copy section. You're a lot more outgoing than she is and used to working on your own. Sandy may not have your leadership experience, but as editor she'll be working closely with me, and I feel this responsibility is just what she needs to develop her own leadership skills."

He gave me a stern look. "I'm counting on you to give her all the support you can, Jana."

Then the stern look eased into one of his grins. "And to give her the benefit of those creative ideas you manage to come up with in such abundance. Imagination isn't Sandy's long suit. Maybe the three of us can sit down this week sometime and brainstorm a bit."

That didn't take away all of the sting, but it eased it a little. Copy editor is a respectable position, even if little fame and fortune come with it. At least it's not a demotion. And he's probably right about Sandy. She's really a nice person and will do a good enough job as editor with Mr. B to back her up. And I must admit that what I know about layout and photography would fit into a teacup. I guess I never looked beyond my own copy section when I was making all those plans for the *QUEST.*

With all that off my shoulders, I can actually start looking forward to the senior class retreat this weekend. Saturday we're going white-water rafting—or actually inner-tubing—on a river near here. Then we'll spend the night down on the ocean and head back Sunday afternoon. Mr. Schneider, who's going along as speaker for the weekend, has informed us that this retreat is to help us bond as a class. Right! I can just see myself having a heart-to-heart with Denise Jenkins. Or Amos Lowalsky with Scott Mitchell. Oh well. It'll be fun either way.

I'm just glad Mr. B didn't realize I was bucking for editor. I still burn red with humiliation every time I think of that temper tantrum I threw yesterday—even if the only person to witness it was me! When will I ever grow up?

*Part Two*

# Saturday, September 14ᵗʰ

I've been asked to write up this weekend's retreat for the school newspaper, so I might as well use this journal for the rough draft. Let me see . . .

> *The sun rose blistering and hostile. The ragged band of humanity might have been alone in the universe, the last survivors in a cruel world swept clean of both man and beast. Terror and adrenaline swept through them with the lashing waves that flailed against their fragile craft. Who were they to pit their puny selves against such a naked force as raw Nature . . . ?*

Actually, we had a great day—though blistering is scarcely an exaggeration. The senior class (minus one or two home with the flu) plus Mr. B, Mr. Schneider and his wife, and a handful of parents along as chaperones, were headed out from the school parking lot by eight o'clock. Even at that hour, the highway was dancing with those shimmering heat waves that look so deceivingly like cool splashes of water. And SCA's elderly school bus is not well known for its state-of-the-art cooling system. Canteens were running on empty before we ever hit the mountains.

But the river was worth it. An unspoiled rush of the wildest, coolest white-water rapids I've ever seen descending a canyon that looked for all the world as though it had never known human presence.

The rapids were wild enough, in fact, that Mr. Careirras, the parent who arranged the trip and the inner tubes, had a hard time talking us into the water. Despite his assurances that they ended in a nice, quiet pool half-a-mile downstream, all logic dictated that we'd be ground to sausage long before we arrived there. It wasn't until Mr. B and Brian Andrews made an experimental foray downstream and returned in one piece that faith overcame logic. By then the heat had made death by washing machine almost preferable anyway, so it wasn't long before most of us were in the water.

Where Mr. Careirras got the inner tubes, I don't know. A semi graveyard, maybe. The biggest was easily as tall as the cab of the pickup in which he hauled them and could hold a whole gaggle of squealing girls. The way it worked was that Mr. Careirras and Mr. B took turns driving the pickup downstream. When everyone who could possibly squeeze onto an inner tube had splashed down into that final pool, the pickup hauled them back upstream. Then the next bunch took a turn. It was the world's best roller-coaster ride, the water a churning froth of bubbles, stomach rushing up into the mouth as a four-foot waterfall dropped away underneath, and just enough genuine hazard in fielding the tube off the rocks to keep everyone screaming in half-exhilaration, half-terror.

That's where the "ragged band of humanity" (see prior introductory paragraph) comes in. We'd been warned to go for cut-offs and old T-shirts rather than bathing suits, and most of us were sensible enough to follow that advice. Still, by the time the rear section of those cut-offs had scraped across a few beds of gravel or got hung up on a boulder, there weren't many who didn't boast a rip or two, not to mention bruises and scrapes galore.

Sally, Annette, and I courageously risked our lives on Monster Tube. The most difficult part was simply keeping from falling through the donut-hole, the thing was so large. We managed to stay on through all those rocks and rapids only to flip over just as we hit the pool at the bottom—right on top of Brian Andrews and Danny Mansilla. They retaliated with a good ducking, Brian for once not serious but laughing and splashing just as much as Danny. Afterward, they graciously offered to show us helpless females how it's done. It was a squeeze, but Sally, Annette, and I weren't protesting, and the five of us rode Monster Tube down the canyon three or four times until Denise called Brian over to stretch out on the bank with her.

Denise was one who had gone for appearance over utility with a bathing suit that just barely missed violating the modesty clause in SCA's dress code. She hadn't, of course, risked that bathing suit in the rapids, and while the rest of us were sunburned and stringy-haired, she didn't have so much as a false eyelash out of place. I don't think I was the only one desperately hoping Brian would have the good taste to turn her down, but he didn't. Danny split after that too, clearly embarrassed at being left on his own with three women. But it was fun while it lasted.

Twilight brought an easing of the heat. One of the school board members had offered the loan of his vacation property on the ocean for the night. It was full dark by the time we arrived to find not the rustic cabin I had expected but an enormous Spanish-style villa right on the beach with a high brick wall running around the property. Unfortunately, as we spilled out of the bus ravenous and more than ready for the barbecue we'd been promised, it was to discover not so much as a single light on to welcome us. Either the owner had forgotten we were coming and gone to bed, or he just wasn't home.

Fortunately, Mr. B did a little snooping and found a note on the gate telling us where to find a key and to make ourselves at home. Unfortunately, the key wasn't under the paving stone where it was purported to have been hidden. Fortunately, Brian Andrews and Danny Mansilla managed to scale the wall. Unfortunately, they discovered man-eating Dobermans on the other side.

So, we ended up drifting down to the beach to sit under the stars, listening to the waves curl in on the sand and singing songs to Hernan Careirras' guitar, a chorus of noisy stomachs adding to the percussion accompaniment. Mr. Schneider was just finishing the devotional message he'd planned on delivering after supper when our host finally showed up with profuse apologies and a catering truck that made it easy to forgive the delay. We spread out sleeping bags on the verandah and dined voraciously on barbe-cued chicken, cole slaw, mashed potatoes and gravy, and hot bis-cuits and honey. You guessed it! Kentucky Fried Chicken to the rescue.

It really was a spectacular day. So why do I feel so empty?

I slipped through the gate (the man-eating Dobermans turned out to be as gentle as kittens) and am sitting on the beach right now, watching the breakers crash down onto the sand in a pale spume of foam. I'm writing in a notebook by the light of a flood lamp on the villa wall. (I'll type this all into the computer when I get home.) Everyone else is asleep, I think, and I feel as though I truly were the only person left alive in the universe right now.

I guess it's that devotional message of Mr. Schneider's I can't get out of my head, which in itself is a note of historical interest. Along with teaching high school Social Studies and AP Psychology, Mr. Schneider also happens to be youth leader at our church so I have the disputable privilege of hearing even more of his discourses than the average SCA student. And not one of them has ever before disturbed my capacity for peaceful slumber. On the contrary; there are few things more highly touted around SCA as a cure for insomnia.

I should interject here that Mr. Schneider is a totally decent hu-man being. He has never murdered anyone, never stolen anything, probably never even jaywalked, most certainly never had a rebel-lious impulse against his parents or any other authority in the days of his youth—if he ever had any youthful days, which is a matter of serious conjecture among his students.

But he's the type of guy who makes you wonder how he *ever* managed to talk someone into marrying him. Hardly into his thirties, he's already stooped and lanky and balding and looks precisely like a middle-aged Shaggy. He even has a dog he drags along to youth functions that bears a remarkable resemblance to Scooby-Doo, an elderly Great Dane that has bald patches of its own and is always scratching, though Mr. Schneider swears he doesn't have fleas (the dog, I mean).

Come to think of it, Mrs. Schneider looks more than a little like that female sidekick of theirs too. Not the Barbie-doll one, the other one with glasses. Do you suppose there was some real-life basis for the cartoon?

Naah, that's too far-fetched!

I shouldn't be so sarcastic. As I said, Mr. Schneider is a worthy citizen if anyone is, and he has plenty of enthusiasm for "working with youth" as he puts it, as though we were some peculiar tribe of aborigines he's been studying. It's just that he has absolutely no sense of humor, and what he knows about the post-twentieth-century teen would fit into the nucleus of a hydrogen atom. Add to that the fact that his devotionals are exceeded in length and dryness only by his class lectures, and the snickers and whispered remarks that punctuated this evening's oration on "class unity" are understandable, if rude.

But long-winded and pedantic though Mr. Schneider might be, there was one story he told tonight that keeps thrusting itself back into my mind no matter how hard I push it away. It was about this person Mr. Schneider knew in college. *Joe Cool* was what they called him—the stone age equivalent of a jock, I guess. He was some big football hero with fans hanging on his every word and girls hanging all over the rest of him.

Mr. Schneider had always detested the guy because he was so stuck-up and always poking fun at him—Mr. Schneider, that is—for being such a geek at sports, not to mention everything else under the sun. It wasn't hard to imagine as he spoke. This incredible-looking, egotistical hunk like Gaston in the Walt Disney cartoon

"Beauty and the Beast" throwing back his head with a roar of laughter as a younger Mr. Schneider trips over his own feet, his black-rimmed glasses flying across the room as they did in World History last week. . . .

Then one night *Joe Cool* committed suicide. The note he left behind said simply, "All I ever really wanted was a friend. All I ever wanted was someone to love me." Mr. Schneider figured this guy had it all—popularity, fame, girls, a future, and all the self-satisfaction having all that can bring with it. But inside that arrogant, smirking exterior was a lonely little boy who felt no one cared about him.

Oh God, that's me! Unloved! And unlovable, too, I guess, or someone *would* love me!

Oh, I'm not denying John 3:16: "For God so loved the world . . ." I've been to church all my life off and on, not to mention that Bible is a required course at SCA. I have no reason to doubt my Sunday school teacher's assurances that from whatever distance God is watching the comedy I'm making of my life, He cares that I don't screw up my part in His plan for the universe more than I already have. But that is hardly personal since God also loves the most vicious serial killer that ever lived or those gang hoodlums rampaging around downtown San Diego. It is scarcely a distinction to make me feel worthwhile.

As for my friends, okay, so I'm fortunate not to be a total reject like some poor souls I could name. I've never had to sit alone in the lunchroom, desperately willing for someone to slap a tray down beside me so I didn't stand out in the crowd. There's always been Sally and Annette at least and the youth group kids I hang around with at church.

But it's all surface. We joke and laugh and talk about everything under the sun from homework to the latest threat to world peace to which new sophomore was seen with Scott Mitchell at the mall last Friday evening. Then we rush off to the next class or the next social event or our ride home, and we never once share what's really touching us deep down inside. And I can't believe that any one of them—even Sally and Annette—would cry too long if I disappeared off the face of the earth tonight.

Like a lot of girls, I suppose, I dream of someday meeting that special *someone*. Someone with whom I can really share all the thoughts and longings and hopes and dreams that make me the person I am. And who will find them—and me—worth listening to. Someone who will love me, not as part of some nebulous section of humanity or because they are my teacher and a good Christian doing their duty like Mr. B or Mr. Schneider, but because they—*he* sees something utterly valuable and worth loving in me. Someone who wants to be with me as much as I want to be with him.

Whether such a person will ever walk into my life—or whether he even exists—I don't know. Right now I'd settle for one single person to whom my continued existence—or lack thereof—would really make any difference in the world. And that goes for my own family most of all!

I've never been the world's most reserved individual, but I don't talk much about my family, not even to those I consider my closest friends. Family loyalty, I guess. Or the fact that any reflection on my family reflects on me, too. I wouldn't even be writing this here if it weren't for that password protection. But sometimes things bottle up inside until they just have to explode out—even onto the blank, uncaring pages of a journal.

Outsiders assume our family's got it all together. And we're certainly not what the social workers call dysfunctional. Both my birth parents live at home. They are both respected members of the community. We go to church just about every Sunday and smile and shake hands with the pastor afterwards. And none of the neighbors have ever had to call the police because of a drunken party or family brawl.

But it sure isn't the Brady Bunch!

When I was small, I used to watch reruns of the Brady Bunch and fantasize that I had their mother. All those kids in the same house, and still she had time to kiss them and talk to them and tuck them into bed. Of course, it makes a difference having that housekeeper. But Annette and Sally's mothers both work, and I've watched how they hug their daughters when they get home from school—even in front of their friends—and the way they let them bring friends home to hang out and do fun things together as a family, and I want it so bad I cry myself to sleep when I get home.

Adults at church and school are always complimenting me on my own mother. All that drive. All that talent. All that concern for the community, the way she runs those committees and hot lines and everything. And that's all true, of course. But we don't see much of that side of her at home. As long as I can remember, my mother has suffered from a bizarre and as yet unclassified health syndrome that allows ample energy and time to do anything she wants, but develops into a sudden migraine any time we suggest bringing a friend home or going somewhere as a family. Or try planning anything at all that wasn't her idea. Maybe that sounds insensitive and unfeeling, but it's the literal truth. Just ask my older sister Julie.

Or Dad, if you'd ever get him to admit it. I couldn't begin to count the times we'd make plans to go somewhere when we were kids—the beach, the zoo, hiking or fishing when we were back in Montana, anywhere. We'd be all set to go with Julie and I awake half the night in anticipation and up at the crack of dawn to pack the picnic lunch so Mom wouldn't have that as an excuse.

Mom had only to stagger from her bedroom to pop the bubble. Julie and I would cringe and hold our breath while she stomped around the house, poking through the picnic cooler and grumbling about the mess we'd made and being too tired and having too much to do and how all this had been planned without considering her needs—our own needs evidently counting for nothing!

Then out would come the "headache." Dad would steer Mom back into the bedroom so we kids didn't have to hear them arguing, and Julie and I would just *look* at each other. Sure enough, in a few minutes Dad would emerge looking sheepish to tell us that Mom wasn't feeling well and that we'd better take a rain check. A rain check when your father is a cop who manages the same day off as you about as often as it snows in San Diego? Sure!

A few times we talked Dad into taking us without Mom. After all, if she's got a headache, you'd think she'd be glad for a quiet house! But then she'd mope around for days, muttering about inconsiderate people "leaving me sick and all alone" and "only caring about their own fun." It was enough to keep the guilt trip stirred up and take all joy out of the experience. So nine times out of ten, we ended up staying home, running sickroom errands and snacks, while Mom lay in bed watching TV and yelling orders about cleaning up crumbs that confirmed our suspicions that she can see through sheet rock.

When I was about eight or so, after an especially bad day with Mom, Julie and I made up our minds to run away. We were going to build ourselves a little cabin in the Rocky Mountains, grow a garden, and live off the land like the "Wilderness Family." Julie was going to be the housekeeper, and I would be the adventurous one and explore and hunt and bring home food for her to cook. Somehow, it never seemed to occur to us what it would put our parents through. I guess we figured Dad had Danny to console him and Mom wouldn't care anyway. After lights out, we'd plan just what our house was going to look like and what we'd need to take. We even had some supplies squirreled away (two Snickers and some gum, if I remember right) when a spat of our own broke up the partnership. Besides, even then we were practical enough to realize it was only a dream without more money than we had.

But Julie escaped the instant she got out of school. She's been a straight 4.0 since kindergarten with her choice of scholarships all over the U.S., and you can be sure she picked the university furthest from home. She's studying pre-law over in Massachusetts now and comes home as seldom as possible. She's even gotten a job over there these last two summers.

All this makes my dad sound like a wimp. He's not. He just likes peace and quiet when he's home, so he usually ends up giving in to Mom. With him being a cop, he's gone most of the time anyway. When we lived in Montana it was different. A small town doesn't have a lot of crime—mostly dragging the drunks off the street on weekends. He'd take Julie and I fishing and come to our school programs. But since we moved to San Diego, he's been too busy saving the world—not to mention worthless street hoodlums who couldn't give a rip anyway!—to care about his own family.

Okay, maybe that's not entirely fair! Someone has to keep the trash swept off the streets if our world is to stay even as precariously balanced as it is. And maybe Dad does care in his own silent fashion even if he hasn't the slightest idea how to show it. I can't even say he's never tried. There was a time before Julie escaped to college when he went through this guilty streak. Pastor Grant had been preaching on the family, and Dad started rumbling about how we needed to spend more time together. So he decided to schedule one night a week as "family night." No TV, no reading books, no volunteer work, just being together!

None of us were too enthusiastic, and Mom gave her own opinion of the idea pungently and loudly enough for all of us kids to hear despite their closed door. But for once Dad put his foot down. We must have spent two months sitting around the table once a week, playing stupid card games and trying to laugh at Dad's painful attempts at humor before he got involved in a big case and gave it up. Julie and I didn't have the heart to tell him it was a little late to start the "family togetherness" thing.

So that's my loving family! A model household on the outside, something else on the inside. I must say with all the quarreling they do—mainly Mom yelling and Dad trying to calm her down—it's puzzled me that Mom and Dad have never gotten divorced. I can't remember ever seeing Mom treat Dad with any kind of affection.

Or any of the rest of us, for that matter. I can't ever remember Mom putting her arms around me and giving me a hug. Oh, maybe she did when I was still a cuddly toddler, but if so, it has been blocked from my memory by everything else. I can't remember her once coming to a school play or concert without complaining about the inconvenience to her schedule, much less ever telling Julie and me how wonderful we were, like other parents we could hear. Or ever in all these years telling me I did a good job at *anything*, no matter how hard I tried!

The truth is, I wonder sometimes how Mom calls herself a Christian. This *can't* be the way God meant families and people to be! There's got to be something more to it than just going to church or running the Fellowship Committee!

But then, who am I to talk? I go to church and youth group. I don't swear or steal or do drugs. I really do try to do all those things I've been taught will keep God happy with me. And sometimes after youth camp or a really good speaker at church (*not* Mr. Schneider!), I even feel like I can do it.

But every time I think I've got things together, I end up falling flat on my face. I shoot my mouth off at my parents or put my foot into it up to my kneecap or have positively homicidal thoughts about Mom or Denise Jenkins and her cronies. And there, I've blown it all over again!

I've often thought that if I were different, maybe things would be better at home. If I could somehow manage to do everything Mom wants and be the kind of person she wants, maybe she'd change and be happy and even love us all a little and want to spend time with us.

But who do I think I'm kidding? I will never be good enough to measure up to whatever criteria Mom expects from me, so there doesn't seem much point in even trying! I wonder, does anyone else snoring up there on the veranda ever have these kind of thoughts behind the laughing faces we've all been showing each other all day? Or am I the only one who ever feels totally worthless and unloved?

## Sunday, September 15th

I hate Mr. Schneider!

I hate SCA and every person in it and all of California!

No, let's be honest, Jana Thompson! It's me I hate!!!

And to think I woke up this morning laughing at myself for all of last night's dramatics and self-pity. The sky was again a cloudless blue, the waves curling in just right to drag out the surfboards, the sea breeze blowing away Joe Cool and all his problems—and mine. The breakfast buffet up at the villa was outstanding, and Sunday morning worship on the beach with the sea gulls crying to each other overhead and the surf beating the rhythm for Hernan's guitar more than made up for another hour of Mr. Schneider's nasal drone.

Things were just fine, in fact, until the final campfire when Mr. Schneider opened things up for a "sharing time." I hate sharing times—especially with this class! It's bad enough to bare your heart in front of your own close friends or your own youth group who are at least church kids and know how these things are supposed to go. It's ten times worse with all the country club and reform school set eyeing the proceedings as though we were a bunch of monkeys in the zoo. And when Mr. Schneider's in charge, as anyone from our church can testify by experience, you can just figure what's bound to happen!

It wasn't so bad at first. Sandy Larson got to her feet, tossed her piece of kindling into the campfire, and shared in her soft, little Southern accent how much God was teaching her in her leadership role in yearbook. A long pause followed while everyone avoided each other's eyes or stared at the ground between their feet as though scared to death Mr. Schneider was going to call for volunteers army-style. Then one of the new girls stood up to say how much she'd appreciated Mr. Schneider's morning message. (Oh, really! And what class is *she* flunking?)

Another drawn-out silence. At last Amos Lowalsky (now, really, what kind of loving parent would saddle their kid with a name like that?) got up to talk about what God had done in his life through some youth mission work he'd been doing during the summer, a speech I tuned out after the first thirty seconds as I'd already heard it once at youth group. Every ten seconds he'd stop to blow his nose, a display of manly emotion that embarrassed everyone but him.

When he finally sat down, Denise Jenkins made a comment about "geeks" loud enough to send a titter around the circle and earn a stern look from Mr. B. Then came another dead silence. This time it dragged on so long it was painful, and a seagull, thinking from our frozen state that we must be an outcropping of rock or something, dropped down to see if there was anything edible about Danny Mansilla's toes. A hail of pebbles and an outraged squawk eased the tension momentarily. Then people started glancing at their watches, and you could just *feel* everyone willing Mr. Schneider to pray or start another song or *something*! But he just stood there, looking around at us with such a disappointed expression on that long, hangdog face of his I couldn't stand it anymore.

So idiot Jana Thompson did what she always does! I jumped up and said something *very* short. I don't even remember what it was. Something about how great the weekend had been and how I hoped God would teach me to be a more loving person. It broke the ice, at least. An audible sigh of relief went through the crowd as Mr. Schneider said, "Thank you, Jana," then quickly closed with another song and prayer.

I didn't think anything more about it until we were cleaning up to go home. I was hauling my stuff over to the bus when Mr. Schneider beckoned me over and asked if he could have a word with me. My heart was sinking even before he edged me over to a quiet spot. I've never known an adult to ask for a "word" that wasn't the precursor to something distinctly unpleasant!

Why can't I just spit it out? Mr. Schneider sat me down on a bench and informed me that he'd noticed I was always one of the first to speak up every time we have a sharing time. Then he went on to give me this fatherly lecture about how being too quick to share spoils the effect of what you say, and how maybe if I wasn't so quick to jump in, other kids would be more open to share themselves. I shouldn't speak up unless I really had something worth sharing. The worst thing was, I think he was actually trying to be kind!

"You've got one of the more outgoing personalities in our youth group, Jana," he finished, "and I know you enjoy sharing your feelings with the group. But maybe you could just tone it down a bit. We really want to encourage *all* the kids to speak up, not just the same few every time."

I felt just horrible! I was so mortified I wanted to sink into the ground. Sure, I didn't have anything to say much worth hearing.

But how could I tell him I was just trying to help? I don't even *like* giving my "testimony," as he always calls it! The only reason I ever speak up at all at these things is because I always feel so sorry for him standing up there with that dejected look on his face, as though we were all letting him—and God—down! And what about Amos and Sandy? *They* always share! Is he giving them the same lecture? Or maybe what they had to say counts as something worth sharing!

Have I really been making such a fool of myself? Is that what everyone's been thinking? I guess I'd always figured the other kids understood what I was doing. Do they really think I've been putting on some super spiritual act?

I feel so utterly humiliated, even more than when I thought Mr. B was going to make me editor. At least then no one saw what a fool I made of myself but me! Sometimes I wish I could just retire from the human race. Maybe dig myself a hole in the ground somewhere and pull it in after me until the world ends. At least then I wouldn't make any more mistakes! Well, Mr. Schneider won't have to worry about *me* bailing him out again. And if he thinks that's going to make the other kids speak up, he's crazy!

## Friday, September 20th

First Mr. Schneider! Now Miss Kitchener! I really doubt if anyone since the world began has ever had the capacity for making a mess of things like I do!

It's not my fault either! It all started with that stupid promise I made to play piano for choir while Miss Kitchener's hand was healing. Can I help it that they had to schedule choir right when Mr. B called for an extra meeting for the yearbook editors to plan out this year's theme and dedication, etc. without the whole crew around? I even found someone to take my place, which wasn't easy considering there's maybe two other students in the entire high school who've ever made it past the First Grade John Thompson piano course. I ended up having to call a parent. I thought Miss Kitchener would be grateful, but she was just upset that the parent showed up a half hour late.

Then today it was the choir's turn to call for an extra practice. I told Miss Kitchener no problem. It wasn't until halfway through last period that it hit me. I'd promised to come home early to baby-sit Danny. Dad's on duty, and Mom's got some seminar on "The Twenty-first Century Woman and Civic Responsibility." When the bell rang, I hurried right to the music room to tell Miss Kitchener how sorry I was. I really did feel bad about it—I know how it is to be stood up at the last minute—and I was about to tell her I'd see about finding someone to take my place before I left. But she gave me such a look! As though I were lying or just making excuses.

"Oh, you!" she snarled in a tone of total disgust. Scooping up her music with her one good arm, she added sarcastically, "Maybe you can let the rest of us know when we can fit into your precious schedule!" And she swept out of the room before I even had a chance to explain.

It isn't fair! It's hardly my fault that Miss Kitchener sprained her wrist or that Mr. B decided on extra yearbook sessions. And it's not like I wouldn't rather be playing for choir than baby-sitting Danny. But knowing it's not my fault doesn't make me any less miserable. I hate having people angry with me.

On top of all that, Mr. B got after me in yearbook yesterday. I'm being too hard on my copy staff—turning back too much of the practice captions they've been working on. He says I need to let them exercise their creativity more even if it's not perfect or exactly the way I would write things. It was the same spiel he used last year, and of course I know he's right. I've been so depressed since the retreat, I guess I've been taking it out on them. Can't I do anything right?

## Monday, September 23rd

I showed up at choir practice today. If Miss Kitchener wanted to act less than adult, I wasn't going to give her the satisfaction of pulling me down to her level. But when I got there, she acted as though nothing had even happened. And after choir, she came over to ask if she'd done anything to offend me. To offend *me*? *She's* the one who got offended!

Well, if she can pretend she doesn't remember, so can I! So I mumbled something about not feeling a hundred percent and left it there. She did thank me nicely for coming in, so I guess I'll just let the whole thing slide. Sometimes I just don't understand adults. I mean, *they're* the ones who are supposed to act mature around here, right? So why do they do things that make you wonder if they're so smart after all?

Oh, by the way, scratch Brian Andrews off my Christmas wish list! It would appear that he has succumbed to Denise Jenkins' curve line like every other male who flutters within orbit of her flame. I thought he had more sense. But what can you expect when a girl as well-endowed as Denise makes an all-out play for a guy? And all that on top of another weekend sitting alone with Danny. This year is not turning out how I'd hoped at all!

## Wednesday, September 25th

I am, at this moment, a new person.

Or if not completely reborn, I have at least been given a new lease on life. Today has in fact been such a turning point in the sorry saga of Jana Thompson that I want to get every last detail down here while it still remains fresh in my mind. No, not just a turning point. The old Jana is gone. Sent into exile. And she'd better not come sneaking back. As Ms. Langdon put it so well, "Today is the first day of the rest of your life, Jana Thompson. So celebrate!"

It is Ms. Langdon who is responsible for my renewed lease on life. A guidance counselor is something new for me. Not that the teachers aren't always handing out free advice, but it has never been a separate office at SCA, though I do remember a school counselor at that junior high I attended those first months in San Diego. That one was a full-fledged psychologist with a wall full of framed diplomas and a physical appearance that fit the stereotype of a mad scientist—tall and gaunt with wild black hair and beetle eyebrows meeting over a genuine hook nose. He terrified me, and the questions he asked during my one session with him about sexual orientation and other matters that were a mystery to me at the time were among the final straws that led Dad to yanking us out of that school.

Still, it was no particular surprise to find a Stick-um on my locker excusing one Jana Thompson from fifth period to report to said counselor. Seniors have been flashing those notes at teachers the last couple of days, and I had no doubts I knew what it was all about. "Guidance counselor" and "senior" usually add up to two things: career choices and college applications.

And I wasn't too thrilled at wasting class time on either. I've already settled on a degree in Communications. I'd like to learn how to write professionally—maybe even for a newspaper or a magazine—and maybe do something with TV and radio as well. As for checking out colleges, that was last year's big rush. My family is too middle-class to qualify for major financial aid while at the same time being too broke to help out a lot with tuition. But I scored well enough on both the SAT and ACT to get my share of scholarship offers. The university here has a good communications program and has made overtures that would permit me to stay out of debt if I lived at home. But that's the rub. I want something a *long* way from home. Maybe near Julie. I did receive an offer of a full four-year scholarship from St. Mary's College somewhere over in Massachusetts. The drawback is that it's an all-women's college. Who do they think they're kidding? But there are a couple of others with not-so-lucrative financial aid packages, and I still have a few months to make up my mind.

All of which I planned to communicate to whichever SCA staff member had been roped in for this counseling job quickly enough to make it back for the AP Chemistry quiz. So it was definitely a surprise to find Ms. Langdon's round face beaming at me from behind the desk in the telephone-booth of an office into which the school secretary ushered me. I know I've mentioned Ms. Langdon somewhere in here back when she put in an appearance at one of those first AP Psychology classes. That she hadn't crossed my mind since is an indication of just how much impact that appearance had on me. She's never been back to class, and I guess I assumed she finished whatever mysterious research she came to do and headed back to where she came from.

Still, being wrong is *no* surprise to me, so I settled unquestioningly into the chair she pointed to. I was mustering my explanations and hoping that hour on chemical equations last night wasn't going to be wasted when I realized that what lay in front of her on the table wasn't a stack of college brochures. It was that temperament analysis test she'd given us. The filled-in little ovals and graph could have belonged to anyone, but I recognized that sloppy *Jana Thompson* scrawled across the top.

Ms. Langdon didn't waste any time on preliminaries. Nor did she even mention application forms or career choices. Tapping the test with one blunt, unpolished fingernail, she informed me, "From what I can see here, Jana, it's evident that you are a highly intelligent and talented young lady. But one thing stands out clearly in these test results. You are suffering from a very low sense of self-worth and self-esteem. That means that you don't think much of yourself," she spelled out as though I were slightly retarded.

Pushing the test away from her then, she rested her elbows where the paper had been and asked, as though she were really curious, "Why, Jana? What is it that you don't like about yourself?"

Well!! I didn't bother reacting to her first statement. I was quite well aware that she probably says that to everyone. But what was I supposed to say to the rest? That a list of academic accomplishments means diddly-squat when it comes to popularity? That my sense of self-worth is low because the worth of that self happens to be nil? That I don't esteem myself because there isn't much to esteem?

I stammered and stuttered and got out something totally meaningless. But when I trailed off, Ms. Langdon was smiling. And not as though I'd just made an idiot of myself. She leaned forward across the desk, and her smile grew so that I could see that her teeth were rather stained and that one front tooth was twisted oddly so that it overlapped the eyetooth next to it. And as she looked down at me hunched over in that old armchair that was a little lower than her own, it was as though she really liked what she saw. Then she asked me a question. I don't even remember what that first question was, but I answered it. And then she asked another and another. Personal ones, too.

And, you know, she talked just as fast as I remembered from Psychology class, and her hands waved just as excitedly. But I guess I'd never noticed how much sympathy there was in her smile or how warm those pale blue eyes could be when she stopped talking and listened. And somehow, I found myself telling Ms. Langdon things I'd never thought to tell anyone in my life. My family. My talent for making every mistake in the book and how depressed I've been lately. Miss Kitchener and Mr. Schneider. The utter fool I made of myself over yearbook. Denise and her pals. Even Brian Andrews and how much I've wanted him to notice me.

The bell shrilled for the next period, but I hardly heard it. Every time I slowed down, she'd prompt me with another question. Her eyes never left mine as I talked, but I didn't see any of the condemnation and criticism or even pity I would have expected in them. I could feel with that extra sense one develops around adults that she was genuinely interested in what I was saying and not just because it was her job to listen to other people's problems.

When I'd wound down for the last time and even she couldn't come up with another question, Ms. Langdon let out her breath and shook her head as though she'd just finished a chapter of some soap opera.

"You do have a problem, Jana, and I know just what it is. The simple fact is that you care too much about what other people think of you. You're trying so hard to please other people and you want so badly for them to love you that you're forgetting the most important person in your life. Yourself!"

Me? Important? Right!

That's when Ms. Langdon pulled out a Bible. I'd heard the verse she read dozens of times; in fact, I've memorized it somewhere along the way between Sunday school and Bible classes. The first and greatest commandments: "Love the Lord your God with all your heart and with all your soul and with all of your mind," and "Love your neighbor as yourself." But I've never heard it explained quite the way she explained it.

"You see what Matthew is telling us here in this verse? God tells us that we are to love other people the way we love ourselves." She was so excited she would have stabbed the page through if her fingernails hadn't been clipped so short. "But if we turn that around and look at it logically, you can see that it's telling us that we have to first be able to love ourselves properly before we can truly learn to love other people. After all, you can't love your neighbor as yourself if you've never learned first to love yourself, right? It's a real problem with our world these days. So many people are suffering from a poor sense of self-esteem and self-worth that they just aren't capable of obeying God's command to love each other. And just look at the mess we've got as a result. That's why it's so important for God's children to have a high self-esteem. Do you understand what I'm saying, Jana?"

Oh, I understood, all right! Always before, I've figured I was to blame when I've been selfish and unloving. I've even felt guilty when I've fantasized deliciously awful things happening to Denise and company like elastic and snaps mysteriously evaporating during cheerleading tryouts, or when I've wished Mom was anywhere but messing up my life. But Ms. Langdon was saying it wasn't my fault. With the poor sense of self-esteem and self-worth I'm suffering from, there's no way I can be expected to really love other people any more than you'd expect a guy in a body cast to pitch in at Annual Clean-up Day in the park. It was a revelation!

"You see your problem, Jana?" Miss Langdon stopped torturing that poor page and stabbed her finger at me like a doctor handing out a diagnosis. "You've never learned to love and value yourself as you deserve. You worry too much about other people and what they want from you and not enough about yourself and your own needs. Take the difficulties you've had these last weeks. You're depressed because people have misjudged your motives. But what difference does it make what Miss Kitchener thinks or Mr. Schneider or Mr. Bradford or anyone else as long as you know you're doing what's right for yourself? After all, *you're* the one you've got to live with the rest of your life."

Reaching into a drawer behind the desk, she pulled out a pad of notepaper that had a lot more pink and perfume than I'd have expected from her and started scribbling. "It's not that I'm saying you should never think of other people. But of utmost importance for you right now, Jana, is to learn to love *yourself*. Once you find your own self-fulfillment and happiness, you'll find it comes naturally to love others."

It sounded good, but I have to admit I was pretty skeptical. "So how am I supposed to go about loving myself?" I demanded. "I mean, I don't even *like* myself!"

"That's easy. Just think of the most loving and attentive boyfriend you've ever had." Her smile managed not to show just how funny it was to think of me with a string of past boyfriends. "Or the one you hope to have someday. How does a man show love to a woman? He thinks of you all the time. He wants to be with you and do things that please you. He pays you compliments and buys gifts and plans special outings just for the two of you. You are the most important person in his life, and your happiness matters more to him even than his own."

Ms. Langdon stopped writing to lean forward, her round face beaming with so much enthusiasm you'd have thought she'd just won the Publisher's Clearinghouse Sweepstakes. "You see, Jana? You need to treat yourself the way that boyfriend would. Pamper yourself a little. Do something more exciting than studies or babysitting. You say you want to get Brian's attention. When was the last time you splurged at a top-rate beauty salon or bought clothes somewhere besides Target or Wal-Mart?"

She looked me over rather critically for someone who probably hasn't spent a cent on beauty treatments or designer clothing herself in recent history. "I'm aware that Denise hurt your feelings the other day, but she does have a point. You are an intelligent and talented individual, Jana, and you could be a beautiful one, too, with a little attention to your hair and makeup. And there's nothing like knowing you're attractive to improve a woman's self-esteem and draw the attention of the opposite sex."

She didn't stop there. "Self-worth" and "self-image" and "self-esteem" and "self-fulfillment" all ran together with a lot of psychological terms I can't even pronounce, much less define, until I began to feel a little dizzy, as though I'd been watching one of those pocket watches swing back and forth too long. But her voice was as warm and sympathetic as her smile, and the stream of words flowing over me was as soothing as tanning lotion over sunbaked flesh, and by the time the final bell rang I *knew* I was beautiful and valuable and the most important person in the world.

The school secretary stuck her head into the office as whistles and shouts and running feet let everyone know that the wild animals had been let out of their cages. Miss Langdon looked annoyed, then shrugged, turned another warm smile on me, and handed me the piece of perfume-scented paper she'd been scribbling on.

"I've enjoyed our time together, Jana," she said as I took the hint and stood up. "I do wish I had time for another session before I leave SCA, but there are so many other students to interview. I expect to be back later on in the school year, though. I'm looking forward to seeing how you get along with my little prescription."

The prescription was on that notepaper. I've got it here and will paste it into my journal when I get this last installation of my journal printed off. It's certainly not much like any prescription any doctor's given me before, but I like it!

1. Make a list of the qualities you like in yourself. Read it over aloud every day.
2. Do something special for yourself every day. You deserve to be pampered, too.
3. Put yourself first in your life. Your wants and needs are just as important as other people's.
4. Learn to say "no." You don't have to fulfill other people's expectations.

I know I've left out a lot, and I am probably horribly misquoting both of us. But that's the gist of it. I'd never thought of that verse in Matthew 22 that way before, but it all makes a kind of exciting sense. At least I know now why I've never been able to feel as preachers say I should about my family and nine-tenths of the people I know—and that it's not my fault. I have Ms. Langdon's word on that.

And it's really okay to think about myself and what *I* want! I'm reading through Ms. Langdon's prescription right now. I think I'll start with Miss Kitchener. She can take those choir practices and shove them down one of those dark and dirty latrines you find in backwoods Montana rest stops. Then I'm going to take out all that money I earned at Taco Bell this summer and go shopping.

PS. Now that the spell of Ms. Langdon's smile and voice is wearing off, I can't help a few misgivings. Will this really give me all that "self-esteem" and "self-fulfillment" she talked about? Will it drag Brian Andrew's attention from a certain flawless, if snooty, profile?

I guess there's only one way to find out.

*Part Three*

## *Thursday, September 26ᵗʰ*

The revolution began today! I told Miss Kitchener off, and it felt great.

I did it politely, of course. "I'm finding myself over-extended," I informed her in a cool, aloof tone, "so I'm going to have to cut the choir sessions. Would you please find someone else to take over effective as of this afternoon?"

Miss Kitchener was so shocked that for the first time I actually witnessed what authors mean when they write that someone's mouth flopped open like a dead fish. "You can't do this to me, Jana!" she spluttered, her voice rising to an unbecoming level for a teacher until she noticed that half the school was parading through the hall where we were talking and staring at her as they passed. "You're the only one in the school who can play these accompaniments besides me. And now that stupid doctor says my wrist is broken after all, and I've got to wear this thing for another two months. What am I supposed to do? I was counting on you!"

She looked ready to cry, and I almost weakened right there. Miss Kitchener isn't a bad person even if she did lose it last Friday. Then I remembered what Ms. Langdon said about always worrying about other people's needs and doing what makes *me* happy and not everyone else. After all, I never asked to take on those choir sessions, and if I hadn't been here they'd have had to come up with someone else. No one's indispensable, right?

So I steeled myself and said as much like Ms. Langdon's own phrasing as I could, "I'm sorry, Miss Kitchener. I understand your position, but I owe it to myself to consider my own priorities and needs first."

Well, she fussed and fumed, but there wasn't anything she could do about it because my playing was totally volunteer and extra-curricular. There has to be some parent somewhere who can come in for a few weeks.

I stopped by the newspaper room next to inform the hapless junior running that chaos that I wouldn't be available to write any more articles. I've already turned in the one on the senior retreat, a much sanitized and strictly factual version of what was in my journal. The other that I'd planned to do this weekend will just have to be reassigned.

"Oh, come on, Jana," he groaned. "Your articles are the only bright spot in this mess. You can't do this to me!"

A refrain that is becoming familiar. He looked even more desperate than Miss Kitchener, and as I looked around at the storm of old printouts and layout sketches, I could see why. *Inkblot* has never been as popular as *QUEST*—partly because the staff advisor assigned to it has never taken any real interest in the newspaper—and it looked like all he had there was a handful of green freshmen. Putting Joel Blumhurst in charge of the *Inkblot* hasn't been much of an improvement. I worked with Joel last year when I was still on newspaper, and even though he has developed reasonable competence at justifying columns of print, he can't write worth a Bolivian centavo and would never have ended up with the job if there'd been any other takers. To keep from patting the poor guy on the shoulder and reassuring him, "It's okay! Mama Jana's here to take care of those horrible, mean articles for you," I had to remind myself of how miserable I'd been before Ms. Langdon got ahold of me.

But I got out of there with one less commitment. Yearbook stays, of course. Copy editor may not be the height of prestige, but it is my only claim to fame at SCA. I don't need *that* much free time.

The first thing I did with those extra after-school hours was head to the mall, Mom, for once, being at home to keep an eye on her offspring. I really hated to spend my summer savings. I had it earmarked for my first semester of college, but this was a national emergency. Besides, I'm counting on those scholarships to cover what I need there. So I stopped at the cash machine, then was left with the question of just how to go about implementing all this great advice of Ms. Langdon. I've never been much for fussing with makeup, and Mom says I've got the style-consciousness of our church missionary closet. What I needed was an expert. So I headed for the most expensive salon in the mall, the one Denise is always bragging about, and picked out the most glamorous-looking operator there.

"Just show me how I can look my best," I begged her. "I don't care how much it costs!"

It took one $100 bill and part of another, but it was worth it! The body perm is one of these new soft and natural ones and makes my hair curl up beautifully around my face and down to my shoulders as I could never get it to do on its own steam. My eyelashes look longer and darker and my lips fuller, and the new eye shadow really does bring out the green in my eyes. As for the new clothes scattered all over my bed, well, I've heard of astrological signs, but I never knew before that people could be "seasons." I'm not even going to write here how much it cost to discover that I'm a "winter," but everything I bought today carefully matches one of the color swatches that was the only tangible item I got to take away from that session. As for that mustard yellow sweater Mom got me for my birthday, new or not, that's going to the Good-Will.

I still can't do anything about my figure (Mom always says I should stop worrying about it because I'll fill out soon enough and wish I hadn't, but I'll believe that when I see it!), and a twinge of conscience is nagging me about the dent I've made in my college savings. But for the first time in my life I can honestly say I look almost as good as Ms. Langdon managed to make me feel. I can hardly wait to unleash the new Jana on SCA High tomorrow!

*Friday, September 27th*

Ms. Langdon was right! There is nothing like knowing you're looking great to raise a girl's self-esteem. The perm and makeup looked almost as good today as yesterday. I wore one of my new outfits, and all the way to school I reminded myself that I am intelligent, talented, and have never looked better in my life.

And it worked! When I sauntered into first-period AP Psychology class with a toss of that perm and a smile—well, no one wanted to be too obvious, but every conversation stopped dead, and there was hardly an eye directed at any other point of the compass as I strolled over to my desk. Denise didn't have a single comment about my hair this time, but her mouth line thinned in a fashion unattractive enough to show that she's going to have to watch the way she frowns when she gets older. The reaction of the others made up for her. There were whistles and catcalls from a couple of the guys as I slid into my seat, and I've never had so much attention from the other girls. Even a couple of Denise's flunkies stopped by to ask where I'd gotten my hair done. Why didn't I do this years ago?

Knowing I look good has given me more self-confidence in other areas, too. Take study hall. As I wrote once before, Denise Jenkins has this nasty habit of making sly digs at the rest of the girls. She can hit off your weakest points to perfection, and if you react, she wins twice because it sounds like you can't take a joke.

Well, she'd been acting like a Rocky Mountain grizzly bear with a sore paw every time she set eyes on me today. So I wasn't too surprised when she came out with a loud—and, I'll admit, funny—comment comparing her own voluptuous curves to my almost non-existent silhouette. On any other occasion, I'd have just sat there, flustered and turning the same shade as my new fuchsia shirt, while everyone snickered. But today I was as calm as ice. Raising my voice just loud enough to be heard by two-thirds of the class without reaching the librarian's desk at the other end of the study area, I answered back in a tone as saccharin-sweet as her own, "Don't take it so hard, Denise! You're so pretty, you're sure to find a husband before your weight gets totally out of hand!"

It wasn't *that* funny, but everyone just roared—at *her*, for a change! Sally, who is always getting teased about her excess pound-age, hissed, "You tell her, Jana!" Scott Mitchell, who was laughing a lot harder than the situation really merited, offered, "You can have me, Denise! I don't mind fat women!"

Now, I've never known Denise Jenkins to change color with rage or embarrassment like us lesser mortals. But as the snorts and chuck-les and whispered repetitions rippled from one end of the library to the other, fire engine red flooded up her neck right to her hair-line, then receded, leaving her face sheet white right down to the pinched lines beside her nostrils. Picking up her books, she stormed out of the library. That's when the monitor finally called every-thing to order. Several of the girls came up later to congratulate me on getting back at Denise. And Scott Mitchell—yes, *the* Scott Mitchell, who's hardly acknowledged my existence since I first fell for him in junior high—actually invited me on a double date to-morrow to see that new movie everyone's been talking about. My first non-youth group date in months. For the first time in my life, I have an inkling of how it feels to be popular!

The one person who doesn't seem too impressed with the new me is Brian Andrews. He was there in study hall doing some re-search on the AP Psychology paper that's due next week, and I know he was close enough to overhear. But he wasn't laughing—I checked. Later on, he walked by me in the hall. He looked as though he was going to stop and talk so I flashed him that smile I practiced in the mirror this morning. All I got was this funny look, almost like, well, maybe he doesn't approve of the change?

But how could anyone like the old Jana better? Oh, well, there's other fish in the sea. I'm not going to let Brian Andrews' poor taste spoil the biggest social triumph of my life!

## Saturday, September 28th

The movie was passable, and Scott and Traynor Davidson, another SCA big-name athlete, were a riot. And not just in the sense of a good time. Traynor's date turned out to be Gloria Williams, one of Denise's regular bootlickers, but she was surprisingly friendly. Yesterday's triumph, I know. Scott and Traynor managed to embarrass both of us, shooting popcorn at people in the dark, then ducking whenever an indignant movie-goer turned around so that it looked as though the two of us were sitting alone. From the hisses, I'm sure more than one victim thought we were the culprits. But it was a lot of fun even if rather juvenile.

Speaking of riots, we had one at home last night. It's not that my parents object to an occasional weekend date, though it has to be double. My dad is a little outdated. (Ha! Ha! Get the joke?) But it completely slipped my mind when Scott asked me out that I'd promised to baby-sit Danny tonight, Dad being on night shift and Mom having another of her perpetual meetings.

I didn't think about it, in fact, until I got home and told my parents I had a date. Mom promptly flew into a rage and told me I'd already made a commitment and how could I do this to her, etcetera, ad nauseam. She had a point, of course. That's the second time in two weeks I've forgotten Danny. I'm going to have to start keeping a calendar. Still, it wasn't as though I'd done it on purpose, and I had every intention of tracking down another baby-sitter for the evening.

But when she started yelling and calling me selfish, I saw red.

After all, Danny is *her* kid, not mine! If anyone is selfish, it's Mom, not me! I decided right then that Ms. Langdon was right. Why should my life revolve around my parents and their needs? What about *my* needs?

I've never raised my voice to my mother before. I've never dared. I mean, she's three inches and fifty pounds bigger than me. But when she told me I'd have to call Scott and cancel, I hit the roof. I told her she could cancel her meeting. I was tired of sitting home alone weekends to be her unpaid baby-sitter so she could run around town, telling other people what to do. I told her it was time she started taking care of her own kid instead of always leaving it to me.

Mom screamed back that as long as I lived in her house, I was going to obey her rules. I wasn't going, and that was final. I don't know what I'd have done next. Maybe stormed out of the house if I was brave enough. No, I'd probably have given in as always, though the humiliation of having to call Scott up still gives me chills when I think of it. But that's when Dad stepped in.

I couldn't believe my ears! He actually said I was right. That he too had been feeling they were taking advantage of me. It wasn't right that I should have to give up my evenings with friends so they could be free to go out. Mom was as stunned as I was.

"Are you siding with her against your own wife?" she screeched.

"It's not a matter of siding." Dad sounded very tired though he'd slept most of the day since he was on graveyard shift last night, too. "I just think she's right. We *have* been making her stay home a lot with Danny. And he *is* our child, not hers."

So I got to go, and it was worth all the fuss, of course. But I do wish Danny hadn't been listening. I didn't mean for him to get the idea that I don't want him around. He's really not such a bad kid, at least compared to some of the rug-rats I've run across. He even cleaned the kitchen when I forgot last week so I wouldn't get in trouble with Mom. He's not much on wiping counters, so I still got chewed out. But it almost made up for the time an individual of the male persuasion actually called last month and Danny told him I was in the shower getting ready to go out with someone else . . . who happened to be nobody more than Amos Lowalsky picking me up for youth group!

And if I'd known Mom was actually chairing that meeting, I'd have tried a little harder to find another baby-sitter. As it is, I got home tonight to find out that Dad had switched his night shift to Sunday. He really hates missing church.

I know I'm doing the right thing for me, but I wish I didn't feel so guilty. I never meant for any of this to hurt anyone. I guess it's like Ms. Langdon said: I've got to learn not to care what other people think. Look at Denise Jenkins. People are always getting mad at her for letting them down or stealing their boyfriends. But it doesn't seem to bother her at all!

## Monday, October 14th

I just realized today how long it's been since I've written in my journal. Life is just so full since I started following Ms. Langdon's advice. It isn't that I'm so busy with school activities anymore. Without choir or newspaper, my after-school schedule is the lightest it has been since I moved into the more rarified atmosphere of secondary education, and I'll admit just between myself and this computer screen that I've cut back to a rather alarming degree on both studying and piano practice.

No, the reason I'm so busy is that I'm actually "in!"

It was that date with Scott that clinched my new popularity. I was rather surprised by this, as I know I never said or did anything particularly charming while on our date, plus I hopped out of the car just as he was about to try for a goodnight kiss. In spite of this, though, he seemed to have a great time, and come Monday lunch, he waved me over to sit beside him. Denise, cuddled up to his other side, looked to be having serious problems with her blood pressure, but she managed to restrain herself to one snide remark. And Gloria, if not as friendly as she had been out of Denise's earshot, was quite civilized. Scott, and Traynor too, made up for any lack of enthusiasm from the female contingent, and by the end of the lunch period, the rest of that crowd had made a tentative decision that anyone with the Mitchell and Davidson seal of approval must have something worth further investigation.

Since then, I've eaten lunch with them every day. It has been a bit of a disillusion to discover that the view is much the same as from anywhere else in the lunchroom, but the prestige value has been everything I thought it would be. In fact, my phone has been ringing off the hook ever since.

Denise has been the biggest surprise. Maybe she respects me for having stood up to her. Or if that's a little far-fetched, maybe it's because I am now, if not as gorgeous as she is, at least able to maintain a pretty good illusion, and she figures that keeping me close is better than risking Scott and certain others of her following wandering off in my direction. Either way, she has grown downright affable, inviting me to join in her study group for last week's American government test and passing me her brand-new fingernail polish to try out during chapel as though I were just another of her crowd. And we've been having a lot of fun together in study hall, trying to top each other's wittiest remarks. She really can be humorous.

Yesterday after school, she even invited me to go to the mall with her, Lisette, and Gloria. It's a sign of my growing self-aplomb that I didn't even blink at cutting yearbook or make any apologies beyond informing Sharon Spinelli that she could fill in for me. Of course I wouldn't have if I'd really been needed, but my copy section is ahead of schedule, and it'll do those kids good to practice writing captions without my looking over their shoulders. The shopping spree made a horrible dent in my remaining college savings, and I had to have a serious session with my conscience before it would shut up. But does Denise know her fashions! I've never been dressed better.

Annette and Sally have sure been acting oddly, though. I know I said I'd help Sally study for that American government test, but it wasn't a contract written in stone! As for Annette, she's been downright rude about my switching lunch tables. It isn't that I don't want to be with them anymore, as I've told them more than once. I'm just making some new friends. As if they wouldn't do the same in an instant if the opportunity were ever offered to them! I guess they're just jealous. And I can understand that. It wasn't so long ago that I was in their shoes.

Scott invited me out again last weekend—Pizza Hut, then bowling afterwards. This weekend we hit Barnum and Bailey's when it came through town with a whole bunch of his crowd. Southwest Christian Academy has some pretty strict physical contact rules on campus, and most of the parents expect them to be followed off-campus as well, including my own, so Scott hasn't shown any real surprise or outrage at the curbs I've put on some of his more enthusiastic advances. If anything, it seems to have spurred on his interest as though any woman who could possibly resist the great Scott Mitchell must have something special.

I don't think he'd believe it if I told him I was genuinely uninterested. The truth is, that junior-high crush of mine hasn't survived a closer acquaintance. Still, even if I could wish Scott had a little more between his ears, he is a real TCD (southern Californian for a Totally Cool Dude), and his attentions are as much an icon of "arrival" among the girls as Denise's are among the guys.

Strolling down the halls at his side and having a seat automatically saved for me in class have done wonders for my self-esteem. It does feel good to be on the receiving end for a change of that battery of envious female stares.

Dad hasn't said a word about my going out so much, and strangely enough, neither has Mom—though she does plenty of muttering under her breath about "selfish" and "ungrateful" when Dad's not around. She even stayed home from the D.A.R.E. rally Friday night when Dad couldn't get another baby-sitter. He must have really put his foot down!

Danny's been absolutely impossible, though. He's been spoiled having me around all the time, and he doesn't seem to understand that things have changed. Besides, it's not as though I actually promised to take him to the circus. I told him I'd think about it because Dad's on some real heavy case and I knew Mom wouldn't get around to it. But there was no way I could drag a seven-year-old along with Scott and his crowd. I can just imagine what Denise would have had to say! It's too bad the circus is only in town for a week. But what was I supposed to do? Anyway, Danny's young. There's always next year.

## Thursday, October 17th

I walked by the choir room on my way out this afternoon. Miss Kitchener was there, still in her cast. I guess she never found anyone to take my place because she was actually playing the piano, her fingers bending awkwardly out the end of the plaster as she tried to reach those treble clef notes. The choir giggled every time she hit a wrong note, and she looked thoroughly hot and very cranky. I waited for a twinge of conscience, but it never came. She should have been nicer while she had the chance.

## Monday, October 21st

I might as well drop this journal for all the time I have for it anymore. But Friday was the first major social event since the senior retreat, and I suppose I should chronicle it here. Actually, it was Field Day, hardly a barrel of thrills for those of us who lack any great athletic talent, but I managed to get some entertainment out of it. Scott and Traynor had all of us organized—our crowd, I mean—to cheer the "losers" over the finish line. Everyone cheers for the winners, right? We decided to give the losers some attention. It was really quite fun. Maybe a bit sarcastic at times, but we were just joking. I did discover not only that losers can't win but also some of them can't take jokes. Especially Marty Hansen, the SCA contender for the Guinness Book of World Records' "Fattest Kid in the World." He has absolutely no sense of humor!

Speaking of funny things, Mr. Schneider called for a sharing time at youth group last night. Not one person spoke up. Not even Amos Lowalsky. Mr. Schneider kept glancing over at me, but I just kept my mouth shut. Well, he asked for it!

My whole outlook on life has changed since that day in Ms. Langdon's office. I look in the mirror and just ooze that self-confidence and self-esteem Ms. Langdon talked about. I've kept up my makeup and hair, just like the stylist showed me, and I even feel better about my figure now that I've seen how Denise and some of the others salivate when I'm sinking my teeth into a third slice of deep-dish pizza.

I'm not the only one who's noticed the change in me either. Saturday, when I was at the rollerblading rink with Scott and some of the others, Scott skated in front of me to take both my hands in his, gazed soulfully down into my eyes, and informed me as though he'd just discovered the principle of gravity, "You know, Jana, there's something different about you."

"Just the new hairdo," I teased, tossing my now-shoulder-length curls back over my shoulders as I did my utmost not to skate into his blades.

"No, it's not that—not that your hair doesn't look great!" he assured me hastily. He shook his head, looking puzzled (as I said, it isn't his brains the girls go for). "No, it's you! You're more, more—" He floundered around for a bit before he got out, "You know, like Denise!"

Thanks a lot! But I know what he means. Now that my self-esteem has improved so much, I can saunter into class, bat my eyelashes, and toss off a clever quip with the best of them. At lunch, I carry my tray over to *the* table without worrying about someone saying, "Hey, these seats are all taken."

I love it! It's like Ms. Langdon said, "If you think you're cool, other people will too." Actually, she used more sophisticated language such as "The poor opinion of others is often a direct reflection of a poor opinion of yourself," but it amounts to the same thing.

The only sore point is that Brian Andrews still doesn't seem to know I'm alive. And everyone's noticed he is alive since the school board stretched a rule to let him play on the basketball team and he promptly sunk thirty points in our first game with St. John's Lutheran. Boy, can he move on a court! And he's so nice, too. He doesn't even seem to notice how popular he is, and he's just as polite and gentlemanly (if that's a word) to the homeliest girl on campus as he is to, well, the prettiest. I like that in a guy.

So why won't he talk to *me*? He can hardly get out a "hi" my direction. And when Denise and I tease him in study hall, he gives me this sober look as though he has no sense of humor, which isn't the case because I've seen him laughing and smiling with other girls. The closest to sociable he's come was a group discussion in English Lit on the connection between the rate of innovations in a society and the availability of good fiction books. No one else in our group had even considered the assignment, and they let us battle out our reports, agreeing on most things but arguing amicably over a few minor points—until I remembered that this was *not* the new Jana and dragged my new persona back into place.

Then he clammed up too and has hardly acknowledged my existence since. It's not as though I haven't given him any encouragement either. Today I even hinted that he join Denise and me and the rest of the crowd for lunch. Instead, he ate with Sandy Larson!

The one consolation is that he's giving Denise the same treatment. Denise, of course, tries to give the impression that it was *she* who lost interest, but she's pretty ticked off about it, especially since Brian has become a big name around campus. What's the deal? Is he scared of pretty girls? Or maybe he just likes the quiet, meek type. If so, Sandy Larson will be right up his alley. I must have dreamed up that day he told me he liked my hair.

Still, there are plenty of other guys who appreciate the new Jana Thompson. I've wasted enough time and thought on Brian Andrews. From now on, I'm going to put him out of my mind—and out of this journal!

## Thursday, October 24th

I missed yearbook again today. Scott invited Denise and Gloria and me over, along with some of the guys, to watch MTV. It was no big deal. I have my crew well trained, and they're doing fine on their own. But when Annette saw me leaving, she really chewed me out. She wouldn't even listen when I tried to explain. What is it with her? I never try to tell *her* what to do with *her* life!

I wish now that I'd stayed for yearbook, though, because Scott's wasn't nearly as much fun as I expected. MTV isn't exactly my taste in music. And those songs are worse in color than on CD. And to be sitting there in mixed company—well, I always thought Dad was pretty prehistoric about the music he lets us bring home, but maybe he's got a point!

The truth is (and I never dreamed I'd ever say this!), I'm getting a little bored with Denise and Scott and their crowd. Sure, they're the "beautiful people" and it makes me look good to be seen with them. But all they ever talk about is clothes (the girls) and sports (the guys) and the latest CDs and movie releases (both). They always seem to be keeping score over who's got the most boyfriends or is the most popular or the prettiest. And if I have to sit through one more conversation on how to keep nails from splitting or how to match your lipstick to your toe polish, I'll scream.

Okay, I'll say it! I miss Annette and Sally—and even my yearbook crew, aggravating though they can be. Maybe they aren't all TCDs. But they're a lot more interesting than this bunch.

### Monday, October 28ᵗʰ

I'm feeling a little down today. I don't understand it. Everything's going great at school, and of course I love being accepted and popular. But it seems that everyone I really care about (or thought I did before I learned I wasn't really capable of loving anyone in my present condition) is mad at me.

Of course, Mom's always griping about how selfish I am. That's nothing new, and since I know how little it means, I don't let it bother me a lot. But now Dad's upset with me. All this last month, since that first date with Scott, Dad hasn't said one thing about my baby-sitting Danny. He's the one who found a junior-high girl from our church to come over after school and on weekends when my parents are both out so that I would be free. But this Saturday she had some big test or project and couldn't come, and Dad asked me to watch Danny so he could take Mom to this SDPD Golf Tournament his precinct's been planning just about forever.

I wouldn't have minded if it was just a couple of hours. But he was talking 8 A.M. until evening! I told him I'd planned to go to the beach with some of the gang. Dad shot back that I'd been going out an awful lot lately, and it wouldn't hurt me to stay home one day. Really! As though I were a freshman instead of a senior.

"But it's one of the last weekends it'll be warm enough!" I informed him with creditable evenness of tone. "And I've already made arrangements. I can't let everyone down now." Then I came up with a perfect solution. "Why don't you just go and leave Mom home with Danny. You know she doesn't want to go."

I still don't know what I said wrong. I mean, it was true! I heard her say so myself. And Dad has said often enough that a bunch of grown men riding around in carts with a kid to carry their gear is the stupidest idea of exercise he's ever seen. I reminded him of that, but he said that wasn't the point and to drop the subject. There was no reason why he couldn't have gone to the tournament, and he's the one who chose to sit at home with Mom and Danny. But I can tell he's upset with me, even though he hasn't said anything more about it.

As for my one-time best friends, they walk by me as though I don't exist—something I really don't deserve. I mean, what have I done to them? I always stop to say "hi" every time I see them and am just as friendly as ever. But Annette stalks into yearbook and off into the layout corner without so much as a greeting. And Sally practically dissolved into tears last week at a little good-natured teasing Denise and I were doing (she's gained *another* five pounds, and there's no denying that her new dress does have some mild resemblance to a flowered tent). I apologized as soon as I saw she couldn't take a joke, but she hasn't so much as looked my direction since. Today I finally decided enough was enough and cornered her long enough to ask flat out what was wrong.

"What is it with you guys?" I demanded. "Why have you changed so much?"

Sally swelled up so red that round face of hers looked like a tomato.

"We're not the ones who've changed, Jana," she snorted. "It's you! You've been hanging around Denise and her pals so much you're starting to act like them."

Funny, that's just what Scott said, but from her, it didn't sound like a compliment!

Even Mr. B's been acting odd. The first time I missed yearbook, he was really nice about it. He even told me I'd gotten so pretty it was no wonder my social calendar was getting too full. But today after English Lit he nailed me and asked me where I'd been the last two sessions.

I told him I'd been busy, but he just shook his head and said, "This isn't like you, Jana. Is something wrong?"

"You wanted me to give them freedom to be creative," I argued, trying to coax him into a smile. But he remained dead serious and reminded me that the first *QUEST* deadline is next Monday. As though I'd forget! The yearbook is divided into five parts, and we have to get each to the publisher who specializes in doing the school yearbooks for this part of the state by a certain deadline. Whether that is absolutely necessary or just an incentive to keep the yearbook staffs—and advisors—from leaving everything to the last month, I don't know. But we have to pay a late fee if we don't get it in on time—or rather, we don't get the discount the publisher gives for keeping on schedule, and the school has gotten used to figuring that discount into their price.

Anyway, my crew is still right on schedule, and I told Mr. B so. But he made me promise I'd be there tomorrow and gave me this little lecture on being responsible and honoring commitments. Me, his best worker for the last three years!

I'd better break this off and go see what's wrong with Danny. He's been in his room bawling his heart out for at least ten minutes, and neither Mom nor Dad have shown up from downstairs to take care of it. I guess Dad's on duty. But Mom should have heard him by now unless her TV show down there is drowning him out.

∾

I just came back from Danny's room. I managed to coax him out from under his pillow—mainly by grabbing it and throwing it across the room—but he didn't want to talk to me. I had to threaten to call Mom before he finally wailed out, "You're always gone now, just like Mom and Dad! Now I don't have anyone to love me!"

I was so dumbfounded I didn't know what to say. Danny's always been the baby of the family, and if anyone's been spoiled and petted around here, it's him. Even if Mom's gone all the time, she lets him get away with stuff we'd never have dared at his age. And she's never let us girls crack down on him either, even when we're baby-sitting. Who'd have thought he could be feeling as unloved and unwanted as I used to feel?

He sounded so heartbroken, I felt terrible! I did my best to cuddle him and tell him I really do love him. But he just pushed me away and said, "No, you don't! All you care about are those new friends of yours. Just go away and leave me alone!" Then he jumped out of bed, recovered his pillow, and shoved his head back underneath. It wasn't worth another tussle so after a little more fruitless coaxing, I left.

I'm so confused! I've followed Ms. Langdon's advice. I've learned to love myself, just like she said. I'm attractive and popular and part of the in crowd. I'm doing what I want and having a lot of fun. So why don't I feel happier?

## Thursday, October 31st

My copy section met its deadline right on schedule this afternoon. Some of it wasn't written as well as I'd have preferred, but at least it's turned in and ready to send off. The photography crew finished on time, too. I have to admit, Amos Lowalsky has done a pretty good job as chief photographer. He never sticks his head out of the darkroom during yearbook sessions, but the pictures he's been sending my way for captions are the best I've ever seen. Wonders never cease.

But layout is another story! I don't know what Annette has been doing these last few weeks, but she is nowhere near ready for that deadline Monday. And after all her fuming about my occasional absences, two of her crew didn't even bother showing up today. Tomorrow is the Harvest Festival, SCA's sanitized version of Halloween, so there won't be any staying after school then. But Mr. B has asked for volunteers to come in Saturday morning to work with layout until the deadline is met. Last year I'd have jumped at the idea. Even besides the fact that Mr. B is a favorite teacher, whenever we get caught in one of these marathon yearbook sessions, we all bring in pop, chips, dip, cookies, etc. and make a day of it. It's still work, but we get a lot of fun out of it.

But not this time. Traynor Davidson managed to talk his dad out of their oversized van for the day, and Scott, Traynor, Denise, Gloria, myself and some of the rest of the crowd are going to a new surf pool that has opened up outside of San Diego. And I'm not the only one with plans for the day. Most of the crew had one reason or another they couldn't come. When it was narrowed down to Annette and Sandy and one other member of the layout crew, S & A defrosted enough to beg me to help. It felt so good to have them on speaking terms again. I might even have relented if Scott and Traynor hadn't poked their heads in on the way back from football practice, all sweaty and muscular and looking more masculine than ever.

"You've got to be kidding, Jana! You're not really going to stick around this dump when you could be catching the surf with us?" was their reaction when they gathered what the discussion was about, and they looked totally dumbfounded that anyone would even waste a thought on such an option.

How could I say yes then? Especially with all those younger girls sighing and looking envious. Scott and his crowd think yearbook is for geeks, anyway, and have been pestering me to quit. Besides, it's Annette's fault we're behind on that deadline, not mine. It would go against everything I've learned these past weeks—and probably not do Annette much of a favor either—if I let her irresponsibility mess up my own life and social activities. So I steeled myself against the look in her eyes and said no. I could tell Mr. B was disappointed, but he was nice about it.

"We could use your help, Jana," he told me with a smile that made up for yesterday's lecture, "but I guess it isn't really fair to expect you to miss an opportunity like this, is it, girls?"

S & A didn't answer that, of course. Their chill factor dropped back down to forty below, and they didn't send another word in my direction. Fine, if they want to be infantile, let them!

## Saturday, November 2nd

The Harvest Festival last night was outstanding; certainly the most exciting social event since I've been at SCA. Or perhaps it is just that my own part in such activities has changed. It was a costume party, of course, since it is advertised as a safer and more wholesome alternative to San Diego's usual Halloween mayhem. But instead of the usual witches, ghosts, vampires, Freddy Kreugers, and even more gruesome kooks you see around these days, everyone had to come as a historical figure. Those students with less imagination or cash tended to go in for the generic Bible characters with plenty of draped sheets and towels. But San Diego has its share of rental costumes, and there were Napoleons and Queen Elizabeths and pirates and Roman soldiers. Sandy Larson looked sweet and demure as the biblical Queen Esther, hardly my own assessment of that spunky lady's character. Denise Jenkins as the mythical Greek huntress Artemis was borderline for school dress code.

I myself splurged and rented a complete Marie Antoinette costume—satin, fake jewelry, hoop skirt, powdered wig, the works. The look in Scott's eyes and on Denise's face made it worth emptying out the last dregs of that college account. The whole evening was easily the pinnacle of my social success with not one moment where half-a-dozen members of the opposite sex weren't buzzing around me. The program was good too—the most hilarious being Brian Andrews' impersonation of a puzzled lion breaking one tooth after another on a rather tough Daniel in the lion's den. Who'd have thought it of reserved Brian?

Worlds of Water today was a lot of fun, too. But it started to turn cold around half past ten, and by noon it was pouring down rain, so we ended up coming home early. I had a hard time concentrating on Scott and Traynor's efforts to keep me up on a surf board, anyway. I kept thinking about Annette and Sandy and that yearbook deadline. I wonder if they ever finished or if they're still over there working?

## *Monday, November 4th*

I've been so stupid!! I HATE myself! I've thought other days were the worst in my life, but this one really is. And it's all my fault, too! I know that now.

Things have been going downhill since I picked up my report card at the school office this morning. I'd already seen the honor roll posted on every bulletin board in the school, and I just couldn't believe that not only was my name nowhere near the top, it wasn't even there. But when I opened my report card! Bs, Cs, even a D! Not a single A! I know I haven't been studying as much lately, but I never dreamed I'd slid that far! I still haven't dared show it to my parents. Can the school possibly revoke my scholarship this far into my senior year?

Then Sandy, sweet, gentle Sandy, who's probably never yelled at a living thing in all her life, practically bit my head off. All I wanted was to find out how things had gone Saturday. So I slid in beside her in Spanish class instead of the seat Scott had saved for me, ignoring her averted face, and determined to be friendly. She wouldn't even look at me while I told her how nice she'd looked Friday and how much fun Worlds of Water had been. But when I asked if layout had met their deadline, boy, did that get her attention!

"No, we didn't finish!" she snapped, finally turning her eyes my way as though trying to decide whether the cockroach in front of her deserved enough personal attention to even bother squashing. "We worked until midnight, then Mr. B had to send us home. Now we're going to have to pay the late penalty, thanks to you!"

I'd sworn not to let her get under my skin, but I lost my cool at that. "Don't blame it on me!" I snapped back. "It was Annette's fault the layout wasn't finished on time, not mine! What's she been doing, anyway?"

I never knew Sandy could look so stony. "It wasn't Annette's fault!" she said so scornfully there was hardly a trace of her usual soft drawl. "If you hadn't been so busy with your new friends, you'd have noticed she was out for most of the last two weeks with the flu. And two of her crew are down right now."

Then she clamped her mouth shut, and I was invisible again. Even when I begged her to explain, she refused to say another word. Then old Mr. Vargas, who has taught Spanish here since some of the graduating class's parents were in kindergarten, was all over us for whispering in class, so I had to give it up. I couldn't believe it! Annette out of school for two weeks and I hadn't even noticed? They could have told me! I mean, I'd never have dreamed of taking off with Scott and company if I'd known they were really in such a bind. Still, I was willing to admit I was in the wrong. So when lunch period came, I skipped my seat at *the* table to look Annette up.

She wouldn't even listen to my apology!

"Just save it!" she practically spit in my face. "You've made your choice. Go back to your 'cool' friends and just stay out of our lives. We don't need your help on layout, and I don't need you for a friend, either!"

I tried to explain about Ms. Langdon, and how I've been learning to be a new, more self-confident person, but she cut off my stammering and stuttering.

"Oh, yeah?" she accused with a bite like a Montana blizzard in her voice. "Well, personally, I like the old Jana better. Maybe she wasn't the beauty queen of the class, and maybe she didn't have all that 'self-esteem' you're talking about. But at least she was human and decent and kind to other people. Now you've got an ego as swollen as a hot-air balloon, and all you care about is yourself. You parade around with all the hot shots, completely ignoring your old friends. You hang around Denise making smart-alecky remarks, and you don't care whose feelings you hurt. Well, you may think you're really something these days. But as far as I'm concerned, what you've turned into is a selfish, stuck-up brat!"

I was stunned. Was that really how my friends saw me? Not sophisticated and charming and mature, but a brat? It was as though she held a mirror up to my face. And when I stopped being furious with her, I knew she was right. I *have* been selfish and unkind and a total jerk! All that sauntering down the hall in front of my friends with my nose stuck in the air. And that joking around in study hall and on Field Day. No wonder Brian Andrews turned so frosty. It makes me cringe to remember the things we said. I never even *liked* Denise and her crowd before this all started, and now I've been so proud of myself for learning to be just like them.

All that self-esteem I've worked so hard at acquiring has just flown right out the window! After all, what difference does it make to have a perm and new makeup on the outside if you're the world's sorriest excuse for a human being on the inside? I just don't understand! I've done everything Ms. Langdon said. So what's gone wrong? I'm sure she didn't mean for things to turn out like this!

*Thursday, November 7ᵗʰ*

I am still confused, but today life almost seems worth living again. It's as though I can make out the smallest glimmer of a light somewhere at the end of the dark tunnel in which I have found myself these last days. It's all been so strange—like an Alice in the Looking Glass version of my session with Ms. Langdon. My mind and emotions so muddled I'm not sure anymore what's up and what's down, and the ground that seemed so solid is suddenly quivering and turning to quicksand underfoot. And yet I can't feel quite as hopeless as I did this morning, or get Mr. B's words out of my mind.

I guess I should go back to that soul-wrenching revelation Annette threw at me Monday. I haven't been able to sleep or concentrate on pulling up my grades, wondering how many others agreed with the ugly picture she held up to me. Speaking of grades, Dad hit the roof almost as much as Mom over that report card, and I'm basically grounded until I can show some improvement. Annette and Sally are still giving me the cold shoulder, and Sandy too, though I never hung around her as much. But I haven't exactly felt like hanging around Scott and Denise and their crowd either. So I've been keeping strictly to myself, sitting in a back corner of the class and not talking unless the teacher calls on me, even skipping lunch so I don't have to face S & A or S & D and company. Scott has cornered me a couple of times to ask what's going on—especially after I turned him down for Friday night. But Denise and her bunch don't seem to miss me. Easy come, easy go, I guess!

I *have* been working as hard as I can on yearbook. I still feel so guilty about having skipped out Saturday that I even stayed behind today to type the new bunch of captions. I was just hitting print when Mr. B stuck his head in the door.

"You're still working, Jana?" he asked with surprise, but smiling and joking, not stern like the last time we'd talked. "We don't need to finish that yearbook tonight!"

I could tell he was remembering that other conversation, too, because he went on while he started shutting down computers, "You know, Jana, you're quite a puzzle this year. First my hardworking, responsible copy editor blooms into SCA's latest beauty queen—and a very pretty one, at that," he added with a twinkle in his eye. "And now, overnight, you've gone from the life of the party to the school hermit. It's good to see you working again, but I hope you didn't take me too much to heart the other day! There's nothing wrong with a smile or even a giggle now and then."

I didn't say anything, but something on my face must have said it for me, because he came right across the room and, not joking anymore, said gently, "What is it, Jana? What's gone wrong?"

That did it! I've always despised girls who cry on their teacher's shoulders every time they want a bit of attention or get a bad grade, so I tried to think of something else. But everything that's gone wrong this year seemed to well up inside, and the tears started making things blurry. Before I knew it, it was all coming out. How stupid I've been, what a mess I've made of following Ms. Langdon's advice, how absolutely everyone that matters is mad at me. Everything!

I'll say this for Mr. B. If he thought I was silly, he didn't say so. He just sat there without saying a word, patting my shoulder now and then. Finally, while I was trying to blow my nose without sounding too revolting, I snuffled out, "And now I'm back where I started! I just hate myself!"

That's where I got a shock, because he just sat there looking at me calmly and said, "You don't hate yourself, Jana. The truth is, you love yourself very much. And that's most of your problem, right there!"

I bolted straight up in my chair. "What do you mean?" I demanded. "I just told you I can't even stand being in the same room with myself."

"Oh, sure, there are things about yourself you don't like," he agreed. "And that isn't necessarily all bad. If you're doing something wrong or that really needs to be changed, then recognizing your weak points can be a real motivation to make some needed improvements. But hate yourself? Never!"

"But I do!" I protested. "I think I've *always* hated myself—except these last few weeks."

"Oh, yeah?" Mr. B was looking skeptical. He leaned back in his chair so that the front legs left the floor, which according to school rules we're not supposed to do. "Tell me, Jana, just how does a person act toward someone he or she loves? One's spouse, for example, or let's say a boyfriend?"

That was easy! I'd been through this with Ms. Langdon. So I told him just what Ms. Langdon had said and added a few more. Compliments. Gifts and special outings. Considering the other person the most important thing in the universe. I was just getting to the part about thinking all the time about the person you love and putting his happiness first when it started to sink in that this was a setup. Mr. B just kept nodding, but I could feel myself getting red, and I started to stutter. Finally I stopped and mumbled, "Okay, I get the point!"

Mr. B put a hand behind his ear as though he were deaf. "I can't hear you, Jana. Could you speak up?"

I didn't want to answer. But he just sat there, and I knew from long experience that he wasn't going to budge until he got an answer, so finally I got out, "You're trying to say I'm always thinking about myself and my own happiness, so that means I really love myself."

He gave an approving nod. "You're an intelligent person, Jana. I knew you'd figure it out."

Well, I knew there had to be something wrong with his logic, and I opened my mouth to tell him so. But just as I was marshalling my arguments, the front legs of his chair crashed down, and then he reached into his shirt pocket and pulled out one of those little pocket New Testaments. I hate it when people do that in the middle of a discussion! I mean, how are you supposed to argue against the Bible? But it was a shock when he flipped it open and I realized what he was reading. It was that same verse Ms. Langdon had read in Matthew about loving your neighbor as yourself.

"You see, Jana, it doesn't say here to love your neighbor *if* you love yourself," he said before I could snap my mouth closed, tapping the page as though I was supposed to be able to read it from where I was sitting. "It says *as* you love yourself. Contrary to a lot of our modern philosophy, God never told us to try to love ourselves. He didn't need to! We were born doing that, and we do such a good job of loving ourselves that we usually don't take a whole lot of time to think of anyone else."

I was beginning to feel like I'd been underwater too long. "But Ms. Langdon said—" I protested feebly.

"Yes, I know what Ms. Langdon said," Mr. B cut in. "I've taken some of the same psychology classes. Self-esteem. Self-fulfillment. Self-worth. Self-love. Tell me, Jana, do you see the common denominator in all these?"

Trust an English teacher to ask that! He waited for me to answer, and when I didn't, he answered for me. "It's 'self.' And that's the biggest problem with this philosophy you've swallowed, Jana. It's just plain self-centered. And I mean that literally. It's all centered on yourself. *Your* self-esteem. *Your* self-fulfillment. *Your* needs. It's certainly an attractive philosophy. You don't even have to try to love other people until you've loved yourself thoroughly—and of course, that could take the rest of your life! Sounds great, doesn't it?"

It was all exactly what Ms. Langdon had said. But from him it did seem a little selfish.

"Sharon Langdon is a nice lady," Mr. B went on. "She really cares about her job and about you kids, too. And I'll admit the philosophy she's advocating is very popular today—even among a lot of Christians. But it's certainly not what the Scriptures teach. You can read the Bible from cover to cover, and nowhere will you find a single passage where we are told to love ourselves or to put ourselves and our own needs first. Always, the emphasis is on loving others and putting them and their needs first."

He flipped the pages of that New Testament to Philippians 2 and handed it to me. "Would you start reading at verse 3, please?"

I read the first two verses: "Do nothing out of selfish ambition or vain conceit, but in humility consider others better than your-selves. Each of you should look not only to your own interests, but also to the interests of others."

Then I stopped because this was getting a little too pointed.

"But is it so wrong to want to feel good about yourself?" I wailed. "To have all that self-confidence and self-esteem Ms. Langdon talked about? I mean, even our pastor and all those youth speakers are always talking about that."

Mr. B's mouth quirked up at that, but it was a kind smile, not as though he were laughing at me. "If you want to know the truth, Jana, the kids I know with the most genuine self-respect and self-confidence are too busy thinking about other things and other people to waste a lot of time worrying about their 'self-esteem.' But let's see what the Bible has to say."

And he lifted the New Testament out of my hands. It's taken me half the evening and the concordance in Dad's office downstairs to find the verse he read, but here it is. Romans 12:3: "Do not think more highly of yourself than you ought, but rather think of your-self with sober judgment."

He slapped the book shut and stuffed it back into his pocket while he went on to explain, "'Sober judgment' means to have an honest estimate of your own abilities—*and* those of others. Not too high, thinking we are somehow superior because of those few things we do well. But not too low either, despising the gifts and abilities God has given us because they aren't what someone else has. It also means to have an honest estimate of both our good points and our weaknesses. The truth is, quite often when we don't like something about ourselves, it is because that something *is* un-likable. And I'm not talking about physical characteristics or per-sonality traits we can't change. Yes, we need to accept that God didn't make any mistakes when He made us as we are—though that doesn't mean, of course, that we can't make the best of the genetic hand God has dealt out to us."

He really did smile this time as he looked over my carefully-groomed hair and makeup and the new outfit I'd carefully chosen this morning. "As I can see you've learned. But if there is something that we—or others—especially dislike about us, more often than not you can bet that's God's wake-up call that there's something we need to work on in our lives. After all, the Bible has a word for people who think they've arrived at perfection and no longer need to do any changing. And that word isn't self-esteem. It's pride."

Every argument I had was withering on my tongue, so I kept them to myself and let him go on. "As to your question, Jana, there's nothing wrong with a healthy self-confidence based on knowing that you're using the talents and abilities God gave you to the best of your ability. Just as there's nothing wrong with admitting that you've got a long way to go in certain areas. But having a good 'self-esteem' as an end in itself has been highly overrated. Take yourself. You've gained a lot of self-confidence and self-esteem in the last weeks. Did it make you a nicer person?"

That was hitting below the belt! I felt myself turning red again. But I didn't have to answer because he went right on without pausing, "I'm sorry to say that I know a lot of wonderful parents who have fallen into that trap. Their children are well cared for, thoroughly loved, and have every possession their parents can afford. The parents sacrifice their own time and pleasures to devote themselves to their children. Their entire home revolves around those kids. And it works! Their kids have great self-esteem. But they are also some of the most selfish, uncaring people I've seen. Why? Because they've been taught all their lives that they are the most important people in the universe. Not once have they ever been encouraged to put anyone else's needs ahead of their own or to love others more than themselves."

I was about to say I'd give anything to have a home like that. Then I thought of some of the kids I know at SCA. Besides, I had this horrible suspicion that maybe he was still talking about me. I was getting angry by then because I'd expected some sympathy, and all I was getting was a lecture. Mr. B might be my favorite teacher, but I was tired of having verses shoved in my face. So I put every bit of ice I could scrape up into my voice. "Okay, I got the point! I screwed up! I was stupid! So what am I supposed to do now? Sit around and meditate on what a jerk I am for the rest of my life?"

Then I wished I could bite it back because Mr. B's face was suddenly sterner than I'd ever seen it. "What you need, Jana," he said, and he wasn't smiling at all anymore, "is to stop thinking about yourself altogether and start thinking about someone else for a change!"

While I was still catching my breath on that one, he added, "And I've got just the prescription for you. I'm involved in a youth center in downtown San Diego most Friday and Saturday evenings. A few of the students from school have been coming along to help out. Why don't you join us tomorrow night? Seeing the problems some of those kids face will make your own seem pretty puny."

A youth center? In downtown San Diego? Where gangs like the Werewolves hang out and muggers lurk around every corner? Right! Besides, this was getting a long way from where we'd started—which was *my* problems!

"You really think helping out in some center for lowlifes is going to make me feel any better about myself than all of Ms. Langdon's psychological junk?" I demanded, putting all the sarcasm I could into the question.

Then I felt ashamed because Mr. B was looking disappointed and a little sad, as though I'd completely missed what he meant. He was quiet for so long I was beginning to think he'd gotten disgusted with the conversation—and with me—and was calling it quits. Then he said slowly, "I can't say if it will or not, Jana. But just maybe you'll find out that feeling good about yourself isn't the most important thing in the world."

That's where the counseling session ended because the janitor stuck his head in the door right then and said we had to leave because he had to lock up. By the time I got home, I wasn't angry anymore. But I couldn't stop thinking about what he said, so I decided to write it all down. And once I began typing, it all started coming back, like I was sitting there listening all over again.

So whose prescription is the right one? Ms. Langdon's or Mr. B's? I wish I could say Ms. Langdon's because I have to admit her advice was a lot more appealing. But look at the trouble it's gotten me into.

One thing's for sure. An inner-city youth center isn't the way I want to find out!

*Part Four*

## *Friday, November 8th*

Mr. B stopped me in the hall today and asked if I'd like to go to that youth center of his tonight. I couldn't think of an excuse fast enough, so I told him I was too busy.

"Are you?" He raised his eyebrows just as he does when someone drags in some lame excuse for not turning in a homework assignment. Leaning up against the wall as though he had all day, he started counting off on his fingers. "Let's see, yearbook is only twice a week. Miss Kitchener mentioned that you're no longer helping with choir. And judging by the report card I saw, you're not exactly busy with your studies. Was there something I missed?"

I could feel my cheeks getting hot because I knew he knew I'd been twice as busy last year with newspaper and choir as well as yearbook. The choir even traveled on weekends when they were doing a concert in some church. And of course he knew I knew that he knew because I'd told him (is this confusing or what?) that I wasn't going out with Scott and his crowd anymore. But I didn't want to tell him the real reason, which is that I just can't stand urban inner-city youth—especially from downtown San Diego. It isn't hard to imagine just what kind of kids would wander into a youth center there. Bizarre clothing, hair painted every color in the book, foul mouths, and ideas so alien either they're from another planet or I am. Not to mention the drugs and all that territorial warfare. I've seen it before, and I have no interest in seeing it again.

It really isn't fair to send anyone from small-town Montana to a big-city junior high school. At least not without a few friends to back him up. My school in Montana had a couple hundred kids in the entire K-12th grade—and that was counting the kids who got bussed in from surrounding towns that were too small to run their own high school. The junior high I attended those few months here in San Diego had four thousand students and was the kind of place where guards had to walk the girls to the bathroom! You passed through a metal detector to get into school, and the number of guns and knives they frisked off the students actually made the news. Right after I left, an eighth grader smuggled in one of those plastic guns and shot a teacher.

My first day there, I got lost in the halls. School had already been going three weeks when we moved to San Diego, and everyone but me knew where to go. I finally blundered into a bathroom, and there was this girl. Purple hair cut two inches straight up, at least twenty gold chains, a skimpy tank top, a black leather jacket, and the tightest jeans you ever saw. Not to mention a dozen or more earrings in her ears, nose, lip, belly button, eyebrow— you name it, it was pierced. She, like me, should have been in class, but there she was sitting on the counter, smoking. Of course there were kids who smoked in Montana, but not many, and I'd never smelled anything like what she had. She must not have liked the expression on my face, because she told me to get out in the kind of terms that would have had my mouth washed out with soap. And since she was several inches taller and thirty pounds heavier than me with a scowl like a Tasmanian devil, I went!

When I finally found my homeroom and stumbled into a chair, guess who turned out to be sitting right behind me! And guess who was assigned to show the new girl around! Next thing I knew, we were behind the gym and she was offering me one of her joints.

I suppose I should have told her that as a Christian and an honest, upstanding citizen, God didn't want me polluting my body with drugs—followed by a spiel to convince her to clean up her own act. But she looked like the kind of girl who'd have a knife stuck down her boot, and I'd already discovered that I was a coward, so I just declined the offer as politely as I could. Not that my civility did any good. She flew into a rage and called me a lot of words I didn't know the meaning of back then.

That was the end of my tour, and I—stupid country hick that I was—assumed that was the end of her. Except that she and a couple of her pals rode the same bus. When I got off—alone, as Julie had some after-school activity I can't even remember now—so did they. I still get a sick knot in my stomach when I remember the rest. They knocked me into a drainage ditch, and every time I'd crawl out, they'd push me back in. By the time they got tired and left, I was soaked and muddy and my new school clothes were ruined.

In Montana they'd have been suspended, at the least. But when my dad called the school, they told him they couldn't do anything about it. It happened off school property, and anyway, such behavior was "within the bounds of normal student roughhousing" (like flushing kids' heads down toilets and bullying them out of their lunch money). I'd have to toughen up and learn to deal with it myself.

I was in that school until Christmas, and I hated every minute! The kids cheated all the time, and I found out only geeks did homework. No one could understand you if you didn't swear at least once every sentence, and three of my classmates were pregnant by the end of the semester. I never did make any friends, and the best part about switching to Southwest Christian Academy was leaving those kids behind.

Anyway, that's to explain to my grandkids why I'm so sour on urban youth (if I ever let them read this, which I'm beginning to doubt). And to explain why the last place I want to help out at is some youth center in gangtown San Diego where the kids are undoubtedly even meaner and tougher than they were at Costa Baja Junior High. As far as I'm concerned, any problems they have, they've earned!

Of course, I didn't tell Mr. B all that. But I did tell him I didn't think my parents would want me around kids like that. After all, that's why they pulled me from public school in the first place. But he just said, "Why don't you ask them, at least?"

That floored me. So I came up with the first excuse I could think of. "Maybe some other time. I have to baby-sit my little brother tonight."

He didn't push me any further, just reminded me that they'd be going tomorrow too, and if I changed my mind, they'd be leaving from the school at six o'clock. I hurried home, worried that maybe Dad was working or Mom had a meeting and that they'd already called a baby-sitter. But for once they were both home on a Friday evening. They both looked stunned when I offered to baby-sit, and it took a lot of doing to talk them into going out. But I could just see Dad running into Mr. B somewhere and mentioning that they'd been home all evening, so I kept pressing. And when Dad saw that I was serious, he actually started to get excited and coaxed Mom into dressing up for her favorite restaurant.

Danny was so thrilled when I told him the evening was his, I thought he'd burst. We played hide-and-seek in the dark and flash-light tag and endless games of Junior Monopoly and checkers, all of which he won hands down. Usually, when I baby-sit Danny, I send him off to watch TV or something so I can study. So I was more than a little surprised how much fun it could be having the brat around. He's really kind of cute! Mom and Dad went to a movie after dinner. When they got back around eleven, Mom was actually smiling, and Dad looked happier than I've seen him in a long time, and I felt this warm glow inside as though I'd finally done something right. Maybe this will make up for disappointing Mr. B about that youth center.

*Saturday, November 9th*

I went!
I never meant to, but by this afternoon the weekend seemed a

century long. So long that I even told Dad about Mr. B's invitation. But instead of the decisive no I'd expected, he thought it was a great idea. "It might do you some good to see how other folks live," was how he put it. I guess I should have figured, being a cop, he'd see it that way.

I still wasn't planning on going. I even volunteered to baby-sit again, since Mom had a meeting. But Dad said that was okay, he'd be home. In my mind's eye, I could see this endless succession of empty Friday and Saturday nights, and I was wishing I hadn't been so quick to turn down Scott's invitation to go skating. It's not that Mr. B's suggestion sounded like an exciting alternative, but when Mom made a sarcastic crack about the popular Jana Thompson having to sit home alone for a change, that decided it!

Dad let me take his car, but the traffic was terrible, and by the time I got to the school, the van was already pulling out of the parking lot. But it backed right up when I turned in, and Mr. B leaned out the window. I was expecting some mildly sardonic comment about changing my mind, but he just commented, "Glad to have you with us, Jana," and told me to park my car and climb in.

So I climbed in—and then almost climbed out again.

Mr. B had said there'd be other students from SCA, but not who. There were six in all—a couple of junior guys and a sophomore girl I didn't know very well. And Amos Lowalsky. Now who would have dreamed he'd ever go in for anything like this? He's never mentioned it at youth group. Or maybe he did when I had him tuned out on one of those long monologues of his.

But the other two! It *would* have to be Brian Andrews and Sandy Larson. After the way I spilled my heart out the other day, you'd think Mr. B would realize what kind of an awkward situation he was putting Sandy and me in! And I wasn't exactly thrilled to see Brian Andrews there, knowing just what kind of an opinion he must have of me after these last weeks. To make things worse, the instant I scrambled into that empty front seat beside Mr. B, everyone started clamoring, "Hey, you can't sit there! That's Karen's place!"

I was so mortified I almost crawled out right then to go home. But Mr. B was smiling and Sandy called, before I could climb out, "Come on back here, Jana! There's plenty of room!" She seemed a lot more friendly than I'd expected, and if Brian's opinion of me was as poor as I deserved, he didn't show it, but said, "Hello, Jana," in his sober way. After a quick mental debate, I decided I'd look more like an idiot if I left than if I stayed. So I crawled in back between Michelle, the sophomore girl, and one of those junior guys, and pretty soon I found out who Karen was.

We'd left the school behind and been driving about ten minutes when Mr. B pulled the van up outside an apartment building. Mr. B honked and a woman—actually more like a girl because she wasn't many years older than I—hurried out. A chorus of "Hi, Karen" informed me who she was. Mr. B didn't say anything, just nodded as she got into the front seat. But the way they smiled at each other—well, I've never thought of Mr. B as anything but a bachelor, but something tells me maybe he won't be one much longer!

Mr. B had barely pulled away from the curb before Karen turned around to welcome me. I still wasn't too excited about this whole thing, and I didn't really want to like her, but I couldn't help it. Like I said, she's just a few years older than me and not much taller with chin-length flaxen blonde hair and a nose that tilts just a little with a scattering of freckles across the bridge. She isn't exactly what I'd call pretty, but you somehow forget about that when she smiles. Like Mr. B, she gives you the feeling that she'd still like you even if you let the social mask slip and let her see the real person lurking behind it.

The others were all talking and laughing and teasing each other with that easiness a group gets when they've worked together in close circumstances, even Brian and Sandy, who are both so quiet at school. I can't say they were deliberately trying to exclude me, but the only topic of conversation was this youth center and people they knew there and things they'd done, and I felt left out and wished I'd stayed home. Then Karen started asking me questions about myself and pulling me into the conversation, and after a while I realized I was almost having fun.

But that was as good as it got. The youth center was a world of distance—well, half an hour, anyway—from the neat suburban neighborhoods around SCA's carefully maintained grounds. The further we drove, the dingier and dirtier the buildings got and the more trash-littered streets and sidewalks and parking lots became. We were threading our way through a maze of grimy, old apartment buildings when a two-story brick building suddenly emerged between two of them like some elderly dwarf squatting between a couple of tattered and disreputable hobos. A sign above the door that must have been the only fresh paint in that neighborhood besides graffiti announced "SAN DIEGO YOUTH AND FAMILY CENTER."

We'd barely pulled into the strip of graveled parking between the Center and its right-hand neighbor when a gang of teenagers mobbed the van. They were just the sort I'd expected—the punk type with hair twisted and teased and painted into a psychedelic nightmare and clothing ensembles and costume jewelry that were not only from some other galaxy but also seemed far too expensive to have been come by legally in that kind of neighborhood. They were all pounding their fists on the windows and sides of the van, and the language coming through Mr. B's open window was as thick as an R-rated movie.

The symbol of one of San Diego's more notorious street gangs painted in bold, fire-engine red slashes on the side of the closest apartment building—not the Werewolves that the SDPD has been having so many run-ins with, but their archenemies, the Devil's Angels—did little to reassure me. I could have sworn we were about to get robbed or murdered or worse, but no one else even blinked an eye. Before I could even suggest that we call 911, the others had all piled out, talking and laughing and even hugging as though these street punks were long-lost relatives.

It was Karen who poked her head back into the van to find out where I'd gone. She laughed at my expression and coaxed, "Come on, Jana, it isn't so bad once you get to know them."

A point I could have disputed when I stepped out of the van right onto something that felt suspiciously squishy. Rather like a mud-filled balloon. I looked down to see my white leather sandal planted smack in the middle of a very full disposable diaper. A dumpster stood against the Center wall, but it was overflowing, and dogs (or something more sinister! The Dumpster Monster?) had ripped open the bags and strewn the garbage all over the street. I almost lost Mom's meatloaf right there, but Mr. B was already calling for volunteers to clean up the mess.

*That* scattered the crowd as though he'd tossed a grenade in their midst. I didn't really expect to see any more of them. But hardly a minute later, the toughest-looking of the bunch—a huge, black kid with cornrows making the weirdest designs all over his head and a gold grill covering his upper front teeth—reappeared with a stack of plastic garbage bags. When he started handing them out with a scowl as big as his face and a jerk of his thumb toward the mess, there wasn't a single attempt at protest.

The clean-up didn't take long with everyone working. I even did my share, picking through the debris for items that were neither slimy nor associated with human waste. It wasn't until we were finishing that I realized that Mr. B and the girls, including Karen, had disappeared. Stacking my sack beside the dumpster for the next dog or alien creature that came along, I trailed Brian and Amos and those street punks up the cement steps into the Center, more than a little put out, I'll admit, over having been dumped.

The noise almost blasted me back out the door. The place must have been an old warehouse, because most of the first floor was one huge, high-ceilinged room that had been turned into a gym. A pack of juvenile gangsters was cheering a wild basketball game at one end, and there was a volleyball net, Ping-Pong tables, and weight-lifting equipment at the other, all in full use.

But that wasn't where the noise was coming from. When my ears had readjusted their decibel intake, I traced the worst of the racket to a makeshift stage at one side of the gym. In the middle of the stage, two speakers taller than me (that would have probably been adequate for an entire stadium) were blaring out a rap beat while a couple of girls in mini-skirts gyrated to the music, chanting karaoke-style into a couple of cordless microphones. Seated so close to the woofers that it should have blown their ears out were a couple guys strumming along on electric guitars. It wouldn't have been so bad if they'd been playing the same chords as the sound track. My piano teacher would have cringed if she hadn't already had a coronary over the style of music.

But the lyrics—at least what little I could catch of them—weren't the gangsta' rap I'd have expected. I caught "God" and "Jesus" both before I gave up trying to figure out that tongue-twisting patter. The soundtrack continued to blast out its beat as we crossed the floor, but the musicians stopped when they saw us, and the two mini-skirts leaned over the edge of the stage and called, "Hey, Amos, get your rear up here and give us some percussion."

Well! I'd already had my share of surprises that evening, but nothing like the shock of seeing Amos Lowalsky, the same guy who can hardly get a girl's name out without stuttering or approach one without tripping over his shoelaces, wave back with a big grin that said this was nothing new, then bound up on stage to settle himself behind a drum set I hadn't had time to notice. I didn't even know he played. But the biggest shock was that he was good! He nodded with a cool authority I didn't know he possessed for the other musicians to take up where they'd left off, then attacked those drums with a flurry of bass and cymbals that had half the gym breaking off what they were doing for a burst of applause. He was like Dr. Jekyl and Mr. Hyde or something! Come to think of it, maybe he hasn't been stuttering so much these last couple months—not that I've addressed myself in his direction enough to really notice.

By the time everyone had turned back to their own activities, the garbage detail had carried Brian and the other guys off into a basketball game, which left me standing with stinking hands in the middle of the gym floor, wishing again that I hadn't come. I couldn't see Karen or Sandy or the junior girl anywhere, and I was ready to storm out and flag down the first taxi, if they had them in that part of town, when something tapped me on the shoulder. I jumped half out of my skin and whirled around. Mr. B frowned down at me.

"So this is where you are, Jana," he informed me as though I didn't know. "I have to rush a patient into Emergency. Consuelo here says she'll show you around and get you started."

Patient? Started?

But Mr. B was in an obvious hurry, his eyes already moving past my shoulder to some point on the other end of the gym. Before I could even ask what I was getting myself into, he'd rushed off, leaving me alone with the girl who had undulated up beside him. Yes, undulated! Just check the thesaurus. There is no other word to describe that thrust-forward, hip-swinging walk.

Consuelo was my age and might have been really pretty—all that wavy dark hair halfway down to her waist and a figure I'd have killed for popping out of those skintight jeans and halter-top. But her hair was all scraped over to one side with a big orange stripe running down the middle like a skunk or the mother on the Addams Family, and there was so much makeup on the one eye you could see, it was anyone's guess what she looked like underneath. The way that eye traveled up and down the outfit I'd found on that last shopping trip made me feel like I was in one of those dreams where you find yourself at a party in your underwear. My heart hit the bottom of my sandals. Hadn't I had my fill of girls like her?

But all she said was, "We'd better find you something to cover that up if you ever want to wear it again." Whatever *that* was supposed to mean!

She really wasn't as bad as she looked. Her language was cleaner than a lot of what I could hear flying around me with only an occasional four-letter word slipping out. Then she'd shoot me an embarrassed glance and apologize. She led me across the gym, popping bubbles with a huge wad of chewing gum and chattering above the music and Amos Lowalsky's drums about how wonderful Mr. B and Karen were and how great it was to have someplace to get off the streets in the evenings. When we got to the other side, she opened a door and hollered, "Hey, Karen! Mr. B says this one's for you."

I saw then what she meant about my clothes. The room on the other side of the door wasn't much bigger than our bathroom back home. But it was set up like a doctor's office with an examining table and sink and cabinets full of medical supplies. Karen had a toddler up on the table, screaming as though he were in the process of being murdered. The mother, in a sari, was trying to hush him in what I guessed to be Hindi while Karen swabbed his arm with alcohol. We had just stepped in the door when the kid puked.

Karen was too distracted to give me much of a welcome. "Thanks, Jana. I can use a hand here," she nodded at me, already wiping up the vomit with some baby wipes. "Sandy and Michelle are in the kitchen getting the refreshments ready, so why don't you wash your hands and help me with these vaccinations."

So that's where the other girls had disappeared to! Consuelo pointed me through another door, and if the office was the size of our bathroom, the bathroom was no bigger than a telephone booth. By the time I'd scrubbed the garbage stink off my hands and backed out, Consuelo had scrounged up from some rag bag an old lab coat that reached to my knees. While I tugged the unsightly thing over my brand-new outfit, comforting myself that at least no one I knew was going to see me in it, she flung open a door at the end of the room. Through it I could see a much larger room packed with women and children and even a few men—all looking "economically disadvantaged," as Mr. Schneider puts it in Social Studies class.

"You want I should send them through?" she demanded loudly, popping her gum again.

That's how I found out that the San Diego Youth and Family Center—or the Center, for short—has a clinic in the evenings and that Karen is the doctor who runs it. And that's how I ended up spending the rest of my Saturday evening swabbing arms and wiping sniffly noses while Karen gave vaccinations and handed out prescriptions and even sewed up a couple of knife wounds. A long way from last week's surfing with Scott and company!

Consuelo disappeared early on. But when I peeked out into the waiting room while Karen was checking one very pregnant Cambodian woman whose three kids we'd just vaccinated, there she was. She was unlike any nurse's aide I've ever seen with that orange stripe and chewing gum, moving traffic along into the examining room with surprising order and helping the patients who couldn't write or spoke only Spanish fill out their forms.

But the big surprise was the secretary or receptionist, or whatever title he was using, who was handling the paperwork behind the battered desk near the outside door. It was that big black kid with the cornrows and gold teeth who had spearheaded the garbage detail. Armal was the only name I caught. He wasn't such an outlandish choice as he looked, though, at least for that neighborhood. The place was noisy with crying babies and adults complaining in half-a-dozen languages and even some pushing and shoving, but all Armal had to do was stand up and flex those massive biceps of his for things to quiet right down.

We'd just finished the last patient—a pre-adolescent who'd gashed his arm playing street hockey, then played macho so that it was going into secondary infection by the time he dragged himself in—and I was congratulating myself that I'd handled the whole gory mess pretty well when there was a sudden commotion outside and Consuelo popped her head in to say, "This one's bad, Karen!"

It was a woman with a baby. The mother couldn't have been any older than Karen, but her shriveled-up face was at least ninety. She was shaking so badly she could hardly hold on to the filthy bundle she had clutched to her chest, and I've never seen anyone so skeleton thin except in news clips of African famine victims.

But that was nothing compared to the baby. It wasn't more than a few days old because the umbilical cord was still attached, tied off with a dirty rag. The dish towel in which it had been wrapped was worn thin, and despite the November chill, its only clothing was an old cloth diaper that stunk like a sewage plant and a toddler's T-shirt that came down over the diaper like a nightgown. There weren't even any plastic pants, so the towel and T-shirt stunk as bad as the diaper.

It was neither cute nor plump like every baby I'd ever seen. Its arms and legs looked thin enough to snap in two with the shape of the bones pushing against the skin. Its eyes were sunk into sockets that looked like dark bruises, and the skin was pulled so tightly across its little face you could actually see the outline of its skull underneath. It didn't look as though it should be alive. But for all its frailty, it was strong enough to scream more than you'd think a newborn could and thrash its tiny arms and legs as though some cruel person were deliberately sticking pins into it.

I was so terrified the baby was going to die right in front of me, I could feel myself hyperventilating. But Karen didn't blink an eye, examining it as calmly as though it wasn't screaming its little head off. It was a girl, we found out when we peeled off those rags, and that dirty diaper had infected the area where the umbilical cord was. Karen gave the baby some kind of shot. Then to my horror, she handed the frail infant to me and told me to clean her up while she took care of the mother, who was still shivering and beginning to do some flailing around of her own.

For the second time that evening, I almost lost Mom's meatloaf. I never did like changing diapers, and this baby was utterly disgusting. It must have been days since it had been changed! I tried to shut my mind off from the smell, but she was still screaming and fighting so hard I could hardly keep a hold on her, much less get her into the tub I was filling with warm water in the sink.

Then Consuelo was beside me, handling that baby with as much competence as she'd handled the waiting room while I worked on the scrubbing end of things. By the time we'd finished the bath and gotten the little thing into a disposable diaper, the mother's own shot had taken effect, and she was no longer shaking but slumped over staring at the reflection of the overhead light on the metal frame of the examining table. Her eyes were wide open and had so much pupil showing it was hard to say what color they should have been. While I dug out some second-hand baby clothes from a box under the medicine cupboard, Karen called Consuelo over and told her, "I'm going to have to take these two to the hospital. You girls close up the clinic and tell Armal that I really do appreciate his help. I'll be back as soon as I can."

Then she was gone, leaving Consuelo and me to clean up the mess. While we scrubbed, I asked Consuelo if she knew what was wrong with the baby. She stared at me as though I were from another planet. "You've never seen a crack baby?" she demanded incredulously. "Where have you been?"

Well, of course I've read about such things. Some junkie gets pregnant, the baby gets addicted to its mother's drugs, then goes into withdrawal after birth. But reading the clinical details and seeing the horror of it are a universe apart.

Things didn't improve greatly after that, either. Consuelo locked the clinic doors, then asked me to give the key to Mr. B before taking off as fast as she could in the opposite direction. Fine, I wasn't exactly begging to hang around with her either. But I'd no sooner returned the key when Mr. B shooed me off to "mingle" and "be friendly."

"It isn't enough just to meet their physical needs," he told me, waving a hand at the budding juvenile delinquents I could see clustered all over the gym. "That's just a temporary fix. What we want is for these kids to know just how much God loves them and the difference He can make in their lives. That's the only way they are ever going to find any real hope for the future."

Sure, I'm going to walk up to these guys and talk Christianity to them! Everyone I saw looked as though they'd be more comfortable at a Halloween party or pulling a switchblade on some crippled old lady than hearing about God!

Mr. B was bustling off again, so I looked around for an SCA face, thinking I could at least hang around behind one of them while they did the mingling. But Brian and the other guys had disappeared somewhere, and the only familiar faces I saw were Sandy and Michelle across the gym behind a long table that was still littered with the remnants of whatever the refreshments had been. There was no way I could head over there with things as they were between Sandy and me. So I stood around, feeling like an idiot and no doubt looking like one too, until a girl in a denim mini-skirt and heels so high she should have been tottering swaggered up, demanding to know in between the unprintable language where I came from and what I thought I was doing there. She looked East Indian, but she dressed and talked pure punk American.

In fact, she reminded me so much of that marijuana-smoking bully from junior high that I was backing up even as I stammered out, not my current address where I'd spent the last five years, but that I was from Montana. I was bracing myself for anything but a peaceful response, so I was totally floored when she asked wistfully if I'd ever lived in the woods. It seems that her favorite TV rerun as a kid was "Lassie" and that she'd always dreamed of living in the country and having a dog.

"'Course, you can't have one around here," she added, pulling out a flaming red lipstick to retouch her mouth. "Someone'd poison it in a week!"

Well! Who'd have thought that these people want anything different than what they've got?

It was eleven o'clock before Karen got back and we were finally able to leave. Sandy and Michelle and the others were all keyed up, talking about the different kids they'd worked with. Amos had to tell all about how one of those guitar players had asked him to explain what it means to be a Christian. Everyone else listened with what actually seemed like real interest, and he didn't stutter once. It turns out that summer youth ministry he kept talking about at youth group and the senior retreat was the Center.

Then Brian dragged out a guitar, and pretty soon they were all singing. They all seemed so alive and happy and—oh, I don't know, in tune with each other. All I felt was exhausted. I don't understand! I grew up going to church just like they did, and I've always done my best to be a good Christian too. But I have to admit, there's something they have that I don't—even Amos Lowalsky.

I asked Mr. B why I got stuck in the clinic while everyone else was out having fun. But he just grinned and told me, "Everyone takes a turn in the clinic. But we like to throw newcomers in at the deep end—just to see if they're going to sink or swim. Karen says you swam very well."

When Mr. B dropped us off at the school, he and Karen asked if I wanted to come again next week. I told them it wasn't exactly my sort of thing. But I'm not sorry I went just this once. Some of it was downright revolting, and none of it was pleasant. But it was certainly educational to see how that other half of the world lives. And I do respect the way Mr. B and Karen—and the others too—give up their time to help those people. I only wish I could be more like them—not that there's much hope of that!

## Wednesday, November 13th

Monday I went crawling to Annette and Sally. I told them I was sorry for being such a jerk and—very humbly—asked for their forgiveness. They were nice about the whole thing. Nicer than I would have been! So I'm eating lunch with them again, and though I still feel a pang of loss when I walk on past the "in" table with my tray or cross glances with Scott's disgruntled glare, I have no real desire to go back. None of them seem to miss me, anyway. Scott's the only one who's even bothered to inquire why I left. I'm afraid most of the high school probably think he ditched me. I don't even want to know how many of those figure it serves me right.

Today, though, lunch was lively enough to make me forget what I've lost. Sandy joined us, and then next thing I knew, Brian and Amos and Peter Ramsey, one of the juniors who went along to the Center on Saturday, plopped their trays down across from us. Amos didn't say much, and Brian talked mostly to Sandy, but Peter did a lot of teasing about my initiation into the seamy side of life, telling Annette and Sally apocryphal tales that had me close to breaking my tray over his head. And after awhile, Brian lost that remote look he's had for me these last weeks and unbent enough to send the occasional remark my way. Maybe in time he'll forget what a fool I've made of myself.

Anyway, it's good to be on speaking terms with my friends again. What I never expected, though, was to have so much time on my hands. I've always griped about my busy schedule, but now that I'm not hanging around with Scott and his crowd almost every afternoon, I've got too much time. Yearbook will get pretty wild after Christmas, but until that next deadline comes up it's just a few hours a week, and this week Mr. B cancelled both sessions to make up for all that overtime people put in on that last deadline.

I am studying again and practicing piano. I have enough time in study hall to take care of most of that, leaving my after school hours and evenings pretty empty, which is the last thing I need as it just gives me more time to think. I was desperate enough last night that I even volunteered to take over baby-sitting Danny again. Dad just about fell out of his armchair in shock, but when he'd recovered, he said no. He was grateful for the offer and might take me up on it sometime, but for the moment he felt things were working out pretty well the way they were. This other girl needed the job, and he wanted me to be free to go out with my friends.

He seemed so pleased with his arrangements, I couldn't tell him my schedule wasn't exactly packed anymore. But I did tell him a little about the Center and the crack baby I'd washed. Then he told me a few stories of the addicts he's had to pull in off the streets. I think that's probably the first time I've sat down and actually talked with Dad in years.

I am still keeping up my hair and the makeup and clothes too, within reason. That was one thing Ms. Langdon had right. I don't have to go around looking like a slob. But I don't get a lot of attention from anyone now that I've dropped the "in" crowd and the Denise-style sauntering and hair-tossing. As for Scott Mitchell, he hasn't spoken to me since I told him I wouldn't go out with him again. I guess it just goes to show it wasn't really me who was so popular, it was that wise-cracking, hair-tossing flirt. Now that she's gone, so's my popularity!

It isn't that I really want to be like that anymore. I listen to Scott and Traynor's smart-aleck remarks in class and Denise and her friends sneering at the other girls and parading their ignorance of every subject on the planet outside their wardrobe, and I wonder how I could have ever thought they were so much fun to be around. I do feel a lot better since I cut loose from them, and it's certainly improved my grades. But I don't really want to go back to the old Jana either—sloppy hair and clothes, always worrying about whether people like me or not, always trying to impress the guys and my teachers.

So who am I now? And what *do* I want to be? I don't really know, but I feel kind of empty inside.

## Thursday, November 14th

I walked by the newspaper room after school today. Joel Blumhurst and the *Inkblot* crew were in there having a meeting, and did they look glum! The first issue came out last week—almost a month late—and Joel was right. My retreat article was the only mildly redeeming feature in the whole thing, and even that wasn't exactly one of my better efforts. Add in all the typos and sloppy layout, and I knew just what kind of ribbing they'd been getting because I'd overheard some of the remarks. Joel saw me standing in the doorway, and his face brightened so much that I found myself being drawn into their council of despair. Before I knew it, I'd agreed to a couple articles for the next issue and even to help them a bit with the layout in my spare time.

I was just leaving there when I ran into Miss Kitchener. She still had that cast on and was juggling her music and purse rather unsuccessfully with the other arm. Unlike Joel, she looked far from pleased to see me, but I swallowed my pride to ask how much longer she'd have the cast and whether she'd ever found someone to take my place.

"Another two weeks," she answered, eyeing me suspiciously as though trying to figure out just what motive I had for inquiring. "And, no, I haven't found anyone to play. I'm doing the best I can, but I sure don't know what we're supposed to do about that Thanksgiving assembly coming up."

Her relief when I told her I'd play for the next two weeks made me feel utterly ashamed. So some of those empty hours are filled back up again. I'd like to think I've made a few things right, anyway.

There was something on the news this evening about some more gang fighting downtown. Just what, I'm not sure because I only caught the tail end. There's always some kind of fighting going on down there, and I don't usually pay much attention. In fact, it doesn't usually even hit the news unless it's been a slow day for accidents, murders, and other mayhem in the city. But the address they were giving wasn't far from the Center, and I couldn't help wanting to know if any of the kids I'd seen there had been involved.

I wonder if that crack baby ever died. I'll have to ask Mr. B to check for me when he goes to the Center tomorrow. How could a mother do something like that to her own child?

*Friday, November 15th*

I caught a girl stealing today!

I suppose I should start with going back to the Center. Little as last week's adventure had appealed to me, sitting home alone again on Friday evening under Mom's knowing smirk was even less appealing. Besides, I couldn't get that crack baby out of my mind. By the time five o'clock rolled around, I was actually pacing back and forth. Dad was home by then, and when he found out just what I was trying to make up my mind about, he shoved his car keys into my hand and almost pushed me out the door.

So I went.

It was a lot different than last week. Brian and Sandy were the only other SCAers who went this time, and though they were as civil as before, I couldn't help feeling a little awkward around the two of them—until we picked up Karen. Maybe she thought we were being too quiet in the back, but she swiveled around in her seat and started telling tales of her med student days. Funny ones too! It's hard to stay at arm's length with anyone when you're all laughing so hard that you're helpless. Mr. B joined in with occasional dry comments of his own, one eye on his rearview mirror and the other on the road. He and Karen are so cute, trying not to make it too obvious how they feel about each other. Honestly, sometimes adults are worse than adolescents! Why doesn't he just propose and get it over with?

But they didn't do all the talking. Once we'd stopped giggling, Karen pulled each of us into sharing some of our own experiences at the Center, and this time I knew what they were all talking about, and I felt like an insider instead of the newcomer. I asked about the crack baby. Karen told me she was doing okay and that the mother had entered a rehabilitation program. Brian looked right at me then to ask about the baby.

"That must have been a tough one for your first time out," he commented when I finished, and even in the dim light I knew I wasn't imagining the approval in his smile.

As for Sandy, she's always so quiet at school I guess I've never really thought of her as having anything to say. But here with just the five of us, she talked as much as anyone, and my ears just about fell off in shock to hear her telling a hilarious experience she'd had last week with one of the tougher female Amazons that hang out at the Center. And she *listens*. When you're telling a story, you feel like she's hanging on your every word, not just waiting for a chance to jump in with one of her own. A trait I could stand to learn from her.

She showed no signs of even remembering that yearbook fiasco. But as soon as I got a chance, while we were carrying some donated secondhand sports equipment into the Center, I apologized to her too. She set down her box to give me a hug along with that gentle smile of hers and said, "Don't even think about it anymore, Jana. We all make mistakes."

Right! As if Sandy could be anything but the perfect lady. I wonder if she and Brian are "pursuing a romantic interest" in each other. I couldn't blame him, she's so pretty and gentle and . . . everything I'm not. Not that they give any indication of being more than good friends.

I learned last week not to dress too suburban. This time I wore jeans with a black T-shirt that has "Jesus Is Lord" scrawled across it in white letters—the easy way to let people know I'm a Christian without having to say anything—plus those chunky cubic zirconia earrings Danny got me last Christmas but I'd never worn because they were so flashy. I still didn't exactly blend into the scenery, but at least I felt a lot less conspicuous. And it's just as well too because Mr. B set Sandy to helping in the clinic, leaving Brian and me to "mingle," as Mr. B puts it, in the gym.

Being out in the gym was a whole lot easier than working in the clinic. But I was soon wishing I was back with Karen. The music was so noisy, and the kids all seemed so mean and tough and just plain *different*. There was no smoking or drinking allowed in the Center, but you could sure smell it on their clothes when they walked in. And language! If those girls have done half the things they talk about—well, I told Mr. B when he came by that I wasn't sure I could handle it, and shouldn't we be telling them that it was wrong to talk like that. But he just patted me on the shoulder and said I needed to let it flow right over me and love the person in spite of his or her language.

"And if it sticks in my head?" I demanded, a little ruffled that he wasn't doing anything to put a stop it. "My parents aren't going to be too happy if I come home from the Center with a filthy mouth."

"Sometimes it *is* hard to keep it from sticking," he agreed, to my surprise. "That's why I like to sing praise songs on the way home. To wash out the filth with something that is godly and pure. But if we're going to wait till these kids talk our kind of language before we share Christ with them, they'll never hear the gospel."

So I gritted my teeth. After a while I got used to it, and the kids didn't seem so bad. After all, once you got past their filthy language and wild dress, they weren't really doing anything different than SCA teenagers. Just hanging out, listening to music, playing basketball, etc. A couple of the girls made challenging comments about that "Jesus Is Lord" on my T-shirt, and I actually managed to get something out. It's strange. I can spout for hours about school or books or politics or anything else I know a little about. But when I try to choke out that I'm a Christian, my heart starts pounding out of my chest and my hands actually get sweaty. Brian makes it sound so easy. He gets out there and talks with the guys, and next thing I know, he's yanked out a New Testament to explain some verse. I don't know why I ever thought he was shy!

At nine o'clock, Mr. B stopped everything for a short devotional time. The canned music died into a blissful silence that lasted as long as it took for a handful of Center kids to join him on stage with guitars and tambourine and even a set of Mexican *maracas*. An Asian girl settled herself behind the drum set, and even if she wasn't as good as Amos Lowalsky, the place was soon rocking with some of the more foot-tapping choruses we sing at youth group on Sunday evenings. Some of the kids around me were grumbling about having to listen to this religious—well, I won't say what they called it. Still, I guess they've learned they have to put up with some preaching if they want to eat because pretty soon they'd all settled down, draped over benches and sports equipment or propped up against pillars or just sprawled out on the floor in front of the stage to listen.

In the meantime, Brian and I set out the food. Different churches around the city take turns providing the refreshments every week, and this time Ocean Beach Community Church had done us proud—a mouthwatering spread of sandwiches, cake, donuts, chips, and even a few pizzas. Brian and I stayed back at the table to keep an eye on things as no one is supposed to touch the food until Mr. B finishes, which isn't as easy as it sounds when half these guys consider any kind of negative a deadly insult to their masculinity. Fortunately, Brian looks tough enough to intimidate most of the two legged scavengers so I concentrated my own efforts in shooing away the winged ones.

And that's how I caught the girl stealing. Or rather I didn't catch her. She got away.

As I said, the Center kids aren't really so bizarre once you get used to them. The regular ones, anyway. And it hasn't taken me long to see that they think the world of Mr. B. They crowd around him so close he can hardly move, and they quote him every other sentence. If Mr. B says it, that's the final word!

All the hero-worship makes them seem more human, somehow. Like little kids wanting a daddy of their own. Maybe it doesn't make sense, but it's kind of made me see that maybe there are real people hiding under all that paint and costume jewelry.

But they aren't all like that. Some of the juvenile delinquents who come in off the street are every bit as bad as anything I ever pictured. Last week we didn't have any trouble—or maybe I didn't see it because I was in the clinic—but twice tonight, before the devotional time, we had teenage thugs in gang paraphernalia stalking in to make trouble. They were drunk, and if there weren't any weapons on display, they were shoving around as though just begging someone to give them an excuse to take the place apart. When Mr. B asked them to leave, they turned mean, and if it hadn't been for the regular Center bunch backing him up, Mr. B would never have gotten them out.

Anyway, the band was just filing down off stage and Mr. B was starting to talk when Brian whispered, "Uh, oh! I think we've got trouble!"

Then I saw what he saw. A pack of Werewolves were sauntering across the gym. The same street gang that was all over the news a few weeks back. The gang with the reputation as the most vicious in San Diego's underworld. There were five or six of them, all with that fanged wolf head on the back of their ragged jean jackets.

One was a girl. She was clinging to the arm of the last Werewolf, and my stomach curled up the instant I saw her. Now this was the kind of girl I'd expected to find in a place like this! Oh, she was pretty enough—maybe even beautiful with those big, dark eyes so many Hispanic girls have and waist-long hair of that shiny black that looks blue in the light. But the way she moved! Like Consuelo, only more so. And it looked a lot worse on her because she was so young—not more than thirteen or fourteen and just starting to fill out.

She looked familiar for just an instant. Like someone I'd met before and not too long ago. Then I realized who she reminded me of. It was a teenage streetwalker I'd seen in a movie Scott and I watched at his house a couple weeks back (okay, so I shouldn't have been watching that kind of movie, but Scott—well, that was when I was still trying to impress him). It wasn't just that hip-thrusting, provocative walk, but the way she stared around the gym as though she were casing the joint. Her face looked a lot older than her body, and not just because of the heavy makeup. It was hard and—I don't know—looked as though she knew things no kid her age ever should, and had been a lot of places she should have never gone.

But right then I didn't have time to think about how much I've always detested girls like her because the pack of Werewolves had reached the back of the crowd. Mr. B was still talking, but his audience was growing increasingly restless, glancing sideways at the newcomers and edging away to give them plenty of elbow space. Then, so suddenly no one could have anticipated it, one of the Werewolves literally flipped out. He started screaming in a stream of foul language that Mr. B had stolen his friend. Now he was going to pay for it. I found out afterwards that one of the Werewolves had gotten his life straightened out at the Center and left the gang.

Mr. B broke off his message, and for one endless moment there was total silence except for that madman's rantings. Then the Werewolf pulled his knife. A long, shiny, and very heavy one, the kind my dad still has tucked away from that year he spent in Vietnam at the tail end of the war. He lashed out with it and lunged toward the platform, his voice rising to a chilling scream.

"That guy's stoned!" Brian said in a grim voice that made him suddenly sound ten years older. "Jana, call the cops!"

And he took off like an Olympic sprinter. The Center kids were screaming and scrambling to their feet as that crazy junkie pushed his way through them toward the platform. A few tried to stop him, including the other Werewolves, but he was slashing around wildly with that knife, and no one dared get too close. Maybe I grew up sheltered, but I'd never seen anyone high on drugs before. I was so scared I could hardly move. But when I saw Brian take a dive at the guy, I managed to tear my feet from the floor and race for the kitchen where there was a phone. My hands were shaking so hard I could hardly punch out 911. If Dad had been on duty, I'd have asked for him. As it was, I just gasped out that there was a lunatic drug addict at the Center and to send the police quickly before someone got killed.

My heart almost stopped when I got back. The Werewolf with the knife was up on the platform. He had Mr. B backed up against the wall with that razor-sharp blade under his chin. Brian and a couple of the other Werewolves were circling around behind him, but keeping warily out of arm's reach.

I wouldn't have dreamed anyone in that position could be so calm. But Mr. B looked as unflurried as though he were having a friendly student-teacher conference. His lips were moving as though he were talking. But whatever he was saying, that crazy kid wasn't listening. He was still screaming and swearing at the top of his lungs and shaking so hard I was terrified he'd slice Mr. B's throat even if he didn't mean to.

That's when it all happened. So fast I almost missed it. Brian lunged in from the side in a tackle that makes me wonder why he's not on the football team. The knife went flying, and an instant later half-a-dozen guys crashed down on top of the junkie.

They were pulling him to his feet, still screaming and struggling, when I heard the sirens. I'd hoped the police would be able to arrest the guy. But when they heard the sirens, the other Werewolves grabbed their friend and hauled him toward the door. No one tried to stop them, not even Mr. B, and maybe he was right. There were still enough of them to get someone hurt. At least it was over.

I let out the breath I'd been holding and swung around to check on the refreshments I was supposed to be guarding. And that's when I saw the girl with the Werewolf jacket. She'd appropriated the big plastic bag with handles on it that I'd used to carry disposable plates and glasses out from the kitchen, and in all the confusion, she was lifting whole platters of that yummy food and sliding them into the bag. While I stood there, mouth dropping to my knees, an entire pizza slid in. It was the one with the taco topping that I'd earmarked a piece of for myself. That brought back my voice.

"Hey!" I called out. "You can't do that!"

The platter clattered to the table, and she swung around to face me, backing up against the edge of the table like one of those wolves at bay. We couldn't have stared at each other for more than a couple of seconds. Just long enough for me to see that her eyes weren't really black but the same coffee brown of a puppy I once had. Then she snatched up the bag and slid off into the mob of Center kids who were still milling around. I suppose I could have shouted, "Stop, thief! That girl's stealing the refreshments!" I'm not really sure why I didn't. But by the time the police crashed into the gym, she was gone.

So that was this evening's big adventure. I really don't know why I started with the girl because the fight with the drug addict was the biggest excitement. Mr. B wasn't hurt much, just a trickle of blood running down his neck onto his shirt. While he talked to the police, Brian and I set out more food. I told Brian about the girl, but he didn't think it was any big deal. There were lots of refreshments left in the kitchen, and it isn't as though there's any rule about how much you can eat.

So why do I keep thinking about her? I mean, the girl's a member of a street gang—a bad one—not to mention a common thief, as I've already seen. And I can just imagine how she keeps alive out there on the streets!

I guess it was those eyes. That puppy of mine came from one of Dad's police rounds. Dad found him washed up on a beach, still tied up in a sack along with a bunch of rocks. He had a broken leg and one ear torn, and Danny and I were the only ones who thought there was anything cute about him. After a month, when he got well enough to start digging holes in the yard, Mom made us get rid of him. But for those first couple of weeks, all he'd do was cower in a corner and shiver when anyone came near, as though he wanted to trust us but had been kicked and shoved away so many times he didn't dare try again. I know it sounds silly, but that Werewolf girl had that same look in her eyes—older than the mountains and terribly sad.

*Part Five*

*Saturday, November 16ᵗʰ*

Her name is Maria.

As usual, I hadn't planned on going to the Center this evening, especially after last night's scare. But Mr. B was treating all the SCAers who have been helping out to dinner at an ice-cream parlor before heading downtown. How could I resist that? So I decided I could put up with the Center just one more time.

There were more SCAers than I'd expected, about ten of us in all, including some underclassmen I'd never met before. And it was fun. The hot fudge oozing down a mountain of vanilla ice cream—my absolute, irresistible favorite—was wonderful. But there was more to it than that. It was that warm feeling of being part of the group. Of belonging.

It's strange. With Scott and Denise and their crowd, I always felt I should be having a good time because they're so popular and all, but I really didn't. Now here's this bunch I'd never have picked out to ally myself with in a thousand years. Except for Sandy as yearbook editor and maybe Brian, none of them are any kind of celebrity at SCA, and I'm not the only one there who'd have a hard time attaching a name to half their faces. But they're interesting and funny and really seem to know what they're doing with their lives.

And they all have that *something* I noticed last week in Sandy and Brian and the others. Something—oh, I don't know, shining and steady under all that typical teen goofing off and roughhousing, of which they certainly do their share. That doesn't make sense, I know. If I could describe it better, maybe I could find it myself.

I must say I was dumbfounded to see staid Amos Lowalsky flipping cherry pits across the table into Peter Ramsey's Coke. And Peter and Michelle sneaking slices of jalapeños into sundaes, then glancing innocently around when their neighbors started spluttering and shooting flames from nose and mouth (yes, this is personal experience speaking). It just didn't fit the mental image I had of young people who would spend their weekends helping the down-and-out.

But for all the fun they have, they're absolutely serious about what they're doing down there at the Center. They really seem to care about those street punks and gang types. I wish I could say my own motives were as pure. I really would like to care about these people the way they do. But I must admit that Brian and Sandy and Mr. B and Karen and Peter and Michelle—okay, and even Amos—and the others, too, are the main attraction for me. I *like* being part of them, even as the newest and smallest cog in the social services machine.

Speaking of Amos, I'm beginning to think it isn't just my imagination that something's brewing between him and Sandy. A month ago, I'd have dismissed the pink that creeps into Sandy's peaches-and-cream complexion every time Amos glances her way, and her nods of encouragement while he's talking, as the delusions of a fevered brain. Sandy may be quiet, but she's very pretty and would have only to direct that honey-sweet smile of hers a little more specifically to have a dozen guys more in demand than Amos Lowalsky jumping to do the honors.

But then Amos isn't the same geek who tripped over his shoe-laces inviting me to the Valentine Banquet last year. I guess I never noticed how much he's grown up these last few months and how his voice (that used to crack at embarrassing intervals in choir) has settled into being a nice baritone. He really isn't such a bad-looking guy anymore, and this Center thing has certainly given him a lot more self-confidence. If he's still on the serious side except when he's behind that drum set—well, so is Sandy. At any rate, whatever is brewing there doesn't seem to bother Brian. In fact, I heard him kidding Amos about her tonight. Maybe he and Sandy *are* just friends.

With all that, we were a little late in getting to the Center. It was less confusing this time with that kaleidoscope of space-age costumes and noise resolving itself into faces and people I actually recognized. A few even waved and called my name as I walked across the gym. I was as surprised as I was pleased. I remembered them from the refreshment line last night, but I'd never have expected any of them to remember me.

For a while, I helped out in the clinic. Consuelo was there again, a green stripe added to the orange and lipstick to match, but keeping that unruly waiting room under control with an iron hand. The way the other girls greeted her, like a long-lost friend, told me she must be a regular there. But with the large group we'd brought, it was soon clear I wasn't really needed, so I wandered back out into the gym. I was watching a whole gang of newcomers flood through the door and trying to work up the courage to walk over and welcome them onto the premises, as Mr. B has instructed us, when I noticed a girl slipping in a little behind the others. The full width of the gym was between us, and she wasn't wearing a Werewolves jacket, but something about that walk and the waist-length shining black hair brought last night's food thief instantly into my mind.

Mr. B strolled into my line of vision just then, and when I glanced around him, the girl was gone. By that time, I'd decided I was mistaken. After all, two-thirds of the kids who come through the Center are Hispanic, and a fair percentage of the girls have long hair.

It's an idiosyncrasy of teachers that they just hate to see anyone standing around without something to do, and Mr. B is no exception. As soon as he discovered I was out of a job, he steered me over to one of the study rooms off the gym. I hadn't noticed these last week. A lot of the regulars here are high school dropouts. The Center encourages them to go back and finish school and even provides tutoring in the evenings. This, at least, was something I knew how to do; I've done enough of it with Sally. I found that East Indian Lassie fan, whose name turned out to be Kami Gupta, at one of the tables and was helping her study for an algebra test when Mr. B popped back in to say that the church that was supposed to provide the evening's refreshments had stood us up.

"There were some leftovers last night," he said. "And we do keep some food in the kitchen for emergencies. Jana, would you check to see if there's enough to put out some kind of spread? If not, I'll have to make a run to the supermarket."

The Center doesn't put out food every night, just Fridays and Saturdays. But Mr. B told me last week that some of the kids who live on the street really count on getting a decent meal there on weekends. I could just imagine the grumbling, maybe even open revolution, if their usual spread wasn't forthcoming. For that matter, the effects of that fairly modest hot fudge sundae were beginning to wear thin, adding some personal interest in the situation. So I said sure, I'd take care of it, and headed to the kitchen.

The kitchen door was kept locked, for obvious reasons with this crowd. But I'd just started to fit Mr. B's key in the lock when it swung open under my touch. And that's when I found out I hadn't been mistaken about that Werewolf girl because there she was! She was at the far counter, her back to me, the cupboard doors, both lower and upper, standing wide open, and it was clear she'd been rummaging through them because there were a couple bags of chips and a box of Twinkies and a loaf of whole wheat bread and other stuff all piled up on the counter. The refrigerator door was ajar too, and I could see she'd even swiped the butter and mayonnaise and leftover sliced cheese we'd used to make sandwiches last night. And right next to all the rest was the one pizza we hadn't put out because there was still plenty of food on the trays.

I was mad! This wasn't just pigging out off the refreshment table as she'd done yesterday. This was barefaced larceny!

"Hey!" I said firmly. Well, okay, maybe it was more like a shout. "Just where do you think you're going with all that?"

She whirled around, flinging her arms out in front of her loot as though to protect it with her own body. Then her eyes widened under those long lashes before narrowing to a slit, and I knew she'd recognized me just as I had her.

"So what's it to you?" she demanded. Actually, that's a fairly loose translation, but since I don't care to use all those asterisks and stars, it'll have to do.

Without taking my eyes off her, I stepped inside the kitchen. I've been scared to death of these gang kids ever since junior high, but this girl wasn't much taller than me and a whole lot younger, and there certainly wasn't any room in the skimpy tank top and skin-tight black leggings for a knife or a gun. Unless she was some sort of martial arts expert, I didn't see what real harm she could do me, especially with a gym full of kids just as tough to call on for backup, as my dad would put it. So I closed the door behind me and placed myself solidly in front of it. That door was the only way out of the kitchen, and she was going to have to get around me to carry off that haul.

"What's it to me? I'm in charge of the refreshments, that's what!" I informed her, exaggerating only a little because Mr. B *had* told me to check on things. "And we need that stuff for tonight. How did you get in here, anyway? And who are you? What's your name?"

"Maria—" she let slip before she stiffened and bit the words off. "It's none of your business who I am," she spit out angrily. "As for how I got in here, if you're so worried someone's going to run off with your pots and pans, you'd better get a better lock than that. A baby in diapers could pick it."

Dropping her arms then from where they were still protecting her loot, she leaned back against the counter as nonchalantly as though I were the thief and she a law-abiding citizen and added with a sneer that curled up one side of that bright red mouth, "You don't need to tell me who you are!"

The look she raked over me was scornful, and I could almost hear her adding up the obviously new shirt I was wearing tonight, the designer jeans I'd bought on that spending spree, and the little gold-and-pearl earrings Dad got me for my sixteenth birthday. She continued with as much icy contempt as Denise herself could have put into her voice, "You're one of those fancy church kids from the other side of town, aren't you? The ones who get their kicks crawling down here to see how the other half of the world lives."

Well, I didn't have much of an answer to that because I'd written something uncomfortably close to it in my journal last week. Besides, I knew she was just trying to distract me from her pilfering. So I took another step into the kitchen and glanced from the pile of food on the counter to a backpack that was sitting open on the floor at her feet.

"Look, I'm not going to call the police or anything," I told her, not wanting to provoke a fight, "but you're going to have to put back that stuff you're stealing."

She gave me the same unblinking stare I've used on Mom when I'm thinking up a quick excuse. Then she lowered her eyes and hunched her shoulders. "Hey, give me a break, I wasn't stealing! I was just hungry, okay? You know what that is, rich girl? *You* try sleeping on the streets for months on end. Going for days at a time without eating. Your stomach twisted up so bad you can hardly walk, and you can't pass a deli without the smell making you gag. You get hungry enough, and you wouldn't be so Miss Holy about borrowing a bit of food from a bunch of high-and-mighty church snobs who've got cupboards loaded with the stuff back home."

She lifted those long lashes to look at me sullenly. "Why should you care, anyway? It's no skin off your nose if that bunch out there have to take a pay cut on all that preaching. I don't bet there's any chance *you'll* be climbing into those pretty, clean sheets of yours on an empty stomach."

It was good sob stuff. But her little-girl face was as hard as nails, and I decided I'd been pretty foolish imagining anything lost or lonely in her eyes. Anyway, I didn't believe a word of it. She was slim, all right, but not starving thin. And she was clean, not as though she'd been sleeping in the streets.

"You don't look that hungry to me," I told her flatly. "And if you are, there's no reason you can't line up for food with everyone else." My hand went to the doorknob, and it swung in towards me. "Look, I don't want any trouble. And I don't want to get you into trouble either. But we really do need that stuff for tonight. If you're not going to put it back, I'm going to have to call Mr. B. He'll know how to take care of this."

"No, wait!" Abandoning her food stash and her backpack, she flew across the room. I braced myself, wondering if I was being stupid not to scream for help. But she brushed right past me to slam the door shut again. Spinning around, she planted herself in front of it as I had earlier. That hard expression on her face had cracked a little, and I actually started to feel sorry for her because even if she wasn't starving, she sure seemed pretty desperate about something. So instead of backing away as I'd intended to, I turned to face her.

"Look, Maria," I said firmly. "That's what you said your name was, right? It's only another hour until we start serving refreshments. You come back then, and I'll make sure you get all you want to eat. I'll even save you some of the pizza." I offered her a smile with that, but didn't get so much as a glimmer of a response so I went on quickly, "Or if you're really in such a hurry, I'll make you up some sandwiches to take with you."

But she just shook her head, her dark eyes flickering from me to that food, as though it were a magnet pulling at her. When the silence had dragged on longer than I had patience for, I let out an exasperated sigh. "Then I'm afraid you're out of luck!" I informed her with stubbornness to match her own. "Unless maybe you want to tell me just why you need our supper so badly."

Her little-girl face twisted up under the makeup as though she really did hurt or was about to cry. But almost before I could be sure it wasn't my imagination, her face hardened again. Her eyes moved from me to the food, deliberately this time, as though she were trying to make up her mind. Then that sneering curl came back to her red mouth, and there was the snarl of the wolf on the jacket she'd worn last night in her voice. "You want the truth? Sure, I'll tell you the truth! You're not going to believe me anyway!"

Actually, none of this is exactly what she said. I'm probably leaving out one word in four as she couldn't even say that much without a heavy sprinkling of the kind of words I don't put in my journal. But it wasn't as though there was anything personal in it. More like it was the only way she knew how to talk. Still glancing from me to the food as though she figured if she could distract me long enough she might be able to make a break for it, she started in, "The stuff ain't for me, see? It's for these friends of mine. They're in trouble."

She was right. I didn't believe a word!

According to Maria, there'd been a big fight this past week between some of the Werewolves and the same gang whose mark—an ugly, red demon-looking creature—I'd seen splashed on the side of one of the apartment buildings the first time I came, the Devil's Angels. I didn't have any problem with that part because even I know that the only gang in San Diego to match the Werewolves for sheer maliciousness and antisocial behavior is the Devil's Angels. Besides there'd been that TV news story a couple days back about a gang war down there to back her up.

But the rest was right out of Hollywood!

This is what she said happened. After a couple days of fighting and busting up cars and smashing in windows and storefronts and all the usual mayhem, which the SDPD always gets to clean up afterwards, the two gangs started counting their wounded and decided to call a truce. A meeting was set up to negotiate peace. Just the two gang leaders and their seconds-in-command. The place: an abandoned warehouse in a neutral zone between the boundaries of the two gang territories. The deal was that each pair come alone. No backup and no weapons. Any tricks and the truce would be off.

There was one minor difficulty. The Wolf, which was the only name the Werewolves leader seemed to go by, had received a serious stab wound early on in the fighting. Who knows, maybe it was even one of those knife wounds I helped stitch up last week. Anyway, he was holed up somewhere mending and, from what I gathered from Maria, couldn't show himself in public until he was his usual, macho self again. That old combination of politics and male ego! So Maria's two friends, Rodrigo and Mick, were selected to go in his place.

According to Maria, her friends were a little surprised at being chosen. Unlike the Devil's Angels, the Werewolves had no particular chain of command. The Wolf ran a tight ship, and everyone else reported directly to him. Rodrigo and Mick had a hot reputation as two of the gang's best fighters. But there were others as close or even closer to the Wolf.

Still, there was nothing remotely suspicious about it either, and being singled out by the Wolf was a step up in their dubious career. So Maria's friends got their orders and hurried off to the rendezvous as agreed, alone and without weapons. They had been waiting some time and were growing nervous about their exposed position when the leader of the Devil's Angels, Abdul, finally sauntered into the warehouse with his second-in-command, Icepick, at his heels. Now isn't *that* a name for a Devil's Angel! They all took turns patting each other down, agreed that the conditions had been met, and began negotiating the truce. But they'd barely reached the discussion stage when Icepick took a step back from the group, kicked over a nearby crate, and snatched up the gun that was underneath.

Rodrigo and Mick were furious that the Devil's Angels had broken the truce. Everyone knew the Devil's Angels were treacherous and deceitful and would stab a surrendered prisoner in the back (I couldn't help wondering here what the Devil's Angels had to say about the Werewolves!). They should have ignored their orders and smuggled in weapons of their own. Or at least given the place a better shakedown since the Devil's Angels must have planted that weapon well in advance.

Still, it never entered either of their heads that this was anything but a trap set up to catch the Wolf, who should have been at that meeting. So they were completely stunned when, instead of shooting them or even taking them prisoner, this Icepick promptly swung around and shot his own leader in the back. Then he turned the gun back on Maria's friends and told them to get their hands in the air. With a cold smile, Icepick informed the two Werewolves that they had broken a truce and committed cold-blooded murder, and now he was going to hold them for the police.

The wilder this story got, the more skeptical I felt. Who's leg did this girl think she was pulling?

"And why would this Icepick want to kill his own boss?" I demanded the instant Maria paused for breath. "How do you know it really *wasn't* these friends of yours who shot him? They could have smuggled that gun in just as easily as the other guys. I mean, even if this Devil's Angel *was* wanting to shoot his own boss, why bother dragging a couple of his worst enemies across town to watch? That doesn't even make sense!"

Maria's eyes shot sparks that would have blistered me if they'd been real fire. "They didn't kill him!" she hissed. "You think I'm stupid? I was there! I saw what happened!"

I shut up and let her explain herself. According to Maria, she'd been with her two friends when the gang fighting broke out. I guess it's kind of like the Israeli War of Independence we studied last year in World History because there was no evacuating of women from the combat zone. Maria didn't say what her own participation was, and I didn't ask, but she stayed with her friends throughout the fighting. When the order came for the truce negotiations, Rodrigo and Mick didn't want to just dump her on the street in case things started getting ugly again, so they took her along. Making sure they arrived plenty early at the rendezvous, they found her a place she could hide until it was all over behind some old crates on the far side of the warehouse.

Maria was obeying orders and keeping her head down when that shot exploded through the building. It scared the daylights out of her, knowing as she did that her own side wasn't packing any arms. So she was as astounded as her friends when she peeked around the crates to see that the person lying on the ground bleeding wasn't Rodrigo or Mick but the Devil's Angels leader. She couldn't tell if he was dead or not, but she could see Icepick holding that gun on her friends and their hands up in the air. There was nothing she could do—she was too far away and unarmed besides—so she could only watch helplessly as Icepick backed her friends right into that puddle of blood, using his spare hand to flip open a cellular phone. She didn't know then that he was calling the police. Icepick was just folding the phone when Rodrigo and Mick made their move.

There was a scuffle during which Maria could only hold her breath. Then she heard the gun explode again. The three bodies flew apart. Then Icepick was down on the floor, flat on his back but with that gun still clutched to his chest and coming up, and Rodrigo and Mick were scrambling out the door. And suddenly Maria was alone in that warehouse with a dead body and blood everywhere and Icepick picking himself up off the ground. If he found her there—

Maria's voice dropped almost to a whisper, and I realized that she was shivering in that skimpy tank top of hers. I shivered too. I was beginning to feel as though I were right there with her behind those crates. Maybe this *was* just a line she'd pulled out of a grade-B movie, but it was a pretty good one.

But Icepick showed no interest in doing any prowling around. He was wiping down his gun with something else that had been under that crate, and when he tossed both down by the body, Maria saw the Werewolves emblem on the back of a jacket like her own. By that time, police sirens were announcing the speedy response of San Diego's finest. Maria huddled down behind those crates as the place started filling up, not just with police, but with people who'd heard the shots and were crowding in to see what had happened. Scrambling out into the shadows, she slipped over to mingle in with the crowd. When the police shooed everyone out, she went too.

That was Wednesday morning. It was afternoon before her friends could make contact with her. Icepick had told his story to the police—that Rodrigo and Mick had ambushed Abdul and tried to shoot him too before his valiant defense and the arrival of the police had scared them off. So now they were on the run, and Icepick was the new leader of the Devil's Angels. The Devil's Angels, of course, were blaming the killing on Rodrigo and Mick, and they wanted revenge. So Rodrigo and Mick were hiding out, not just from the police, but from the other gang. They'd been holed up for two full days when Maria took advantage of that Werewolves junkie to swipe them some food off the refreshment table.

"I'm the only one who knows where they are, see?" she concluded, managing somehow to look half terrified, half proud at the same time. "That's why I needed your stuff. I don't got no money, and they're dead meat if they hit the streets."

It sounded good. But I could see some holes in her story big enough to drive a truck through. For one thing, if this Rodrigo and Mick were such hot stuff among the Werewolves, why did they need some kid playing hooky from junior high to do their sneaking around for them?

"So where are your Werewolf buddies in all this?" I demanded skeptically. "I mean, you guys are supposed to be one big happy family, right? Why aren't you going to them for help instead of sneaking in here?"

Her stare told me I was mentally handicapped. "Because the whole thing was a setup!" she hissed out furiously. "And maybe it was one of the Werewolves that set them up. That jacket didn't come from the Angels! My friends can't trust anyone. Just me! I'd do anything for them, see? They were the ones who got me into the Werewolves when I'd been on the street for months."

Okay, so maybe she did know what it was like to go hungry. Her story was incredible, but she was so intense about it, I was beginning to believe her in spite of myself. So I said, "Look, if all this is really true, it isn't food you need. It's the police. Let me call Mr. B. He'd be glad to help your friends. Once you've testified to the police that it was Icepick and not your friends who killed that guy, they'll be free, and so will you!"

"Are you crazy?" Maria knocked my hand away from the doorknob. "The police wouldn't believe me any more than you do. And Icepick would kill me if he knew I was there!"

It was the panic in her voice that convinced me. Dashing across the kitchen, she snatched that open backpack off the ground—still empty. "Look, I'm out of here. You can keep your stupid food if it's such a big deal. And if you go repeating this stuff to anyone, I'll—well, I'll make you wish you hadn't, that's all! I don't know why I told you any of this, anyway! I must have been out of my mind!"

I was wondering the same thing myself. Why *did* she tell me, a complete stranger, all this stuff? Especially if it's true! I guess maybe when things get bad enough, you get so desperate you've just got to talk to someone. Even me!

So, did I get taken in tonight by a teenage con artist or was she telling the truth? I don't know. But I couldn't just let her go after all that. Refreshments were pretty skimpy, and Mr. B ended up having to run to the mini-mart to buy a few things. But I'm not sorry. I think maybe she *did* need that stuff more than the rest of us.

## Tuesday, November 19ᵗʰ

I asked Dad this morning what he knew about a gang shooting involving the Devil's Angels and Werewolves. I don't know why I didn't think of it earlier except that Dad has never talked much about his work—maybe because Mom always says she feels safer when she doesn't know what he's doing. Dad gave me an odd look and asked where I'd heard about it. The gangs' week-long smashing bash had made the news—that must have been the clip I'd caught the tail end of—but not the shooting. I told him a girl at the Center had mentioned it.

It turned out Dad knew all about it. He wasn't on the case, but one of his friends was involved in the investigation. Yes, it was true that the leader of the Devil's Angels had been shot, but not during the fighting. The police were looking for the two Werewolves involved, but that was gang turf down there, and the odds of finding them were pretty slim.

The truth was, Dad admitted, a gang killing wasn't a top priority for San Diego's overworked forces of law and order (with the hours Dad puts in I can testify to the "overworked" part!). Sooner or later, the two Werewolves would have to come out of hiding, then the police would pick them up.

"But how can they be so sure these Werewolves were the ones who killed the guy?" I protested. "What if they're innocent? What if they have someone who can testify that someone else did it?"

"I'm sure they do!" Dad answered dryly. "These guys can always find someone to testify anything they want! But the police have a pretty good case this time. They have the weapon involved as well as some other solid pieces of evidence. *And* a witness. Not to mention, the footprints and fingerprints the perps were kind enough to leave all over the scene for I.D."

Dad gave me another of those odd looks. "It sounds like this girl you mentioned knows a lot about what's going on down there. Is she involved in either of those gangs?"

I didn't know what to say, so I shrugged. After gazing thoughtfully at me for an endless minute with what Julie and I call his "cop stare," Dad shrugged too. "Well, if you see this girl again, tell her that her pals would be smart to turn themselves in. According to their police records, they're both juveniles with nothing but misdemeanors against them until now, so they probably wouldn't get too hard a break—especially if they came in voluntarily. But the Devil's Angels are on the rampage over this killing. If they find out where those kids are holed up before the police do, it's unlikely they'll ever get a chance to tell their side of the story!"

So Maria was telling the truth. Not just about her friends, but about the police believing her. I was tempted to tell Dad the whole story. But right then Danny poked his head in the kitchen and shouted that the bus was coming. By the time we got home from school, Dad had already left for the precinct. Now I'm not sure I should tell him. After all, I don't know anything that could help the police, and if they're not going to believe Maria anyway, I'd sure hate to get her into more trouble.

## *Thursday, November 21ˢᵗ*

When Dad got off duty tonight, he told me he didn't think I should go back to the Center. Things looked to be brewing up to another turf war between the Devil's Angels and Werewolves, and he didn't know what Mr. B was thinking taking SCA kids into that part of town.

The funny thing is, I'd already decided not to go back. It's been a busy week with yearbook and playing for Miss Kitchener again. Plus, I've got a lot of studying to do if I'm going to make up for last quarter's slump, not to mention a Social Studies paper to polish up this weekend. Besides, I'd never planned on making this Center thing a regular deal.

But when Dad said that, it was like a blow. *Never* go back to the Center? That's when I realized I really do want to go back. I want to see how Sonya, my drug baby, is coming along. I like being with Mr. B and Karen and the other SCAers and even Consuelo. And I want to find out what's happened to Maria. Maybe even pass on Dad's warning, if I can. Quitting now would be like losing a book halfway through the most exciting chapter!

"Come on, Dad, it's not that dangerous!" I wheedled. "It's not like we're out on the streets, and Mr. B always watches out for us. And you said yourself that the Center's been good for me. Please? I really want to do something to serve my community—the way you do, Dad!"

Now that last was a master of parental psychology, and I knew right away I'd won my case. Dad's big on civic responsibility. But it had hardly jumped out of my mouth when I realized that I actually meant it. I guess I've grumbled a lot about the Center and its less appetizing aspects in this journal, but it really did feel good to see those mothers light up when their babies got their vaccinations or when they got to see their new little one on the screen of the sonogram machine. And I was almost as excited as Kami when it finally dawned on her just what a differential equation was. Is this what Mr. B was talking about?

## Friday, November 22nd

Maria didn't show.

There's no reason why I should be disappointed. It's not as though I really expected to see her again. But I couldn't help wondering all evening where she was, in what abandoned building Rodrigo and Mick might be hiding, whether they had food to eat. The food I sent with her couldn't possibly have lasted them all week. Or maybe she never came by for more because the Devil's Angels already found their hiding place.

But I couldn't just sit around wondering. I wasn't the only one with a Social Studies paper due, so the group was pretty low tonight—just Brian and myself besides Mr. B and Karen. So I ended up in the clinic with Consuelo.

Consuelo really upsets my ideas about street punks. She certainly looks like one and can talk like one, too, when it comes to dealing with some bully trying to shove his way in front of a little *Latino* granny waiting for her flu shot, though she does try to keep the language toned down. But when she's helping Karen in the examining room or filling out forms, she has all that teeth-breaking Latin medical terminology down pat. She works like a galley slave and never loses her cool—or her grin—even when things are at their most revolting. The clinic is considered the "grunt" job, so while everybody takes their turn, they're always glad when it doesn't land on them. But I've never seen Consuelo anywhere else.

Tonight we were wiping down the bathroom after an addict in withdrawal had spewed his meager supper all over. At least he made it that far. They don't always! In an effort to distract my stomach from following his example, I asked Consuelo why I never saw her out in the Center with the other kids.

"If I didn't know better, I'd swear you really like doing this stuff," I said, waving my hand around at that filthy bathroom, "cleaning up after junkies who'll never change anyway."

She was silent so long I was afraid I'd put my foot in my mouth again. But after sluicing another bucket of Pinesol and water over the walls, she answered, not with irritation or defense, but thoughtfully, "I was one of those junkies myself once. If it wasn't for Mr. B and Karen, I'd still be on the stuff. I guess I figure it's my turn to pass that help on to someone else. Besides, I'm going to be a doctor myself someday, and this is good practice."

Well! Consuelo a doctor? With that skunk stripe and clothes bright enough to read by in the dark? Some of my shock must have showed because her thoughtful expression changed instantly to the one she reserves for the more disreputable characters who push their way into the clinic, and she demanded, "You don't think I can do it, do you?"

"Oh, no, sure, of course I think you can!" I stammered out. She gave me an unbelieving look, but went back to work. Later on, when Karen had sent me out to ask Mr. B for another box of gauze from supply, I asked him about Consuelo. I couldn't believe it when he told me that Consuelo had received one of the top SAT scores in the city and was hoping for a scholarship to medical school next year. She already has plans to be the first brain surgeon ever to come from that San Diego barrio.

"You can't judge people by their outside, Jana," Mr. B added a little sternly. Well, I guess not!

Just glancing back over these last journal entries, I see I've made it sound as though Mr. B and Karen are the ones who run the Center. But that isn't so. The San Diego Family and Youth Center is open during the day too, and they have nutrition classes and counseling for teenage pregnancy and who knows what else. The kids come in all week to toss around a basketball and study, and different volunteers come in to help tutor. Mr. Jefferson, a retired high school teacher with a grandfatherly manner and woolly hair that looks white as snow against his chocolate-brown face, actually runs the place and has an office upstairs. Every once in a while, he wanders in to see how things are going.

But Mr. B is in charge of the weekend youth program, and he's there most Friday and Saturday nights except when something's going on at SCA. He drops by during the week, too, as often as he can and is tutoring Consuelo in AP physics and calculus. It turns out she's taking those by correspondence in the evenings as well as a whole load of regular classes. I guess that makes her a lot smarter than me!

Karen runs the clinic three nights a week. She is specializing in pediatrics and is still a resident—or whatever it is when they call you doctor but you haven't quite finished training. She'll finish her residency in June but has no future plans, yet. Or so she says. I'll bet Mr. B has some ideas for her!

While we were cleaning up, Consuelo told me a little bit more about how she ended up at the Center. She was higher than a kite the night she wandered in during one of Mr. B's devotional talks two years back, but not so high she couldn't get the general idea of what he was saying.

"He said God loved me!" She shook her head over the counter she was scrubbing as though it was the most incredible news in the universe. "You know what that did to me, Jana? I ain't never had no one to love me before, not since my ma took off when I was still in diapers and my pop set me to raising those brats of his next woman. I started on the hard stuff just to get away. I think I was hoping it would kill me. And then Mr. B tells me there's a God who even knows my name!"

She finished the counter and started on the trash can full of bloody swabs and disposable syringes and used specimen containers. "I ain't never touched the hard stuff since that night. Not even when Mr. B and Karen had to hold me so I wouldn't hurt myself wanting that next fix so bad. It was seeing them cleaning up after I lost it and never once getting mad at me that made me believe that all that stuff about God loving me could really be true."

"Yeah, well, God loves the whole world," I murmured as she paused to tie the garbage sack shut, and I added before I could catch myself, "The whole crawling planet of us."

"No, I don't mean that whole world stuff," she cut me off impatiently. "He loves *me*, Consuelo Gonzalez. Like He's my best friend. Like I'm His. I ain't never going to be alone again, see? That's why I don't need that poison no more. I got Someone who's caring about me even when my pop and step are screaming bloody murder on the other side of the wall and the little ones are clawing each other's heads off. And I'm going to spend the rest of my life making up for a little of all that dying on the cross and stuff God did for me. You just wait and see!"

And I'm the one who's been to Sunday school half my life! Consuelo was blowing bubbles with that wad of hers the whole time she was talking, which should have spoiled the effect. But it didn't, and I found myself suddenly envying her so much my throat hurt. *Her*, a girl who lives in a three-room apartment with a couple of boozers as parents and a pack of squabbling half-siblings whose welfare supplements are the family's only income.

Oh, God, do You really love like that? So much that it doesn't matter if anyone else ever will in the rest of my life? And so *personally*? Me, Jana Thompson, out of this whole world of people clamoring for Your attention?

On the way home Brian talked to me.

I know Brian's wandered into this journal often enough in the last three months. He's attractive and intelligent and nice and basi-cally meets every requirement I've ever come up with for a man. I've done my share of daydreaming about him and even indulged in a few entire mental conversations.

But I guess I've never thought much about him as a *person*. You know—not just a good-looking member of that mysterious half of humanity commonly known as the opposite sex, but as an actual human being with real thoughts and ideas. I've never really con-sidered what his life is like outside of school and my imagination. What he's really feeling inside.

Until tonight.

It isn't that we've never talked before. Brian has unthawed a lot these last couple weeks at the Center and at school too, and some-times I've even wondered if maybe I wasn't getting a little bigger share of that smile than some of the other girls. But we've always been in a crowd, and there's always a lot more joking and teasing than serious talk.

But tonight the others weren't there, and though Mr. B and Karen were their usual sociable selves, it was clear to anyone with half a brain that those two wouldn't mind some private time up there in the front of the van. And somehow, back there alone in the dark, it was easier to talk in a way we never would have if we could have seen each other's faces. We talked as *friends*, not with that awkward maneuvering that seems to make up much of man-woman conversations.

I don't know how the conversation shifted to Brian's family. Some prying question of mine, I'm sure. But he didn't seem to mind. I had no idea that he has a younger sister, Patty, and that she is a student at SCA. But then, the junior high crowd doesn't mix much with the high school.

Brian's parents are divorced, and I guess it's been rough on his mom raising Brian and Patty all on her own. His father's a lawyer, so you wouldn't think there'd be financial difficulties. But he took off across state lines as soon as he married his secretary, and now he's got an expensive new family. With him being a lawyer and Brian's mom not having two dollars to rub together to hire one, he's done what he wants as far as child support. That's why Brian had to drop out of college this year. And the fact that he's helping with Patty's school bills played a role in his dropping out too, I guess, though he tried to gloss over that part.

Brian hasn't seen his father since the man showed up two days late for his eighth grade graduation. He wasn't complaining, just sharing quietly about how he and his mom were trying to give Patty a stable home life. But even in the dark I could feel the hurt still lingering underneath. He's certainly got every reason in the world to hate his father, but there was no hatred there.

"I don't know *what* I'd do if my dad took off!" I told him. "Want to boil him in hot oil, I guess."

Brian didn't answer right away. I could see the glitter of a street-light reflecting off his eyes, then he turned his head to look out the window so all I could make out was the shadow of that strong jaw of his. "Yeah, it hasn't been easy," he said after such a long pause I thought he wasn't going to answer at all. "But I guess maybe God's taught me a lot of things these last years I might never have learned otherwise."

You know, I really like that guy!

## Saturday, November 23rd

What am I getting myself into with these people?

It shouldn't have been such a shock. Ever since I started at the Center, I've seen posters all over advertising *YOUTHQUAKE* in these great, jagged letters meant to symbolize, I suppose, some impending catastrophic event. I did gather it referred to some special Center-sponsored youth festival over the Thanksgiving break, but since I never figured on hanging around that long, I didn't pay much attention. If I thought at all about it, I assumed there'd be the usual out-of-town Christian band and guest speaker . . . until we were driving home from the Center tonight.

Most of the regular SCA crowd was there, and Mr. B started talking over his shoulder about plans for the youth festival and our own individual participation, and it suddenly sank into my brain that *we* were supposed to be putting this on! The SCA volunteers, that is, along with a few of the Center kids. No outside, professional, or expert help at all. They've got to be kidding!

Mr. B will be doing most of the speaking, of course. But everything else from the advertising to the music to the program is supposed to come from the rest of us. No one else seemed to be panicking. It turns out that Amos and a couple of underclassmen along with some of the Center crowd—that karaoke bunch I saw that first night?—have been working Saturday mornings and some weeknights to put together a band. Others will be doing drama, and a few will be sharing their personal testimonies. I made myself smaller in the back corner of the van when Mr. B started calling out names for that, petrified mine was going to surface. But it didn't. Just Brian and Peter and Michelle and a few of the Center kids themselves. And the drama teams were all made up long before I joined the Center group. So I started breathing again . . . until Mr. B announced that *everyone* is to help pass out invitations in the neighborhood around the Center next weekend. With Werewolves and Devil's Angels and who knows what else prowling around out there? What is Mr. B thinking?

The whole thing seems pretty high risk to me. I mean, these kids are raised on the streets! Why should they want to listen to us? They're likely to show up with a stash of rotten tomatoes and sulfuric eggs—or worse—if they show up at all! But Mr. B insists we can do it. He says these street kids will pay more attention to their old pals whose lives have been turned around than to some imported group that doesn't know where they're coming from. Maybe he's right. At any rate, if the others are going to do it, I'm not going to wimp out, as nervous as I am at the prospects of setting foot outside the solid brick walls of the Center.

At least the food should be a big drawing card. The churches are all getting together on this one, and they've promised nachos; turkey sandwiches and casseroles from all those Thanksgiving leftovers; apple, pumpkin, mince, and every other kind of pie those church ladies can dream up—the works! I'm just hoping maybe Maria will see the posters and show up.

Speaking of Maria, Mr. B suggested we each choose someone we've met at the Center to pray for while we're getting ready for this youth festival. I thought right away of Maria. Could my praying really make any difference? I don't know, but I guess it won't hurt to try.


*Sunday, November 24th*

I asked Dad tonight when I got home from youth group if I could be involved in *YOUTHQUAKE*. One condition Dad put on my helping in the Center was that I couldn't neglect our own church or youth group. That hasn't been any real hardship because, despite my griping about Mr. Schneider, our church youth group is pretty good, both in size and range of activities, and has always been my main—more like only—social outlet before these last months. There is a younger couple, honest-to-goodness Generation Xers, who leaven out some of Mr. Schneider's more antediluvian ideas. Tonight, for example, we had a cookout. Not hamburgers or hot dogs or anything else in the common way, but Middle East-ern shish kebabs and unleavened bread followed by the staging of a synagogue meeting circa the time of Christ, complete with the women's gallery and head coverings. The kids from our church re-ally like John and Heather and flock out on Sunday nights. The group is big enough, in fact, that it was never a problem dodging my only SCA classmates, Amos and Sandy. Maybe that's why I never found out how much fun they can really be.

Interestingly, the whole bunch seem a lot more fun these days. Truth is, I've been finding youth group more than a little juvenile since I became a senior. I mean, some of these kids were still in grade school when I started! Scott and Denise and their crowd wouldn't be caught dead at anything so pubescent, and only my reluctance to start another battle at home has kept me faithful. But I've actually enjoyed these last couple of weeks, and I find myself looking at that rowdy adolescent crowd with their enthusiasm and puppyishness and *innocence*, not with proper seniorly disdain, but hoping they'll keep it for a long time to come.

But I'm still not talking to Mr. Schneider.

Anyway, since *YOUTHQUAKE* will be running through Sunday evening, the Center team will have to forego their own evening church services that day. Amos and Sandy already have the green light from their parents, and after leaning back in his chair to pon-der in his usual deliberate fashion, Dad agreed that one miss at church and youth group wouldn't quite constitute a breach of my contract. Actually, what he really said, rather dryly, was that it was a better investment of my holidays than couch potatoing in front of the TV. He wasn't so enthusiastic about SCA students canvassing the neighborhood down there, but that gang war the police were expecting between the Devil's Angels and the Werewolves never did materialize, and I assured him that Mr. B will be sending us out in groups, not alone. So he told me I could go with his blessing and even made a joke about getting extra patrol cars assigned down there. At least I think it was a joke.

He seemed in such a good mood, I went on to ask him if he'd heard anything new about the Werewolves and the Devil's Angels leader who'd been killed. He raised his eyebrows at that, and I guess he had reason to. I haven't paid this much attention to one of his police cases since I was still in grade school and thought my daddy was the biggest hero in the world. He hadn't heard anything new, but he said he'd check it out with his friend for me.

If Dad's pleased about the Center, Mom isn't. Tonight I overheard them arguing in the kitchen. That baby-sitter hasn't turned out to be as reliable as Dad hoped, and Mom doesn't want me going out so much. I heard Dad say, "He's your child, not hers. Maybe you should consider giving up some of your own volunteer work."

That's when Danny came into the living room and crawled on my lap. "Why do they always have to fight?" he whispered into my ear, wrapping his arms tightly around my neck as Mom's voice escalated in the kitchen. "Don't they love us?"

I didn't know what to say to that so I carried him off to bed and read him a story. Ever since that night I found him crying, I've been trying to pay him a little more attention. I'd hate to have him grow up like Julie and me, thinking no one loves him. It's too late to hope Mom's ever going to change, so I guess it's up to me.


*Monday, November 25ᵗʰ*

Glancing back over the last few entries, it seems that the Center is taking up a rather inordinate percentage of this journal. I guess maybe it has become the most important thing in my life right now. But that doesn't mean nothing else is happening. I've been studying hard, and my grades are back up to where they should be.

Thanks to those SAT and ACT scores, I've received several more scholarship and financial aid offers. One of them is just what I want and clear across the continent. I'll probably end up taking it, though I have yet to send in the form. I guess I should mention that the U right here in San Diego has been trying to tempt me with a full four-year scholarship. But I don't really count that one as I'm not even considering anything that close to home.

I wrote an article about the Center for *Inkblot* (oops, there we go with the Center again!), and both Joel Blumhurst and the newspaper's much absent staff advisor loved it. It's going to be the front-page headline for this next issue. And I'm still playing for Miss Kitchener, at least for another week or so. She really isn't such a bad person, and I've long forgiven that stupid blowup of hers. Maybe I'm just starting to understand her better. She's the high-strung type, and when she gets under a lot of pressure—like that day I couldn't make it to choir—she blows up. But she doesn't really mean it, and she does apologize afterwards. I used to figure that once you were an adult, you had an obligation to act mature at all times. I'm learning better. After all, I will very shortly be of age to vote, and look what a long way *I* have to go! As long as I make allowances for Miss Kitchener to have bad days too, we get along just fine.

And it's great to be friends with Annette and Sally again and Sandy, too, now that we've gotten to know each other better at the Center (see, I just can't get away from it!) and even in youth group. It's still hard to get together much outside of school. But now we have our own regular lunch table, and I don't even glance at the "in" table when I walk by anymore because I think we really have a lot more fun. In fact, a couple of times lately, when the giggles at our end have gotten a little out of hand, I've even caught Denise casting our way what, from anyone else, I'd take to be envious glances. Though that's probably just wishful thinking.

It isn't that we're exclusive like Scott and Denise and their crowd.

If anyone wants to join us, they're welcome. But most days Annette and Sally and Sandy and I end up with Brian, Peter, Amos, Michelle, and a couple of the other regulars from the Center. And the Center does tend to come up a lot in conversation. It would be just perfect if only Annette and Sally could get involved, too. But they bus from clear across the city, and their parents don't care for them out alone so late at night.

## Tuesday, November 26th

Dad was on night patrol last night, and when he got home from his shift this morning, he had some news for me. Mom was still asleep, and I was making myself and Danny some toast and scrambled eggs so I stirred in a couple of eggs for Dad and poured him a cup of coffee while he told me what he'd found out.

The police still haven't picked up Rodrigo and Mick, but Dad did take a look at the police report. The weapon has been positively identified. It was one of a dozen registered as stolen during a Werewolves raid on a downtown gun shop. My heart sank to my toes at that because if that gun really had belonged to the Werewolves, then Maria had been lying after all when she said that it was Icepick who did the shooting.

But Dad hadn't finished. Identifying that weapon had still left the police with several unanswered questions. For one, the gun had been wiped clean of fingerprints. And all indications were that it was the Werewolves jacket tossed carelessly on the warehouse floor beside the gun that had been used to wipe it. What they were trying to figure out was why the two Werewolves assassins would take the time to wipe down the murder weapon and yet be so stupid as to leave both gun and jacket behind? And why would the Werewolves shoot the leader of the Devil's Angels, but leave Icepick alive as a witness?

There was something else interesting, too. Some of that blood on the warehouse floor wasn't from Abdul. It was of a totally different blood type. If Rodrigo and Mick had shot Abdul and then escaped, leaving not only the gun and jacket but also an uninjured Icepick to call in the police, whose blood was it? Sure, there'd been fighting going on down there earlier in the day, but the traces of another blood type they'd found were as fresh and wet as Abdul's own when the police arrived.

"Are you saying that maybe one of the Werewolves got shot too?" I asked Dad. Maria hadn't said anything about one of her friends being hurt. Then I remembered that second explosion she'd heard just as Rodrigo and Mick were escaping.

"It could be," Dad admitted cautiously.

The problem was, if that other blood type belonged to one of the two killers, then who shot him and with what? The police hadn't been able to hold onto Icepick as there were no charges against him, and the new Devil's Angels leader had evaporated from public view just as soon as he'd made his statement to the police. But there'd been just the one round missing from the murder weapon when the police had found it, and that matched the bullet recovered from Abdul's body. The police had of course considered the possibility that Icepick or Abdul might have indulged in some shooting of their own. And though the crime area had been searched thoroughly, no second weapon had been found, and the first police response had been too quick on the scene for Icepick to have ditched a gun beyond the search area and then returned to where they found him. All of which backed up Icepick's story that he and Abdul had been unarmed at the time of the shooting.

Which meant that if there *had* been a second gun involved, the Werewolves must have taken it with them. But then, why not take the murder weapon as well? Besides, Icepick had never said anything in his statement about a second shot, even on the part of the

Werewolves. As neatly as Icepick's story fit the evidence, it just didn't explain those extra traces of blood.

That was when I started to get excited, because if Maria's story was true—and I was beginning to think maybe it was, after all— then there *was* an explanation. It would have been easy enough for Icepick to slip an extra bullet into that gun before wiping it so that it would seem there'd only been one shot, maybe not realizing that blood samples would show there'd been two shootings.

Of course that scenario left questions of its own. Such as that the police hadn't found any extra ammo on Icepick. But then, maybe he'd only had the one extra bullet. Or he'd swallowed any left-overs. Weren't pushers and druggies always doing that kind of thing? As to why the gun had been registered as being stolen during a Werewolves raid, hadn't Maria said her friends were sure they'd been set up by someone within their own gang?

Anyway, according to Dad, the police still had an APB out for Rodrigo and Mick, but at least they weren't so completely convinced anymore that Icepick was telling the whole truth about Abdul's killing. Like I said, a gang shooting wasn't exactly a top priority in the SDPD, but at least the blood analysis had raised enough questions that Dad's friend in charge of the case had decided to check out Icepick's story a little further.

Dad cocked his eyebrow when he'd finished, giving me that cop look of his. "Now, are you going to tell me why you're so interested?"

I mumbled something about being curious after running into those Werewolves at the Center. Which is the truth, as far as it goes. But I'm wondering if I shouldn't tell Dad the whole story. If the police really aren't so sure anymore that Rodrigo and Mick are guilty, maybe they'd be willing to listen to Maria's story. Maybe they'd even arrest this Icepick and fix things up so Maria and her friends wouldn't have to be on the streets anymore.

But then again, maybe they won't believe her. And I don't know how to find Maria again, anyway. All I could tell the police is what she said about her friends hiding out somewhere around the Center. And if the police go barging down there to ask around for them, it isn't going to be two minutes before the Devil's Angels know they're supposed to be in the area. And they don't have to worry about search warrants and proper procedure. I know where I'd put my bet as to who'd find Rodrigo and Mick first. I've got to think about this a little first.

I wasn't paying much attention to Danny sitting there wide-eyed over his scrambled eggs and cocoa. But when we got on the school bus, he asked me anxiously, "Is there really a war down where you go at night? Do you want to borrow my gun?"

That gun, a black plastic UZI machine gun with sound effects, is Danny's prized possession, so I knew he was really worried about me. I said thank you, but no, and not to worry. But I did tell him a little about the Center, including the story of the Werewolf who'd jumped Mr. B. By the time I finished, putting in a good plug for "Just Say No" while I was at it, Danny's eyes were bigger and rounder than when he's watched too many Saturday morning cartoons.

"Wow, that's awesome!" was his opinion. Then his wriggly little body grew unusually still, and after a moment's silence, he looked up at me and said, "I guess you're just like Jesus, Jana!"

That staggered me! "Why?" I asked.

"Well—" He rubbed his finger up and down the side of his nose as he does when he's thinking those profound thoughts the smallest kids can surprise you with. "My Sunday school teacher told us how Jesus went out and made friends with poor people and bad guys, not just the people who went to church. Just like you're doing."

He was so cute with his serious expression, I had to give him a big hug, though I didn't try to disillusion him. Me like Jesus? If he could only see my inside!

*Part Six*

## Thanksgiving Day, November 28th

Thanksgiving was bad!

I used to love Thanksgiving when Julie and I were still small back in Montana. Driving up the winding gravel driveway to the sprawling log house that Grandma and Grandpa Thompson built up in the Rockies when they retired. All the aunts and a few of the uncles tripping over each other in Grandma's huge kitchen, basting turkeys and beating cream for pies. Sneaking around playing spy games in the woods with cousins and second cousins and even a few thirds until we were called in for dinner. Even Mom was always at her best with that many people to keep organized.

This year there were just the four of us. With things going so much better lately, I guess I'd begun to harbor delusions of a nice, storybook family Thanksgiving. I should have known better! Maybe normal families can handle being alone together all day, but in our house it's not a good idea. Mom was in one of her moods, and nothing Danny and I did was good enough. We cleaned the house and polished Mom's wedding silver and china as though the President were coming for dinner instead of just us. I really didn't mind all the work, even if it *was* supposed to be a holiday. And Dad even pitched in to do the vacuuming. But no matter how hard we tried, Mom could always find a dust streak we'd missed or a speck of skin on the potatoes.

I honestly tried to bite my tongue. But when she started in on Danny for a spot on one of the spoons so microscopic I couldn't even see it, that's when I lost it. Mom was carrying on as though Danny had robbed a bank, and Danny was crying hysterically, and I just couldn't take it anymore.

"Hey, give the kid a break!" I muttered just loud enough to cut through the storm. "He's just a baby!"

It wasn't respectful, and I admit it. But at least it drew Mom's attention from Danny to me. While she started in with the "Who do you think you are to talk to me like that?" routine, Danny managed to slip away.

By the time the table was flawless enough that even Mom couldn't find anything else wrong, no one was very hungry. Dad gave an impressive—and, I think, even sincere—grace, thanking God for His many blessings throughout the year, while the rest of us sat there with closed eyes and stony faces, not feeling thankful at all. Then he dragged out a few of his timeworn jokes as he flourished the carving knife and fork over the turkey. He was trying so hard to make it a festive occasion that I played along, though I was still seething inside. At least we could make it a special time for Danny. But Mom managed to point out that the steaming, perfectly browned holiday fowl was a little too crisp on the outside and the potatoes too lumpy and that I'd carelessly let the pumpkin pies burn. They were a little brown on the edges, not burnt at all!

After dinner, Mom retired to bed with a headache, saying that she'd slaved all day in the kitchen and now we could show some gratitude by doing the cleanup. Dad volunteered to help me, trying to make a joke out of it. But the disappointment on his face as he started to load the dishwasher did something to me, and it just exploded out, "Dad, why haven't you and Mom ever gotten divorced?"

If Dad and I hadn't started talking more lately, I know I'd never have let that slip out. And I sure never expected him to answer me. But he set down the stack of plates he was rinsing. In that deliberate, thoughtful way of his, he said, "Jana, when I married your mother I made a commitment to her before God. That commitment wasn't just for while things were going good. It was for life."

Walking over to where I was furiously scraping turkey bones into the garbage, Dad put his arm around my shoulder, something he hasn't done in a long time. A month ago, I'd have shrugged him away. But after a startled moment, I relaxed and let him hug me.

"I know you kids haven't always had it easy with your mother," he said. "And maybe I haven't stood up for you as much as I should have. I'm sorry for that. You'll find when you're an adult that it isn't always as easy as you think to make the right decisions. Your mother is my wife, and I've tried to back her up as a husband should. But I know it hasn't always been fair to you girls."

"But why is she like that?" I wailed out the question I've been wanting to ask for years. "She's supposed to be a Christian, but she doesn't act like she cares about us at all!"

Dad sighed and let go of me. "Your mother's a Christian, all right. I was there when she asked Christ to be her Savior at a youth campaign not so different than the one you're going to tomorrow. But I guess maybe you could say she's a defeated one."

Picking up the dishcloth, Dad started wiping not too expertly at the counter while he tried to explain.

"I know your mom doesn't like to talk about her childhood, but there are some things you're old enough to understand now. Your mom hasn't always had an easy life. She's a brilliant woman—it's from her you girls get those brains, not from me. She dreamed of college and doing great things. Just as I've seen you do, Jana. But she was only nine years old when her mother died and her father turned to drinking. She spent her teen years kicked around from one relative who didn't want her to another. And when her father died too, leaving only a pile of debts, all hopes for college went out the window."

It seemed strange, and rather wonderful too, to be talking like this with Dad. Like two adults rather than the father-daughter thing. I held my breath for fear he'd stop. But he went on almost as though he was talking to himself.

"She was beautiful on our wedding day. Absolutely radiant with happiness. Thrilled to finally have a home of her own. But things didn't turn out the way she expected it. You girls came along before she ever got that chance to go on to college. Not having grown up with a mother, she didn't always know how to handle three kids of her own. Then she didn't realize how often a policeman has to be gone. And I'm not a very outgoing person. I guess I've failed her there. Over the years, she's let bitterness and anger drown out the joy of her Christian life. It's only since she's gotten involved in this volunteer work that she's found any real enjoyment and an outlet for her talents and abilities. That's why I've never interfered with it."

His eyes focused on me again. "But I certainly didn't mean for you girls to end up with more than your share of household duties. I guess I've been gone too much. I didn't even notice what was happening until lately. I'm sorry, Jana, and I ask your forgiveness."

I nodded, a warm glow filling me inside. But that's when his face turned stern. "But you've got to admit, if you're honest, Jana, that it hasn't all been your mom. You girls haven't always been as kind and loving as you could be, either. You've done your share of talking back, and I haven't been blind to the way you and Julie have always stood together against her—even when she was right!"

I wanted to defend myself, but I couldn't. Mom *is* selfish and unreasonable often enough. But it's true, too, that Julie and I have gotten into the habit of rebelling against *anything* Mom says. Like last year when she pointed out a serious flaw in logic in my history paper on the Civil War. I was so furious at her sarcastic remarks I wasn't about to admit she could be right, even when I got the paper back with just those points marked off.

But Dad had moved on past my shortcomings. He patted me on the shoulder as if to cheer me up, then walked over to the sink to rinse out his dishrag as he went on, "I came to terms a long time ago with the fact that I can't change your mother. But no matter what she does or says, she's my wife, and I've pledged to love and cherish her to the best of my ability. We had some good times once, and I try to remember those and pray that some day your mother will be that woman again. Maybe if you can do the same, Jana, you might just be able to forgive her for the way things are now."

Well! If Dad had only talked like this to me a few years ago, though I doubt I'd have been in the mood to listen. None of what Dad said makes Mom's behavior right. But at least I think I understand her a little bit better. You don't think of your own parents as people with hopes and dreams and disappointments of their own.

And Dad! I've always thought he was kind of weak because he never stood up to Mom, and it's always surprised me how many awards and even medals he's gotten for being an outstanding cop. But I guess there's more than one way of being strong. Maybe Dad isn't the Superman hero I thought he was when I was a kid. But somehow I respect him more tonight than I have for a long, long time.

After we'd finished cleaning the kitchen, we spent the rest of the afternoon watching football and playing Candyland and Life and other table games Danny could play. I just tucked Danny into bed with a story, and now I'm lying on my bed with the computer keyboard propped up on my pillow, trying to remember some of those good times Dad talked about. I've had to go back a long way because Mom's never been the cuddling and kissing sort of mother, and even in family pictures, she's never looked happy.

But I do remember—maybe clear back in kindergarten—how Julie and I used to sit on the piano bench with Mom, singing these goofy nursery rhymes Mom learned from *her* mother before she died. And there were those matching frilly dresses Mom made one year for Easter, the prettiest dress I ever had. I have a vague memory of Julie and I twirling round and round like Cinderella at the ball. And Mom smiling as she watched. . . .

I'm going to end this now and pray for Maria as I promised— wherever she might be tonight. Maybe I'll even add in a prayer for Mom.

## Friday, November 29th

One of the phrases Ms. Langdon threw out at regular intervals during our session together was "emotional roller coaster." It grabbed at me because it sounded like a good part of my life. And has this day ever been one! Angry and terrified and happy and tonight flying right up into the skies. More than once in these last months I've felt that my life was tossed upside-down, but tonight I can say beyond the shadow of a doubt that it will never again be the same.

It began once more with the Center. Or rather, it began with Denise Jenkins showing up in the SCA school parking lot to accompany us to the Center. Okay, so Brian or anyone else has every right to bring along anyone they choose. But *Denise*? Since when has she ever displayed the slightest interest in getting her hands dirty on behalf of someone else? A pang of unease twisted my stomach the instant she stepped out of Brian's beat-up station wagon looking like she just stepped out of the pages of a fashion magazine. Her high heels and skin-bearing outfit were more appropriate for an evening of dinner and dancing than the Center in downtown San Diego. Brian is such a special person. The thought of him falling under her predatory spell was a disturbing one.

No, that isn't being honest as I swore to be in this journal. The truth is, that stomach-knotting pang was neither unease nor concern for Brian. It was sheer jealousy. The Center bunch are *my* friends. We've become a team. And over these last couple of weeks, I guess I've been thinking of Brian as a rather special friend. Denise has her own crowd. Why should she have to horn in on what I've made for myself here?

I pretended I didn't see Brian scoot over with his slow smile so that I could slide in beside him on the opposite side as Denise, crawling instead into the back of the van where I could ignore his occasional puzzled glances. The sight of Denise batting her false lashes at him and somehow managing even here to turn herself into the focus of attention made the acid rise into my throat. I could have sworn Brian had seen through that beauty-queen facade months ago! He'd certainly shown enough cool disapproval when Denise and I were still hanging out together during those weeks I'm trying so hard to forget.

Fortunately, everyone else in the van was too excited about the upcoming youth festival to notice my own uncharacteristic silence. Except for Mr. B. We were unloading the flyers he'd had printed to advertise *YOUTHQUAKE* when he asked me why I was so quiet. That man has eyes in the back of his head! I didn't answer. I couldn't say, "It's because I'm afraid of what will come out if I unclamp my lips."

This was still early afternoon. The festival didn't begin until 7:30 P.M., but there was plenty to do before then. The evening's drama team had to practice. So did the band. That still left a good-sized group as even the more irregular SCA volunteers had turned out to help with the festival along with a fair number of the Center regulars. Mr. B assigned us all to canvassing the neighborhood and began naming us off into teams of three, intermixing male and female and SCAers and Center kids. The idea was to keep us suburban types from being out there in that concrete jungle on our own.

My own enthusiasm was less than marked, I'll admit. But Denise was furious, especially when she found out that she couldn't pair up with Brian, who was staying behind to help Mr. B set up the lighting and sound equipment. She promptly volunteered to help him, though I can testify by eyewitness account that the girl can hardly plug in a toaster. But Mr. B vetoed that just as promptly, saying that she'd be of more use passing out flyers. There was no answer to that without a public admission that she hadn't come to be of any use, so Denise subsided sulkily to wait for her assignment.

Now as I said, it was a good-sized group with at least a dozen other girls. So what were the odds I'd end up with Denise? I still don't know if Mr. B did it on purpose. It would certainly fit his sense of humor! But Denise's glare had hardly time to do more than scorch me when Mr. B named off the third of our trio—Armal, the big, black kid with the cornrows and a gold grill on his teeth who helps in reception at the clinic.

Armal is really a nice guy and as gentle as he is huge. But I can still remember my own panic the first time I saw him, so I wasn't completely unsympathetic to the horror and distaste that widened Denise's baby-blue eyes when he loomed up beside us with a stack of flyers. Still, she didn't have to make it so obvious. When her eyes narrowed to slide down over him as though he were something to be scraped off those expensive Italian sandals, I elbowed her in the ribs and hissed, "Stop staring!"

She stopped staring, all right. In fact, she didn't cast so much as another glance in his direction, and as we trailed the rest of the crowd outside, she made good and sure I was between her and Armal as though he might at any moment show his true colors as a serial assassin. Armal on his part was looking just as uneasy about this haughty, new female who might have just stepped out of a TV commercial. That left me to try to get our assignment underway. Not an easy task with Denise pretending that Armal was The Invisible Man and speaking to me only when unavoidable, while Armal, eyeing Denise as though she were some exotic jungle fowl that wandered into the barnyard, responded to my attempts at conversation with a uniform grunt that could mean either *yes* or *no*.

In the end it didn't really matter, because Armal wasn't with us for long. He wanted to start with his own apartment building, which was fine with me as I was curious to see just where and how he lived. So we left the other teams to scatter out to nearby apartment complexes and threaded our way through a dozen side streets and two narrow gravel alleys before Armal called us to a stop in front of an old brick building maybe ten stories high. By then I was so turned around I could never have found my way back to the Center on my own.

The building had definitely seen better days with graffiti sprayed across the brick in black and red and neon orange as far as a step ladder would reach and at least half the windows boarded up where the glass had been broken out. There was garbage in the gutters and not so much as a tree or flower pot or even a blade of grass thrusting its way through the cracked sidewalk. Even considering the holiday, the number of kids on the steps and in the street was overwhelming; they were all sizes, right down to toddlers in danger of every car and bike going by. Kids on skateboards and roller blades. Kicking around a soccer ball. Or smoking—and not just the older ones, either!

Armal must have been some kind of a local hero because everyone crowded around to listen just as soon as he climbed the steps. While he made a plug for the campaign, Denise and I passed out flyers. Or rather, I did. Denise's idea of handing out a flyer is to lean gingerly up against the cleanest spot on the banister and wait for someone to come over and ask for one.

There were a fair number of flyers wadded up on the ground even before Armal finished. But some of the kids seemed interested, especially when he laid it on about the food. One, a wiry, olive-skinned *Latino* about my own age with hair raked back into a greasy ponytail and a tattoo of a scorpion on one cheek, asked if there'd be any beer. When Armal said no, he spat with disgust on the ground. But then he swung around to rake his black eyes over Denise and me and leered, "Sure, Armal, if the chick's part of the show, I'll give it a shot!"

I didn't need to be told which "chick" he was referring to. That seductive outfit stood out even among the psychedelic hairdos and circus-clown clothes. A barrage of catcalls and wolf whistles and ruder remarks drowned Armal out, and Denise brightened up for the first and only time in the whole afternoon. But her haughty look returned immediately when Scorpion-Cheek and a couple of the others began to saunter our direction. I looked around fast for our bodyguard.

That's when I noticed the boy. He was no more than ten or twelve, and once I gave him a good look, I realized I'd seen him once or twice at the Center. But only now that he and Armal were standing together did I see the resemblance. He was an Armal in miniature, right down to the cornrows. Armal was bent down while the kid whispered urgently into his ear, and it was clear he'd forgotten all about us. Denise was looking at Scorpion-Cheek now exactly as she had earlier at Armal, and I was getting a little nervous because I knew that whatever those perfectly outlined red lips were opening to say, it wasn't going to be too politically correct. But before the explosion hit, Armal straightened up, scattered Scorpion-Cheek and pals with one wave of his enormous hand, and trotted down the steps.

"I got some business to take care of," he informed me, ignoring Denise as completely as she had him. "It won't take a minute. You and her," the flicker of his eyes acknowledged Denise's existence for the briefest of moments, "can wait here."

Then he seemed to take in for the first time that catcalling mob and Scorpion-Cheek's watchful eyes. "No, maybe you better come with me."

The building didn't look any better from the inside than from the outside. It would have been impossible to say what the original paint shade had been between more graffiti and dirt and what looked suspiciously like food stains. There was an elevator, but an "Out of Order" sign had been nailed across the door, and the nails were actually starting to rust. Denise balked when she saw the stairs, and I couldn't really blame her with those high heels. But I'd already started up after Armal, and she wasn't about to stay downstairs alone, so after a few choice phrases more common to the Center than SCA, she started climbing. Armal's little brother brought up the rear.

We must have climbed all ten flights of stairs before Armal pushed open a fire door and motioned us into a long hall. A wave of earsplitting music greeted us. Every apartment must have had its stereo on full blast, and the resulting mixture was horrendous— like some of Scott's CDs! But it wasn't loud enough to drown out the angry voices as Armal stopped in front of a door halfway down the hall.

"Oh, no!" Armal exclaimed, pounding one huge fist into the other. He swung around on his younger brother. "Why didn't you tell me he was here?"

But the boy was already backing away, his dark eyes rolled back with fear so that only the whites showed and his skin paled under the dark pigment. Before Armal could make a grab for him, he turned and scurried away as fast as his little legs could carry him.

"Is it your father?" I asked Armal, eyeing the apartment door anxiously as a male roar rose behind it.

"No, my step!" he said curtly. It was the look on his face that told me something was seriously wrong. Armal is so big and dangerous looking that even the worst of the gang troublemakers back off when he strolls up behind Mr. B. But just then he looked as scared as his younger brother. Neither Denise nor I put up an argument when he ordered us to stay outside.

I got a quick glimpse of the apartment as Armal eased the door open. It wasn't just shabby and small. It was filthy! Beer cans and take-out food containers and dirty laundry scattered all over the floor. A tattered couch with a couple of preschoolers bouncing on it. There was a woman with the pure, high-cheeked features of all those pictures of Queen Nefertiti in the history books and the saddest eyes I'd ever seen. And the Voice!

He was huge, bigger than Armal with a belly that showed where all those cans on the floor had gone. And he was mad! The phrases spewing from his mouth would have stunned me if it hadn't been for those weeks at the Center. Grabbing Armal by the arm, he yanked him into the room with an ease that showed how much muscle was under all that padding. The door slammed behind them, and that angry roar started to rise again. I could hear kids and, I think, the mom crying.

Then the door edged back open, and Armal's stepfather thrust his head out. "Git!" he snarled. "The kid won't be out again today."

The door slammed again, and Denise and I were left staring at each other in the hall. Poor Armal! He's always so cheerful and uncomplaining and *tough* at the Center. I never dreamed he came from a home like that! I hated to leave without making sure he was all right. But there was nothing two girls could do, and Denise was in a hurry to get out of there.

Armal's younger brother hadn't gone any further than the other side of the fire door. He clattered down the stairs in front of us, not so much as glancing over his shoulder, but staying close enough to make it clear he wasn't just running away but was serving as our escort. I was grateful for this when we emerged to find Armal's mob of acquaintances still loitering at the bottom of the steps. The catcalls erupted again as soon as they saw Denise, and Scorpion-Cheek and his pals immediately rearranged themselves so that there was no way to get past without physical contact. But when our juvenile escort turned a scowl on them so like Armal's it made me want to laugh—or maybe even cry—they moved back, letting us through with no more than a little jostling and what I'm sure they considered appreciative comments.

Our escort evaporated at the property line, but we continued on another block, Denise taking the lead for a change, walking so fast despite the high heels I could hardly keep up with her. That lasted as long as it took to turn a corner and leave Armal's home and friends out of sight. Then she dropped down on the closest set of steps under a dilapidated sign that read "Mamita's Burritos." Dumping her almost untouched stack of flyers onto the concrete step beside her so that I had to grab at them to keep the breeze from scattering them into the street, she kicked off her high heels.

"That does it!" she announced, shaking out a pebble that had to have hurt. "You drag me through a hundred miles of slum with a reject from the Addams Family, get me practically assaulted by your buddy's punk friends, then almost get us both killed in that domestic violence sitcom back there. And now look at my feet! And I've got a broken nail. I ought to sue you!"

She wasn't carrying a handbag, and that tight outfit of hers didn't exactly allow room for storage, but from somewhere a cell phone suddenly appeared in her hand. "And maybe I will, too," she informed me, "just as soon as I call Brian and tell him to get down here and pick me up."

Just how I was supposed to be responsible for forcing her into the last hour's activities, I have no idea. But what really got me was the way she talked about Brian, as though he were some dog on a leash she only had to jerk to bring him running. Maybe because in part I was afraid it was true.

"Brian's got things to do," I enlightened her coolly. "He can't just drop everything to keep you from having to walk a few blocks." From where I was standing, I could see another apartment building on the next block with people lounging around on the steps and in the streets. "Look, we came here to do a job! There's no reason we can't at least finish handing out these flyers. Then we'll *walk* back to the Center."

Denise was already playing with the cell phone's control panel. "Be my guest! But if you think I'm taking one more step in this filthy neighborhood, think again! And why should I? Or you either. Let's be real, Jana! No one's going to know if those stupid flyers end up in a dumpster instead of wadded up on the street. Not unless *you* tell them. As if it makes any difference, anyway!" The look she gave her surroundings showed exactly what she thought of the neighborhood and everyone in it. "Do you really think anything's going to change down here just because a few of these lowlifes show up at some stupid preaching campaign?"

You'd think I'd have learned the futility of arguing with her by now. But keeping my cool around Denise has never been one of my strong points, and it hurt that she'd sneer like that at all the hard work Mr. B and Karen and the others—and even myself, a little—had put into the Center and the festival.

"No one forced you to come," I reminded her in a voice that was tight because I was holding onto my temper by one thread. "Why did you bother anyway if you didn't want to help?"

Her buffed and polished fingertips paused on the key pad, and I could see from where I was standing that the number she'd summoned up from the directory was the Center's. Brian's thoughtful foresight, no doubt! She lifted her shoulders in a shrug that managed to convey both elegance and boredom. "Oh, I don't know. You guys are always going on about this precious 'Center' of yours. I just figured I'd come and see what the big deal was—maybe get a look at the wildlife outside Southwest Reform School."

"You mean, you were trying to impress Brian!" The accusation came out of my mouth before I could stop it. But it didn't phase Denise. She just laughed—that cool, utterly self-possessed laugh that Scott Mitchell once described in an unoriginal attack of poetry as fairy bells, but to me has always had the same effect as the grating of fingernails across a blackboard.

"Yeah?" she said softly. "And just who are *you* trying to impress?"

That shut me up like a slap across the mouth. After all, haven't I admitted more than once right in this journal that my own motives for coming to the Center aren't much better? Denise was looking me over with that superior stare she does so well. I could feel the dampness under my hair from running those stairs, and streaks of dirt and even a few cobwebs had somehow found their way to my T-shirt and probably to my face as well, judging from her smug expression. But she still looked as though she just stepped off the cover of *Vogue* magazine, and I couldn't help thinking what a contrast we'd make for Brian when he showed up. My chest was hurting with that hot, frustrated feeling you get when you want to strike back but just can't think of anything smart or crushing enough to say, and the palms of my hands hurt where my fingernails were biting into them. I wouldn't, of course, really have gone so far as to strangle her, but I'm not sure I'd have volunteered much in the line of defense if someone had shown up just then to do the job for me.

Denise showed no awareness of my homicidal reflections. Punching the SEND key, she raised the phone to her ear and her plucked line of an eyebrow in my direction. "Well?" she said sweetly, and the tone made it a challenge.

There must have been any number of considered and mature reactions I could have displayed. I chose none of them. I'm not totally sorry for what I did because of what came of it later, but it was still incredibly stupid!

"Fine!" I snapped, snatching up her stack of flyers along with my own. "Go ahead and call your boyfriend. I'm going to finish what we came to do!"

And I left her.

I had no worries for Denise. There was always that Mexican café for shelter while she waited for Brian to ride to the rescue. But it didn't take me long to realize that wandering around the streets of that neighborhood with a bodyguard like Armal was one thing. It was another to be out there alone—and female.

The apartment building on the next block wasn't too bad. I caught some of the same jostling we'd run into at Armal's (so maybe it *wasn't* just Denise's outfit), but a pair of elderly *mamitas* out on the steps, catching up on the latest barrio scandal while they supervised the youngest crowd, were quick to shout at the hecklers to remember their manners and leave the *señorita* alone. And to my surprise, they promptly did. I got rid of a dozen flyers and left a stack with the *mamitas* for the rest of the building's inhabitants. I continued on, feeling a sense of accomplishment that now that I'd made my point maybe I'd earned a dignified exit back to the Center.

It wasn't until I rounded the corner and walked a few more blocks, then turned another corner, that it began to sink in that maybe I was in over my head. I could have sworn I'd headed back the same direction Armal had brought us, but nothing was looking familiar. The low-income housing projects with their peeling paint and crumbling plaster and screaming mobs of kids in the streets had vanished, and in their place were old, squat brick buildings, some a full block long, that looked as though they might have been warehouses. But there were no trucks or cars in the parking areas to show they were still in use, and even the huge metal loading doors were boarded over. A creepy feeling was prickling between my shoulder blades as though all those blank windows were eyes watching me, and I'd have given almost anything just then to run into another living, breathing human being.

Then I saw movement behind a window about three stories up across the street and changed my mind. Consuelo had told me stories over cleanup sessions about runaways and street gangs and dope pushers hanging out in old, abandoned buildings not far from the Center, and it didn't take a genius to figure out this must be the area she was talking about. I made a sudden decision that going back to Denise and helping her call Brian wouldn't really be such a loss of face after all. Then I took one last step to peek around the corner before heading back—and tripped over someone's legs!

The corner led into an alley rather than a street with the back end of a couple of those warehouses forming a solid wall on either side. There must have been twenty of them, all teenagers or maybe even a little older, sprawled out in the November sun that made a stripe down the middle. The air was hazy with smoke, and judging by the sickly smell and spaced-out expressions, I didn't think it was tobacco in those rolled-up tapers. Half-a-dozen crates of beer in tall, dark bottles were stacked against one brick wall, most of them empty from the looks of it.

But the pair of legs I'd stumbled over were sober enough. I'd landed full length on the concrete, the flyers spilling out of my hands. By the time I scrambled up, scooping the flyers back into my arms, he was on his feet, a stream of precisely enunciated obscenities pouring out of his mouth. I started backing toward the corner, stammering an apology, but he moved to cut me off, a long knife appearing out of nowhere in his hand.

He wasn't very tall and was a bit on the wiry side, but he moved incredibly fast and smooth like those ninjas in the movies—or a good cat burglar. And the easy way he held that knife, point down and handle first, told of plenty of practice using it. His head was shaved bald, and at least a dozen gold chains glittered against his chest, which was bare under the jean jacket that was missing both sleeves. More gold gleamed from the earrings that made a semicircle up each earlobe.

Then as he swung around to hiss what I knew to be Spanish and guessed from his tone to be an order, I saw the back of his jacket. A fanged wolf! That's when I knew just how much trouble I was in. I'd stumbled right into the middle of a Werewolf hangout.

Baldy wasn't the only one on his feet now. Half of the bunch on the pavement were too stoned to react to his order, if that was what it had been, but the rest were up and fanning themselves out in a circle around me. My stomach knotted into an icy ball, and I'd have traded every one of my scholarship offers for one of those extra patrol cars Dad had joked about to come cruising by right then. My mind was so blank I couldn't think of a thing to do except what I'd come for, so I launched into a shaky explanation of *YOUTHQUAKE*, holding those flyers out in front of me as though they were a shield. But not a hand moved to take one. Their faces were blank and cold under those unnaturally dilated pupils, and I knew right away I wasn't going to find any takers here.

But it was Baldy who scared me most. He was smiling at me, but it wasn't a smile of goodwill or friendship. He looked like something that had crawled out from under a rock! And those unblinking black eyes belonged to some cold-blooded species, like maybe a rattlesnake or a Gila monster. Stepping forward in the middle of my stammering presentation, he slapped the flyers from my hand to the ground and sneered, "Forget it, baby! I can think of a lot better ways to party with a pretty girl than reading that trash!"

He'd been moving closer and closer, but I guess I was just too naive to understand just what he meant until suddenly his free arm snaked around me and I found myself pulled tight against the full length of him. I'd never allowed a guy to touch me like that, and I was so terrified my teeth were chattering and I could feel myself starting to hyperventilate. So it's odd the way my brain took the time to register the smells. That bare armpit pressing against my face had been eons without soap or deodorant. His breath was absolutely rancid. Cigarette smoke and stale cologne permeated his jacket. I guess those abandoned buildings don't go in a lot for bathing and laundry facilities—or maybe he thought he was too macho to use them!

But I didn't dare pull away. One arm was occupied around my waist, but the corner of my eye could still see that knife hanging casually point down from his other hand like the fang of a saber-toothed tiger. And if I managed to pull free from him, there were other Werewolves all around me. Spaced-out or not, I couldn't doubt that they were as dangerous as they looked.

Baldy's face was coming down, and I just knew I was going to be sick, when the sudden and loud creak of a door jerked his head up again. He loosened his grip enough that I could lift my head to see what he was turning to look at. In the brick wall of the warehouse behind Baldy was a narrow side door. You could still see the splintered ends of the boards that had once been nailed over it. The door had opened, and stepping out from the dimness inside into the afternoon sun was . . . Maria!

"Maria!" I called over Baldy's shoulder, actually dizzy with relief—or maybe just the exhilaration of being able to breathe again.

But she showed no signs of sharing my excitement. For one horrible instant, I even thought she was going to duck back inside and pretend she hadn't seen me. Then she strolled out into the alley.

"Yeah, what do you want?" she said as stonily as though we'd never met.

Baldy loosened his hold another fraction, his narrowed black eyes going from me to her as he registered that I knew her name. "You know this chick?" he demanded.

Maria hunched bare shoulders above the same tank top I'd seen on her last time. "I've seen her around. She's one of those Jesus freaks from the Center."

She sauntered over, her glance telling me to keep my mouth shut. Pressing her slim body up against Baldy on his knife side, she slid an arm slowly up his chest and started doing things on the back of his neck with her long fingernails. "Hey, come on, Luis. Let the girl go!" she coaxed in a throaty voice I couldn't believe was coming from a girl too young to be in high school. "We don't need no more trouble with the police."

While she breathed into his ear, she kept squeezing herself further and further in between us until Baldy had to let me go. Whether she did it on purpose, I don't know. But I didn't really care, it felt so good to be free from that creep. He didn't complain, just pulled her tight against him and kissed her. With that breath I'd have gagged, but she endured it until he came up for air, then did a little dance on his chest with those fingernails and cooed, "You want to party, Luis, we'll party. Just let me get rid of the girl."

The look that accompanied her promise made me blush. My dad would lock me up and throw away the key for a month if I looked at a guy like that! But at least it distracted Baldy's attention from me. There was a dazed expression on his weasel features as she unwrapped herself from his grip, and he made no protest when she jerked her head at me to follow; he just stood there with his eyes glued to the sway of her walk as she pushed me toward the corner. Nor did any of the other Werewolves try to stop us. They were already sinking back down onto the pavement to resume work on their half-smoked joints.

The high fashion model pose lasted only until we were around that brick wall. With just a glance over her shoulder, Maria broke into a run, not slowing until we were around the next corner. As she skidded to a stop, she wiped the back of her hand across her lips so that what little lipstick Luis had left unsmeared transferred itself to a red streak against her olive skin.

"Pflah!!" she spat out as though to rid herself of his taste. "I hate that jerk!" Then she rounded on me to hiss, "What do you think you're doing down here? Are you crazy? Do you know what could have happened back there if I hadn't come along?"

I have an adequate imagination. I started thanking her for rescuing me, an even bigger deal than I'd thought if she really detested the guy as much as it seemed, but she cut me off before I'd finished the first sentence. "You gonna tell me why you're snooping around down here?" she demanded. "You ain't been tracking me, have you?"

Her expression was so hard and unfriendly, I was taken aback. I guess I've been thinking so much about Maria, and praying for her too, it never occurred to me she might not be feeling equally friendly toward a girl she'd only met for a few minutes and not exactly under the best of circumstances. I was itching to ask her about Rodrigo and Mick, but her hostile glare wasn't encouraging. So I handed her the one flyer I'd managed to hang onto and explained about *YOUTHQUAKE*.

"The food's going to be great and plenty of it," I hinted. "Why don't you come? If you still need supplies for your friends, I can get all you can carry."

"My friends are just fine! They don't need your handouts," she retorted sharply. As clearly as though I could read her mind, I knew she was kicking herself for ever having spilled her heart to this nosy stranger. But then her eyes slid away from mine, and just for an instant I saw there a terrible worry and sadness that brought back that memory of a lost and beaten puppy. No matter what she said, things *weren't* fine.

"They didn't find them, did they?" I blurted out.

Even to myself I sounded as anxious as though these were friends of my own we were talking about. Her eyes came back from wherever they'd gone to give me a strange look. "No, they didn't!" she snapped out. "And they're not going to!"

That she was in a hurry now to get away from me was obvious, and I couldn't blame her. After all, she didn't really know me from Adam, and I guess she'd probably learned long ago not to trust strangers. But I'd been waiting a long time to pass on Dad's message—the one about Ricardo and Mick turning themselves in before the Devil's Angels caught up to them. I could do that at least before I removed myself from her life.

But I'd hardly launched into it when Maria broke in, "You're telling me your pop's a cop?" Her fists clenched up, fear and anger both showing under all that makeup. "That tears it! How *could* I have been so stupid!"

I could see her muscles tensing to make a run, and I knew that in two seconds I wasn't ever going to see her again, so I got in quickly, "Hey, I haven't dragged the police down on you so far, have I? I haven't even told my dad, really, I promise!" That made her pause long enough for me to get in what Dad had told me about the police not being so sure anymore that Rodrigo and Mick were guilty.

"Don't you see, Maria? That means they'd probably listen if you'd just tell them your story," I urged her. "Dad says it's dangerous for your friends to keep hiding out. He says the Devil's Angels are going to avenge their leader. If they catch your friends, they'll kill them!"

Maria gave me a look that said she didn't need some backwoods suburbanite explaining the facts of inner-city life to her. "Tell me something I don't know!" she said scornfully. "Besides, it's been two weeks, and there hasn't been no fighting at all!"

She hesitated, her little-girl forehead suddenly developing wrinkles. Then she went on, slowly and thoughtfully as though she'd forgotten who she was talking to. I held my breath, willing her to keep talking.

"That's what's freaking me out. It's really weird, man! The Angels should have hit us hard after Abdul. It's an honor thing, see? You can't just let it slide when another gang takes out your leader. Then no one's gonna have no respect for you. But the Angels ain't been seen on the streets at all. Like they've gone soft or something! And Icepick's got the word out that all he wants is Rodrigo and

Mick. He'll back off the fighting permanent if the Werewolves will just turn them over to him."

"But no one would do that!" I exclaimed, shocked into interrupting. "Not their own friends!"

Maria gave this bitter laugh. "Are you kidding? Half that bunch back there would sell off their own mother for a fix. And that lowlife that had you, Luis, he's never liked Mick and Rodrigo. Now that they're gone, he's real hot stuff with the Wolf—maybe even the hottest. If it wasn't that he's got it in for Icepick like nobody's business, I'd start thinking he set the whole thing up just so Rodrigo and Mick would take the fall! But that doesn't make no sense because everybody knows Luis'd really like to be the Wolf. Getting rid of Rodrigo and Mick doesn't make no difference there. Still, don't think Luis wouldn't be talking to the Angels in a minute if he got any notion of where Rodrigo and Mick are! And maybe the Wolf would too if it means a truce—all this fighting's bad for business."

"Then you've *got* to bring them in," I urged her. "My dad's a good cop. He'll make sure they get a fair deal."

She was shaking her head, but the worry and sadness was there again—and something more. Maybe desperation. I could sense she was weakening so I pushed a little. "Look, if you won't let me help, at least come to the Center tonight."

But that's where I lost her. Her eyes suddenly narrowed on me, and the indecision on her little-girl face tightened to suspicion and hostility. "Why?" she demanded flatly. "So you can have that cop pop of yours waiting to pick me up?"

"Of course not!" I protested. But she wasn't listening. "Look, what's in all this for you, anyway?" she swept on. "Why should you care if I show up at this Earthquake thing? You making commission, or what?"

"What do you mean?" I put in feebly.

Maria jerked her thumb back towards the Werewolf hangout. "You think I'm stupid? You saw how we live back there! And Rodrigo and Mick—you want to know how I got food for them? I made some friends. Nice, respectable men friends. You know what I mean? I even lifted their wallets. I'm not exactly the kind of person *you* hang out with, Miss Suburban!"

Her eyes were hard and unfriendly again. "So what makes you so worried all of a sudden about me and my friends? Since when does someone like you care what happens to a girl like me?"

That's a good question! Why *do* I care? I really don't know! She's as well as admitted she's a prostitute and a thief. A month ago, I wouldn't have stood in the same room with a girl like her. And it's not as though I'd choose her for my college roommate even now. I guess maybe all that praying's made me feel responsible somehow.

If I'd been Mr. B or Karen or even Brian, I'd have known just what to say. A nice little sermon about how God loved her and so did I. But me being me, I just stammered out, "Because I do!"

That hard glare studied me for a long moment. Then suddenly the breath went out of her, and she hunched her shoulders. "Yeah, well, maybe I'll come and maybe I won't! But not for you. For the food. And you'd better not be setting me up, or I'll make you wish you'd never been born."

We were facing each other like two opponents squaring off in a boxing ring, her eyes boring into me as though she were trying to read what was actually written on the neuron paths of my brain, me doing my best to exude sincerity and trustworthiness. So when she went on to mutter, without her gaze shifting so much as an inch, "Here's your ride," I thought it was a trick and didn't even turn my head until a familiar and very stern baritone called, "Jana!"

I spun around. "Brian!"

He was striding down the sidewalk so fast he might as well have been running. I'd never seen Brian angry before, but it wasn't hard to read that clenched jaw and the pinched white lines on either side of his nostrils. Or the grim line of his mouth. Maria jerked a thumb as his furious steps ate up the remaining distance between us. "He'll take you the rest of the way. I'm out of here."

Then she swung around to face Brian. "Next time don't let your girlfriend out alone around here, okay?" she told him harshly without a hint of the come-on she'd used on every guy I'd seen her around. "You should know it ain't healthy for girls like her."

The next instant she was off at a run, and Brian and I were left staring at each other. I didn't know what to say, especially after that "girlfriend" crack. But there was no need to rack my brain for an introductory remark because Brian waited only until Maria had rounded the corner before he exploded.

"Are you out of your mind, Jana? Taking off alone in Werewolves territory? What were you thinking? Don't you know you could have been mugged or killed or—who knows what? I swear, you're not safe to be let out of the house on your own!"

He was being so severe and dictatorial about the whole thing I couldn't help smiling just a little—especially as I'd seen that first expression of utter relief on his face when he'd seen me standing beside Maria unhurt and in one piece. For some reason, this seemed to infuriate him even more.

"What's got into you, Jana?" he demanded. "Denise said she begged you to wait when she hurt her foot. But you insisted on taking off. How could you leave her on her own like that? She was practically bawling when I got there."

I'd actually forgotten about Denise! And what was this about a foot injury?

"It wasn't quite like that—" I started to defended myself. Which isn't so easy when an unwritten law says you can't tell a man unpleasant truths about another woman—*especially* his own date. But Brian was losing the grim expression as his breathing slowed, and when I mentioned meekly that this was the first I'd heard about a foot injury, he cut in, "Yeah, that sounds like Denise. I sure didn't see anything wrong with her feet that a pair of low heels wouldn't cure!"

That's when I realized he wasn't quite as ensnared as I'd feared. He went on, "When Denise called up to ask if she could come along, I told her jeans and sensible shoes. Women!"

He grinned down at me, his gray eyes showing approval of my own jeans and tennis shoes, and I grinned back, too relieved and happy to care if maybe I was showing more of my own feelings than I meant to. But I had to admit, "She was right in a way. I did know it was stupid to go off alone. I was just too mad to care at the time."

His glance was more understanding than I'd have expected from a member of the so-called less perceptive gender. "Yeah, well, she always did like to get your goat!" was his only comment. And that was the last I heard about Denise or my own delinquency. As we started back to the van, which I could now see parked just a block or so up the street, he asked companionably, "So who was the girl? Haven't I seen her before?"

"Sure, that was our klepto," I answered. He slowed his long strides to match mine while I told him about Maria and my run-in with the Werewolves pack. And though I filled him in about that second meeting in the kitchen, I left out Rodrigo and Mick and why she was stealing food in the first place. If I tell anyone about those two, it'll be Dad first.

After all that, I sure didn't expect Maria to show. Denise was still fuming when we got back to the van, but there was a limit to what she could say with Brian listening, and as he made it clear he was more interested in the Werewolves than her complaints, she soon subsided. Back at the Center, she disappeared, presumably to nurse that mysterious foot injury. But the other propaganda teams were starting to filter back by then, and we all pitched in together, setting up chairs in the gym and helping with the food that kept pouring in from the churches until we ran out of room to put it all. Mr. B wandered through the chaos as calm and unruffled as ever, but everyone else was wound tighter than a pocket watch, and I know I wasn't the only one on pins and needles, wondering if many people would show up.

We needn't have worried. By the time Amos Lowalsky rattled out the opening drum roll, the place was packed! Every kid I'd ever seen walk through the door of the Center must have been there and a whole lot more besides. I didn't see any fanged wolf heads, but there were plenty of other gang jackets. Someone had obviously done a better job at handing out flyers than I had. The most exciting thing for me was to see Armal bound in at the last minute, his little brother and a whole pack of his buddies on his tail, including Scorpion-Cheek. I guess his stepdad let him out, after all.

The rest of the evening was flying up into the skies. To my shock, the music was *good*! I go more for mellow instrumental than for steel drums and electric guitars—all that classical piano training, I suppose—and I did catch an occasional wrong chord or flat note. Or maybe that's just the way those songs are meant to be played. But the lyrics packed a real message, and Kami Gupta and Consuelo and the others had obviously done some serious practicing since that first karaoke session I'd walked in on. Then when Armal of all people got up there to belt out a rap version of "Amazing Grace," the whole mob was on its feet, screaming and whistling.

I sat in the back to keep an eye out for Maria; I'd been praying all week for her. So it shows something about the state of my faith how surprised I was when she slid into an empty seat beside me just as Brian strode onto the platform to give his testimony. I was so happy to see her I wanted to reach over and give her a hug. But she'd perched herself on the very edge of her seat and looked so nervous and edgy I was afraid she'd spook like a startled deer if I touched her. So I just leaned over and whispered, "I'm sure glad you decided to come."

She made no answer to that. "Is your pop here?" she hissed, her eyes roaming across the gym as though she expected undercover cops to jump out of the walls.

"Of course not!" I whispered back indignantly. "I haven't even seen him since I talked to you."

She relaxed into her seat just a little, then whispered, "I gotta talk to you."

That's when I really looked at her for the first time. And what I saw startled me. I'd only seen Maria three times before but, unlike Luis and some of the other Werewolves I'd caught a whiff of, she'd always been neat and washed with that long hair shiny clean, the tons of makeup flawlessly applied, and her clothes spotless, if a bit on the skimpy side.

But now her hair was all tousled and her makeup smudged into black circles as if she'd been rubbing her eyes or maybe even crying. There was a rip in her Werewolf jacket that hadn't been there the last time I'd seen it. And wherever she'd been since I left her, it wasn't a shower!

"Right now?" I asked, a little reluctantly because Brian was talking now and it was worth listening to. Besides, I did want her to hear the preaching and all.

Maria shrugged. "Naah, after the show's fine." She swept the gym with another quick scan, then allowed her shoulders to touch the back of her chair.

Consuelo was up to the mike after Brian. It was the first time I'd heard her full story. She told how she'd been a runaway and a member of a street gang until she was so wasted on drugs even the gang didn't want her around. When she wandered into the Center clinic, she was so sick from hepatitis and malnutrition, she thought she was going to die. While Consuelo shared how God had turned her life around and how she hoped to go to medical school next year, I watched Maria out of the corner of my eye. She was listening, all right. But if it was making an impact, you couldn't tell from her expression.

Amos and the band ripped out a couple more roof-raising numbers. Then Mr. B got up.

I've heard Mr. B preach before, but not like that. Or maybe it was just that I wasn't listening. It was as though God were speaking right to me. Me—small, insignificant Jana Thompson! Pretty soon I forgot about Maria and the sour sweat smell of the gang kid who'd slid in on the other side of me and Denise cuddled up to Brian in the front row and everything else but what he was saying.

Mr. B talked about how everyone has this hole in their lives. This longing for something bigger and better and more meaningful than what they've got. They think they can be happy if they can just fill that hole. So they run around trying to stuff it with pleasure or money or drugs or a more exciting job or the latest car, boat, or other toy. Or they try to fill it with human love—friends, popularity, that significant other in their lives. But pretty soon the party's over or the latest boyfriend's let them down, and they finish up just as lonely and unhappy and empty as they started.

Then Mr. B told how only God can fill that emptiness and give us a life that's worth living because that hole was meant for God in the first place. The reason it's there is because clear back in the Garden of Eden with Adam and Eve, the companionship that was meant to be between God and man was cut off when man decided to disobey God. And until we stop trying to fill that hole with our own selfish wants and let God fill it with Himself and His love, we'll never feel complete. The best part is that He will fill that hole if we ask him, no matter how many mistakes we've made or how bad we've screwed up, because God's own Son, Jesus Christ, died on the cross of Calvary to give every one of us a new start.

Maria hadn't so much as shifted in her seat since she'd settled in, not even clapping or stomping for the music like the rest of the crowd. But when Mr. B finished, I saw her brush her jacket sleeve across her face as though maybe she were wiping away tears, and though I tried hard to blink them back, my own eyes were hot and stinging. Mr. B hit it right on! Oh, sure, I haven't done any drugs or maybe messed up as much as Consuelo or Maria. But it's like Mr. B said that day in the yearbook room—my life has been so full of me! And I'm so tired of me and the mess I've made of running my own life!

Right there while Mr. B was talking and the tears were threatening to spill over onto the makeup I'd repaired when I got back to the Center and that whole echoing gym with hundreds of kids was so quiet I could hear Amos Lowalsky accidentally drop his drumsticks in the front row, I closed my eyes and asked God to empty that hole of me and start running the show in my life. It's Saturday morning now—almost lunchtime. It's taken me that long to write all this down. And even with all the usual letdown after a big night and the fact that I didn't get more than four hours sleep last night, I'm feeling happier than I've ever been in my life. Did I ever really know before in all these years of going to church and Sunday school and even a Christian school what it meant to be a Christian? I'm not sure, but I know now!

It isn't that everything is so different. Mom snapped at Danny at breakfast, and I had to bite my tongue to keep from snapping back. But I feel so peaceful inside. And I know at last just what it is that Mr. B and Karen and Brian and Consuelo and the others have because it's in me too. It's like Consuelo said, I'm not alone anymore. And I never will be again. I have Someone in my life so awesome and wonderful that all that being jealous of Denise and wanting Brian's attention and the problems here with Mom and just hurting so desperately for someone to love me—none of it seems to matter anymore.

After the message, Mr. B gave an invitation for anyone who wanted to pray with him to come forward. What a shock to see Scorpion-Cheek bound up there before anyone else. Armal jumped right up beside him, and they both started hugging and crying. I was back there just crossing my fingers that Maria would go forward too. But she didn't, and she ended up slipping out before I even got a chance to talk to her.

I wish now I'd gone after her even if it was the closing prayer. I don't think God would have minded. I guess I just figured she'd wait for me at the back, but when I went to look for her, she was gone and no one had seen her. I found out later from the kitchen crew that someone had run off with a couple bags of tortilla chips, a turkey ham, and a whole cherry cream pie. So at least her friends got a decent meal tonight.

So what did she want, I wonder? Well, maybe I'll find out tonight. If she comes back. I've been praying that she does. There's something else I need to do, too. Dad's out on a case right now, but as soon as he gets home, I'm going to tell him all about Maria. I know she's scared stiff of the police, and I certainly don't want to get her or Rodrigo and Mick into trouble. But she looked so—well, desperate when she came in last night. I think she needs more help than I can give her, and I'm just going to have to trust that Dad will be Dad about it and not just Sergeant Dave Thompson of the SDPD.

*Part Seven*

## *Saturday, November 30ᵗʰ*

*YOUTHQUAKE* was as great tonight as last. I watched the door all evening, but didn't see any sign of Maria. And Dad was still out on that case when I left for the Center so I never did get a chance to talk to him about her. Okay, so maybe it's no big deal. After all, what do I know that could help the police track down her or her friends? I just can't help feeling that something's really wrong!

I did try to track her down after the festival. There were no Werewolves that I could see, but other gang jackets were hitting the refreshment tables, and I started asking if any of them knew Maria. I don't know what good I thought it'd do. But they had only to take a look at my unadorned clothing, original hair coloring, and general air of being from some foreign territory to clam up tighter than the California State Bank's time vault. Finally in desperation, I roped Consuelo into helping me, letting her do the talking. Black hair, dark eyes, and an olive complexion isn't much of a description in downtown San Diego, but there was that Werewolves jacket and the age, and at last a couple of girls admitted they'd seen her around. Not in some time, though.

I couldn't tell Consuelo what was so urgent about finding Maria, and by the time I finally gave up, she was shaking her head over this crazy Anglo. "Look," she told me shortly, "if the girl didn't show, it's because she didn't want to. Besides, don't you think you're getting in over your head on this?"

"What do you mean?" I asked.

"You say this girl's a Werewolf," Consuelo explained patiently as though dealing with a sub-human I.Q. "Don't you know how that bunch keep alive out there? Stealing, drug dealing, not to mention prostitution. Your Maria's no angel if she's hanging out with them. Those guys don't go feeding no one for free!" .

"I don't care," I retorted, angry because I'd have thought Consuelo would understand if anyone did. "She's in trouble, and she needs our help!"

Consuelo gave me a long look, then she said, "You know, Jana, you've sure changed!"

"What do you mean?" I asked again, not really paying much attention because I was trying to figure out what to do next.

She hunched up her shoulders. "I remember when you first started coming here. You'd walk in that door with your nose wrinkled up like you were smelling something rotten! And now you're going out of your head worrying about some streetwalker from one of the meanest street gangs in the city."

Was I that bad? Have I changed so much? But that doesn't matter now. Maria's out there somewhere tonight, and I just know she's scared and in trouble!

## Sunday, December 1st

I'm not really writing this on December 1st. Too much has happened, and these last weeks have been too wild to even think about my journal. But now that everything has simmered down, I want to go back and write it all down before I forget—as if that were possible! And since Sunday is when it started, I'm going to start there and put it all down in the order it happened as though this were all a book or something. Truth be told, this whole affair has been closer to an improbable suspense novel than I ever thought my life would be.

I never did get to talk to Dad. He came home while I was at church Sunday morning after a drug bust that made the twelve o'clock news. But he went straight to bed and still wasn't up when I left for the Center that afternoon.

When we got to the Center, the whole place was going crazy.

Denise hadn't showed up again after Friday, and no one was surprised, not even Brian. But there was school on Monday, and some of the other parents hadn't been as understanding about missing their own church activities, so the SCA contingent had been reduced to a handful—Brian, Sandy, Michelle, Amos, and myself, besides Mr. B and Karen—and even a number of the Center regulars we'd counted on were missing. The food still hadn't showed up. Two of the band members and one of the main performers in that evening's drama were down sick, and with the whole thing starting in an hour, the rest were going into hysterics. And just as we started to get them calmed down, Brian informed us that Peter, who was supposed to be sharing his testimony that night, had come down with chicken pox. At his age!

That was the only part in all that chaos that really concerned me. Mr. B got on the phone and rattled some chains about the food. The band and the drama group managed to rearrange their numbers minus the missing members. But when Mr. B asked me to take Peter's place, I almost bolted into the street. Me get up in front of that huge mob who even after all these weeks still seemed at times like aliens from another planet? Besides, I hadn't forgotten Mr. Schneider's lecture.

"I don't do testimonies anymore, remember?" I said more sharply than I'd intended. Then I was ashamed because Mr. B looked so disappointed.

"Are you going to let one person's comment keep you from sharing God's love for the rest of your life?" was all he said. But I felt about two inches tall, and I knew I was acting more juvenile than Danny. So I agreed, "Okay, I'll do it. But it's going to have to be short because I haven't a clue what to say."

I only had fifteen minutes before things started. Ducking into one of the study rooms, I started thinking—*and* praying! After all the testimonies I've given at youth groups and camps, it should have been easy. But those were fake, and I didn't want this one to be like that. I don't have a wild, exciting past like Consuelo. And I'm no great athlete like Brian Andrews. Why would any of these people want to listen to me?

I finally decided just to tell the truth. My hands were sweaty and icy at the same time as I climbed that rickety board platform and looked out across that mass of faces floating hazily beyond the floodlights that had been rigged for the occasion. But once I started talking, the words came out as though they'd been written by someone else.

I told them how I'd gone to church and Sunday school since before I could walk, but how I'd never let God run my life and how unhappy I'd been with myself. I admitted how I'd hurt my friends and family trying to be popular, and how Mr. B'd had to tell me to stop thinking about myself all the time and start thinking about others. I told how I'd started coming to the Center and working in the clinic. I even admitted how terrified I'd been of all of them until God showed me they were people just like myself and helped me to love them.

I really have no idea what all I said or what kind of reaction I was expecting. Maybe some hisses or a dead silence; certainly not the cheering and whistling and stomping feet that followed. But none of that mattered because just as I was sliding the microphone back in place, I saw who was standing straight as an arrow across from me in that rainbow sea of painted hair and jewelry and bright clothing. Maria! She was leaning up against the door that leads into the clinic, her hands were behind her back and a look of concentration was on her face as though her full attention was on what I'd been saying.

The cheering was still raising the roof, and I could hear Consuelo whisper how much she liked my talk as she stepped forward to take the mike for the next number, and Mr. B was patting my shoulder with a smile of approval that warmed me to my toes. But I was in a hurry to get down off that stage. I wasn't going to wait till after the meeting and have Maria disappear again.

But by the time I reached the back of the gym, Maria wasn't there. I threaded frantically through the knots of teens who preferred to stand, searching every face. I couldn't believe I'd lost her again!

I'm not sure what made me try the door to the clinic. For obvious reasons, it's kept locked when the clinic is closed. The drugs Karen keeps in stock might be medicinal, but they could be sold or even mixed for a quick trip if some junkie got ahold of them. But a sudden picture flashed into my mind of an open kitchen door and Maria's hands behind her back and countless TV shows of policemen and detectives and bad guys picking locks in just that way.

My instinct was right. The door was unlocked. Maria was so far removed from any of the junkies I'd seen at the clinic, I'd never dreamed she might be into drugs. So when I saw her across Karen's office with those syringes in her hands and a pile of medicines and First Aid supplies on the examining table, actual nausea rose into my throat. Here I'd been fantasizing about Maria coming to me for help, and all she'd been waiting for was a chance to steal drugs.

It was like a replay of the last time. Maria's head jerked up as I stepped into the office, her hands freezing on a roll of bandages she was pulling out of the cupboard. I was too stunned and disappointed to move, so for a long moment we just stared at each other. Maria had cleaned up a little since I'd seen her two nights earlier, but her eyes were sunk deep into dark smudges, and their expression was so wild that for the first time I could believe she might be on something.

"Maria!" Ungluing my feet from the floor, I managed a step forward. But Maria was already reacting. Scooping the stuff on the table into that backpack of hers, she slammed past me and out the door before I could even finish her name. I was right behind her.

This time it wasn't food she was taking, and I couldn't let her get away with it.

But I *had* to stop and lock that door. The gym was too packed with outsiders to leave those precious medical supplies unguarded even for a minute. And though it took only a second to push in the lock button on the inside doorknob and pull the door shut, Maria was already halfway across the gym to the big double doors of the entrance. I didn't bother calling "Stop, thief!" or shouting for back-up. The cymbals were clashing and the drums and electric guitar were so loud no one would hear anyway. I just pushed after her as fast as I could through those clapping, stomping teens.

The backpack slowed her down or I'd never have caught up to her. By the time she scrambled down the front steps of the Center, I was right on her heels. Just as she reached the first corner, I managed to grab her arm.

"No, Maria!" I cried, yanking her to a stop. "This isn't right!"

Heads were turning along the street so I lowered my voice, trying to keep it calm and even the way Karen does when she's counseling a patient. "Drugs aren't the answer to anything, Maria. Please, just give me the backpack and come on back to the Center. They'll get you some help."

I'd expected resistance, but to my shock, she started laughing. Wild, hysterical laughter that held no humor at all, and I was more sure than ever she'd been taking some drug. Even in the dim light of the streetlamps, she read my expression. "You think I'm on something, don't you?" she gasped out. "You think I stole this stuff for a cheap high? One shot to suicide?"

She broke off that terrible sound as suddenly as she'd started. Pulling out a handful of bandages from her backpack, she shoved them into my face and hissed, her voice as harsh and flat as though she'd never been laughing, "I didn't take the stuff for me, okay? It's for my friend Mick, remember him? He's dying, see? Dying!"

That's when I realized it wasn't drugs, but worry and fear and despair that made her eyes so wild, and I knew I'd been right. Something had gone terribly wrong! "What do you mean, he's dying?" I demanded. "Did the Devil's Angels find them?"

She gave her head an impatient shake. "Look, you did me a good turn once, and I ain't forgotten it. But that don't give you no right to mess around in my life. Just back off!"

Ripping her arm away from the grip I'd made the mistake of relaxing, she took off again into the night. I didn't try to stop her. Sure, with that backpack weighing her down I could probably catch up to her. But I wasn't strong enough to drag her back to the Center, and in that neighborhood, I couldn't exactly call for help.

I stood on that street corner for maybe as long as it took to count to five. It was all happening so fast! There wasn't time to think, and my head spun with trying to make a decision. There were gangs and muggers and who knew what else out there in the night. I'd had that pounded into me by more than Friday's adventure. And I'd already gotten in trouble once for taking off alone. But if I went for Mr. B or Karen, Maria would be long gone. And she seemed so desperate, no matter what she said. How could I let her vanish from my life again without even trying to help?

Then it was all clear in my mind, and I started running. But not with the stupid thoughtlessness of the last time I'd taken off alone. I knew full well there could be danger out there in the blackness beyond the comfort of the streetlights and the warm twinkle of apartment windows. It wasn't that I was being brave either. Truth was, I was scared stiff. But if there's anything I learned that night, it's that you can't always step away from danger. Sometimes you've just got to face it. Dad's taught me that lesson every time he steps into the street as a cop—just because *someone's* got to do it. And right then this was something I had to do.

Even with that backpack, it took me four blocks to catch up to her. Outside the dim circles of light that were the streetlamps, the night was full of odd shadows and spooky noises, and I wished desperately I was anywhere else. Once I could have sworn I heard a scuffle of feet and quick breathing as though someone were right behind me, but when I whirled around, no one was there, and when I spun back, Maria was out of sight.

I sprinted to the corner, afraid I'd lost her for sure this time and was alone out there in the night with those spooky noises and the dark human shapes I could see here and there leaning alone or in groups against walls or in doorways. But when I scanned both directions, I caught a glimpse of a hump disappearing around the next corner. She must have thought she'd lost me because when I rounded the corner, running as hard as I could, she'd dropped to a slow plod. Before she'd gone another half block, I was cutting around in front of her. I don't know whether she was more astounded or furious to see me. It was too dark there halfway between two streetlamps to see her face, but the general and carefully edited gist of what she had to say was, "How dare you sneak around after me? Who do you think you are sticking your nose into my business? Why can't you just stay out of my life? If I wanted your help, I'd ask for it!"

Now that I wasn't alone, the night didn't feel so spooky. Planting myself right in her path, I told her firmly, "Because you need help—whether you want it or not! If this Mick friend of yours is so sick, then *that* . . . " I waved my hand at her backpack, " . . . isn't going to do him any good at all. Not unless you know a lot more about what you've got in there than I do. *Please* come back to the Center with me. Karen's a doctor. She knows what she's doing. She'll help. Or we can call my dad. He can have an ambulance out here in no time flat."

Maria didn't bother to argue. She just walked right through me, her backpack shoving me aside. I scrambled into step beside her.

"I'm not leaving you!" I said to her stony profile. "If you're not going to come back with me, then I'm coming with you."

"It's a public street!" was all she said, walking even faster. I stretched my legs to keep up, almost slamming into a lamppost when she— deliberately, I'm sure—steered me too close. If I had to chase her all over the whole city, I wasn't going to lose her again. Still, I must admit I was beginning to feel a little foolish and depressed too, wondering if maybe I'd done the wrong thing, chasing alongside a girl who very clearly wanted nothing to do with me.

But it was only a few more paces before she spoke abruptly. "If you're going to tag along like a can on a cat's tail, you could at least spit out your name."

That startled me. Hadn't I ever got around to telling her my name? I reviewed our brief acquaintance. I guess not!

"Jana Thompson," I informed her warmly, only too pleased that we were finally communicating. "What's yours? The rest of it, I mean? I know your first name is Maria."

"Jimenez."

So much for communication! She lapsed into total silence again, and after a hesitant clearing of the throat, so did I. By then I was wishing I'd brought a coat instead of the pretty pullover that was all I'd figured I'd need at the Youth Festival. Even with all the exercise, I was getting cold. This might be only a nice fall evening in Montana where I can remember sledding at twenty below zero, but for San Diego, it had to be setting new winter records. My breath was making little gray clouds in the glow of the streetlamps, and the wind whistling between the tall buildings bit through my sweater. How could Maria stand it with only that skimpy tank top under her Werewolf jacket?

After another half block of no sound but our own footsteps, it burst out of me. "How in the world do you live out here? I mean, this is awful!"

Maria slid me a long and considering sideways glance. Then she shrugged. "Nobody said it was easy. My first winter on the streets, I thought I was gonna die. I might have, too, if Rodrigo and Mick hadn't come across me. You gotta find a gang of your own if you want to survive."

It was as if she were trying to explain what had brought her to join the Werewolves. I thought of those teenage goons sprawled in blissful indolence outside that abandoned building like Mr. Grasshopper in that old fable. No jobs, no one even thinking of working that I could see. "But how do you keep warm?" I demanded incredulously. "Or buy food to eat? Or clothes? Besides, uh—"

I broke off as I realized what I'd been about to say. But Maria finished for me. "Prostitution?" She shrugged again. "There's other things. Hubcaps, car radios, wallets, drugs—not that I've been stupid enough to touch that, whether you believe me or not!" she added, giving me a hard look, and I knew she still hadn't forgiven me for my earlier blunder. "'Course you've got to turn everything you make over to the Wolf. He's real mean if you hold back. If he knew I'd been scoring some hits for Rodrigo and Mick, he'd skin me alive—and that ain't no joke either! But if you're loyal to the gang and don't go slacking off your share, they'll take care of you. Keep other gangs and the cops off your back."

If she was trying to shock me, it didn't work. In movies they make street gangs, if evil and violent, at least exciting. But this all sounded so squalid. Camping out in cold, dirty abandoned buildings! Having to beg some teenage hoodlum for everything you had to eat or wear! Maria couldn't be more than thirteen or fourteen, and from everything she'd said, she'd been with the Werewolves at least a couple of years. Why would a kid who should still be playing with dolls choose to live on the streets? I mean, I'd felt like running away at times. But I'd never choose this!

"Do you *like* living like that?" I asked her, honestly curious to know. I don't know what I expected, but not what I got.

"I hate it!" came out in a low, fierce voice. "Do you know what I'd give to live in a real house again? With a real bathroom? Maybe even a garden and a puppy and—and school?"

Then, like a flood bursting through a dam, "The Werewolves are bad, you know! Oh sure, some are just trying to make it on the street like me. And some are so spaced-out all the time they don't even know what planet they're on. But the others!" She gave a sudden shiver, and it wasn't from the cold. "They really *like* hurting people. Rodrigo and Mick are the only ones who've ever treated me like a human being."

"So why don't you leave? Go home?" I waved my hand toward the massive dark blocks with their twinkling galaxies of windows that were the apartment buildings of the housing projects. "Anything's got to be better than this! Your parents must be terribly worried."

I knew I'd said the wrong thing before it finished clearing my lips. Maria whirled around on me so suddenly I slammed into her. We were right under a streetlamp, and the glare in her eyes said that she hated me. Or maybe she was just looking through me at a memory.

"Home!" She spit it out as though it were a dirty word. "You want to know why I don't go home? Okay, I'll tell you! I never knew my pop. But I had a mom once. Sure she drank a lot and she slapped me around a bit, but I could handle that! Everyone's got their problems. I didn't blame her. But her boyfriends—that was something else! When I was a kid, she'd make me call them 'uncle,' but I knew they weren't no real uncle of mine. And when one of them tried to shift his slimy hands from Mom to me, I decided to get out. 'Course, if I'd known the streets would be the same thing, maybe I'd have stayed."

Maria started walking again, fast and furious. "I never figured it'd be for long. It's not like I did a very good job of hiding. I figured the police would catch me in a day or two. Maybe my mom would even be sorry and get rid of her boyfriends so it'd be just the two of us again. But they never did. I found out later my mom didn't even report me missing."

Maria hunched her shoulders as though she didn't really care. But she didn't fool me because that lost puppy look was back in her eyes. "I haven't seen her for two years now. She's probably died of AIDS by now if the booze didn't kill her first!"

This time I *was* shocked. More, I was stunned! Here I'd been talking Prodigal Son, and she was talking Greek tragedy. I mean, what kind of a sick world do we live in where a child no more than eleven or twelve has to run away from home to be safe from her mother's boyfriend? What kind of mother would just let her go? And I thought I had problems!

I tried to think of some kind and comforting words, but I choked on them. What was there to say? All I could see in my mind was that lonely, little girl trudging through the streets of San Diego, getting hungrier and colder and hoping desperately that her mom would care enough to call the police. So she'd learned to survive the only way that had come to her. Would I have done so much better? Maybe I'd have gone off, too, with the first person who seemed to care.

For all those weekends at the Center, I don't think it ever really hit me until right then that the ugly, vicious, cruel world out there I'd so self-righteously despised every time I'd seen it on the news and TV and down in the housing projects held an awful lot of innocent victims who'd never chosen or deserved to be there any more than I'd chosen or deserved my own warm, comfortable, *safe* berth in life. And yet I'd had the nerve to judge those victims, watching complacently from my safe perch as they swept helplessly along like wreckage on some filthy tidal wave of sewer, fighting and kicking and, most of them in the end, drowning.

I didn't realize I was crying until a drop rolled down my nose and I sneezed. I wiped a quick sleeve across my face, horribly embarrassed and hoping Maria hadn't noticed. But when I glanced over, she was staring at me, and there was none of the scorn I'd expected, but wonder, and she reached out to touch a teardrop I'd missed. "You really *do* care!" she whispered incredulously. "All that stuff you were saying back at the Center—"

I nodded, too choked up to talk, fumbling in my pocket for a tissue. And that's when Maria smiled. A *real* smile, the first I'd ever seen from her. It was like a rainbow peeking out of a storm cloud and made her look like the little girl she should have been. She grabbed my hand, and she looked, well, not exactly happy, but as if maybe there was still one small ray of hope left in life after all. "Okay, Jana. You want to help me, come on!"

She didn't try to lose me again, and as we walked, she filled me in on Mick and Rodrigo. They'd been safe enough these last couple of weeks as far as the Devil's Angels were concerned—*or* the police. Even with the word out all over the streets, neither Icepick, now the new leader of the Angels, nor the Werewolves themselves had managed to pick up so much as a hint as to where they'd vanished. Maria herself was careful never to go near them except at night. She didn't elaborate, but I got the impression that it was both normal and expected for the Werewolves to scatter after dark, presumably for whatever nefarious businesses kept the gang coffers full. At any rate, Maria hadn't had any difficulty slipping away on her own.

But the police report had been right about that blood on the warehouse floor. Some of it *had* belonged to someone besides Abdul, and that someone was Mick. That second shot Icepick had fired during Rodrigo and Mick's getaway, whether deliberately or an accidental discharge during the scuffle, had caught Mick in the shoulder.

There'd been no way, of course, to take Mick to a doctor. Even Karen at the clinic had to report bullet wounds to the police. And though he'd lost a lot of blood, it hadn't seemed serious, just a flesh wound that hadn't broken any bones. The three of them had bandaged it as well as they could, optimistically hoping it would heal on its own. Only now infection had set in, and nothing Rodrigo and Maria had done was helping. In desperation, Maria had broken into the clinic, lifting not just the medicines and bandages I'd seen, but also Karen's *Physician's Desk Reference Encyclopedia* in hopes that something in there might tell her what in all that pile she'd grabbed would cure Mick. No wonder her backpack looked so weighed down! I'd seen that book on Karen's shelf, and it was a monster.

We turned into a narrow alley, then around another corner. Suddenly it was three shades darker with no twinkle of lights anywhere on the squat, black buildings that loomed over our heads. It wasn't difficult to deduce we must be somewhere in the neighborhood of all those abandoned warehouses where I'd run into the Werewolves two days before. I hadn't noticed anyone but ourselves on the streets for a few blocks, and I certainly saw no sign of life out there now, but all those blank, dark windows over our heads felt even more like watching eyes than they had during the day. I didn't like it at all, and for a change, Maria seemed no less nervous. She kept "shh"ing, though neither of us was saying a word anymore, and every third or fourth step she'd stop to check over her shoulder.

But it was too dark now to see anything but the moon glowing weakly through the smog high overhead and the few scattered streetlamps that hadn't had their glass busted out. I strained my ears to listen, but all I could hear was my own heart pounding so loudly a mugger could have picked it up ten yards away. Maria paused at the mouth of another alley, this one wider and paved. She stood for a long moment tensed and motionless, scanning the night in all directions, her nostrils flared as though she were sniffing the air for danger. Then she tugged at me to follow her, and I found out just why she was being so cautious. *And* why neither the police nor the Devil's Angels or Werewolves had managed to find Rodrigo or Mick in two long weeks.

Not a single streetlamp lightened the blackness of that alley. I'd have been stumbling all over if it hadn't been for Maria's tight grip on my hand, but she threaded her way as confidently as a blind man in a house he's got memorized. When she stopped, it was so suddenly I bumped into the backpack. She released my hand, and I could feel rather than see her stoop down. The tiniest metallic clatter in the dark said that she was lifting something. Then she shoved it into my hands, and the feel of bars and cold steel told me just what she was doing. She'd raised one of the grates through which the water poured off the streets when it rained.

I couldn't believe she really expected us to go down into that hole. But the humpbacked shadow that was Maria and her backpack was already lowering itself down while I, too stunned to protest, held the grate off the ground. Then she tugged at my ankle, and after an endless hesitation during which I told myself I'd been absolutely crazy to come this far, I followed.

With the grate lowered back in place, there was barely room for the two of us and that backpack to squat down there. Then suddenly I could breathe again. I groped panic-stricken in the dark. But Maria was gone and where she'd been was a hole in the rough cement under my hands barely wide and high enough for a full-sized human to slither into.

"Come on!" the hollow echo of her voice hissed from somewhere inside.

I came, but it was the hardest thing I've ever done. There were terrifying moments after that, and I certainly wasn't in any great danger right then. But that tunnel was the worst part of that night.

I've never cared for closed-in places or being alone in the dark, and this was far worse than either. I was so scared that somehow the bad times that came after that didn't frighten me quite as much as they should have. If I could survive the horrible, claustrophobic blackness of that tunnel, nothing could ever be quite so bad again.

It went on forever, never widening more than a few inches beyond my shoulders and so low I had to hunch myself forward on my belly, my nose almost touching the cold concrete. I could hear Maria somewhere up ahead of me, swearing under her breath as she pushed that backpack ahead of her, and I kept telling myself that she had to know where she was going. But it didn't help. Even in a dark alley or windowless room at least some glimmer of light sneaks in. But this was the blackness of a cavern buried far beneath the earth, so black I couldn't even see the fingers I held in front of my nose, and the air was musty and hard to breathe as though we were running out of oxygen. Once a chunk of rock or plaster fell from the ceiling onto my back, and I just *knew* that the entire sewage system and the street above were about to come tumbling down on us, leaving us buried so completely we'd never be found. I remember babbling a mental prayer that God would at least let my parents find out what had happened to me.

Now, when people who know just a little of what happened come up to tell me how brave I was, I remember those minutes that seemed an eternity but probably weren't more than five, and I don't allow myself to get overly inflated because I know exactly how brave I was. I think I was on the verge of shrieking, maniacal hysterics when I heard Maria tumble out somewhere ahead of me with a thud that echoed back down the tunnel. Then a light went on.

It was just a pencil flashlight but bright as a floodlight after that blackness, and in its comforting glow I could see the end of the tunnel just a few feet away. My heavy breathing started to slow and the pounding at my temples to recede. Then I tumbled out after Maria.

We were still underground, I discovered to my dismay, but now that I could see, it wasn't so bad, and as my heart rate spiraled downward to normal, I regained my self-respect enough to feel ashamed of my panic. I glanced around. The tunnel had come out at a right angle into a huge concrete drainage pipe tall enough that I could stand up straight. This stretched away from the glow of the flashlight as far as I could see.

But the smell! Not even sewer rats would have put up with that smell! It hadn't rained in days, and the tunnel we'd crawled through had at least been dry. But there was water here. Filthy, slime-coated water that ran down the center of the drainage pipe and smelled like a mixture of sewer gas and dirty socks. It was the same odor I'd caught a whiff of Friday night, and I knew now where Maria had been before she showed up at the Center. It might have been Chanel #5 for all the reaction Maria displayed.

While I was still gasping for breath, she stepped across the stream of sewer water and turned the flashlight onto a service ladder that rose to the top of the drainage pipe. By the time I'd cautiously picked my way over to her side, she was already climbing, silently, with each foot placed carefully on the rungs so as not to clatter, the flashlight dangling down in her hand so that I could see to grab the foot of the ladder. Once I pulled myself just as silently onto the first rung, the beam of light turned upwards to show a metal hatch above Maria's head on the ceiling of the water conduit.

She tapped twice against the steel trapdoor, the small clink echoing so loudly along the drainage pipe I could see why she was making such an effort to be quiet. There was a pause that must have been as breathless for Maria as myself. Then two more taps echoed back, and I knew we'd found her friends. The hatch creaked open, and I scrambled up after Maria toward the light.

If sewer rats would have turned up their noses at the smell, they'd have turned down the living accommodations altogether. This place wasn't high enough for even my petite frame to stand up straight in, and it was only a few paces from any one wall to the other. Valves and pipes and other things I couldn't identify festooned both walls and ceiling.

I still don't know what the place was. A crawlspace, maybe, for getting at the sewer system, because there was another hatch at the far side that had to lead out somewhere. This one was bigger than the one Maria and I had come through—more like a small door— and it had been boarded over from the inside. Both the boards and a mattress tucked into one corner were so old and dilapidated that it was clear eons had passed since the place had been used for its original purpose.

It was clear too that this wasn't the first time someone had used the place for a hideout. A lightbulb hung down from an electrical wire that had been strung across the ceiling to disappear behind a metal pipe. In its sixty-watt glimmer, I could see a tattered throw rug that looked like a rescue job from a garbage bin, a rusted tool chest, and a chaotic jumble of empty chip bags, juice bottles, and wrappers. In one corner, I recognized the box Ocean Beach Community Church had sent their pizzas in. But I didn't really have a lot of time to study the furnishings because most of my view was being occupied by a *very* angry young man.

He wasn't any older than me and good-looking in a dark Latin style with hawklike, thin-lipped features, a high-bridged nose, long-lashed eyes that were really gorgeous when they weren't narrowed with fury, and a slim build as tight-muscled and graceful as a jungle cat. Still, I must admit I'd have been scared to death to meet him without Maria along. It wasn't that he looked so mean. Not like that Luis guy back at the Werewolves hideout. He just wasn't—well, *tame*. You could see him more as a battle-scarred young warrior than as a student sitting in some San Diego high school working on his Lit assignment. Maria flew into his arms as soon as she was up the ladder, and the reunion scene that followed was as emotional as though she'd been gone for a month with hugging and kissing and even crying. So I was able to pull myself all the way out of the hatch before his eyes landed on me. Then did he explode!

Even after five years in San Diego I still don't speak much Spanish, but I got the gist, which was that he wanted me out of there and not necessarily with all my body parts. He was swearing in both languages, and Maria was pleading, clinging to his arm as though the weight of her slim body could possibly hold back that volcano in the making. But they both lost me right then because I heard a low moan and saw the pile of blankets on that old mattress move. I crossed over, stooping a little because of the ceiling. The instant I saw the young man lying there under those blankets, I knew Maria had been right. This guy was sick! Very sick!

Mick was bigger than Rodrigo, at least six feet with heavy muscles and built like a linebacker. A tangle of longish blond-red hair and the straggly start of a beard that was coming in even redder than his hair gave him the look of a pirate or a Viking, and like Rodrigo, I wouldn't have wanted to encounter him alone in a dark alley.

But right then he didn't look dangerous at all. He was lying with his eyes shut, not even moaning anymore and so motionless I had to check twice to see that he was still breathing. When I touched his face it was burning up with fever, and when I pulled back the blankets I almost gagged. No wonder Maria hadn't blinked at the smell out there in the sewage pipe because this was ten times worse! Like meat that had been rotting in the hot sun for a week. A bandage that might have been part of a flowered sheet had been wrapped under his armpit and up over his shoulder. I couldn't guess when it had been changed last, but the cotton roses and tulips were stained with palegreen, and where the bandage didn't reach, thin red and black lines like little veins shot along the puffy flesh down his arm and up into his neck. The whole mess was swollen and hot and oozing. Even at the clinic, I'd never seen anything this bad.

Rodrigo and Maria were still arguing furiously in a jumble of English and Spanish. "She's the one I told you about from the Center," I heard Maria say. "Her *papá* is a cop. She says he'll help us."

The revelation wasn't exactly calculated to calm him down. Some of the phrases that followed I hadn't heard even at the Center. Maria kept trying to shush him, and with reason, as anyone down in those pipes on the other side of the walls must have been able to hear him a block away. He looked furious enough to hit her, and I was having nightmares of Mick's shallow breathing stopping altogether under my hands while they shouted, so I interrupted with a sharpness that cut right through Rodrigo's tirade. "Look, if you two want your friend here to die, just keep arguing."

That did it. Rodrigo broke off abruptly and crossed over to kneel by the mattress. He spread his hand gently over his friend's nose and mouth, and I knew that he was checking to see if Mick was still breathing. Then he looked down at me, and his eyes were as cold and hard as black marbles, and his order when it came was as harsh as though I were a slave or his prisoner, "Do something now, you little—!" But the language that followed didn't bother me because I could see the desperate worry that had drained the fury from his muscles.

Maria was beside me now, dumping out the contents of that backpack. I rummaged through it, trying to look as though I knew what I was doing. There were bottles and plastic containers with pills and plenty of those little glass bubble things with liquid inside that Karen uses for shots. And that *Physician's Desk Reference*, of course, not much smaller than a complete *Webster's*. But the book wasn't much help. Most of the medical terms on the containers had nothing to do with bullet wounds, and though I did figure out that one of the glass bubbles held an antibiotic of some sort, there were no instructions on how to get it from the bubble into the syringe or from there into the patient. Besides, I'd helped Karen enough to learn that you're supposed to test for allergic reactions before pumping anyone full of antibiotics.

Still, there were clean bandages, a whole tube of first-aid cream, and even a pair of scissors. With Maria's help, I peeled back that filthy bandage. This had glued itself into place so badly I was glad Mick was unconscious as we tugged it loose. What was underneath was even worse than I'd expected with the black, swollen hole where the bullet had gone in swallowed up by the bloated, stinking flesh around it. I didn't even know where to start. I rocked back on my heels, only too conscious of Rodrigo and Maria's hopeful eyes on me, but all I could think to say was, "We'll need some clean water."

Rodrigo hurried to carry a bucket over from the corner. It was half full, but the water wasn't fresh, and there was a Twinkie wrapper and crumbs of some sort floating in it. I looked from the water to the mess under those bandages and Mick's motionless body sinking deeper into a coma even as we watched, and my heart sank into the pit of my stomach. I found myself grabbing at Maria's arm, and then I was babbling, "This isn't going to work! He's going to die! Please, we've got to get help! He's going to die!"

Tears poured down Maria's cheeks as she stared down at Mick, and I knew she too was seeing what I saw. She jumped up so fast she banged her head on the ceiling pipes. Then she whirled around defiantly on Rodrigo. "We gotta do it! If Jana says they'll help us, then I say we gotta take the chance. Mick would do it for you!"

I held my breath as I waited for Rodrigo's response. It didn't come right away. His gaze went slowly around that awful cubbyhole, then back down to Mick, the lines of his face so hard and angry I was sure what the answer would be. But I guess maybe it wasn't Maria or me he was angry at because he shrugged at last, his eyes not moving from his friend's face. "Yeah, why not! We're done with this place anyway."

In the end, it was Maria who went for help. I couldn't go alone because I'd never have managed to find my way to the Center and back even without the other two's unspoken addition that I was too green and lacking in street smarts to make it out there on my own. I could have gone with Maria, and that's what I'd intended. But Rodrigo's softening of heart didn't extend quite that far. Whether he thought I'd evaporate on them or just bring in a dozen police cars to have them arrested, I don't know. But he insisted I stay with him—as a hostage, basically—and as the thin-lipped set of his jaw made it clear he was done bending, I didn't try to argue but wrote out my home number for Maria to call Dad and told her who to ask for at the Center.

It's certainly a unique experience and not one I'd recommend, sitting in an underground crawlspace with a critically injured man and a street hoodlum who looks as though he'd prefer having you on his lunch menu than indulging in any of the social graces. I must admit that for those first minutes after Rodrigo lowered the hatch behind Maria, I couldn't do anything but crouch beside that mattress almost as still as Mick, nervously following Rodrigo's every move and wishing I could read the intentions written behind those stormy black eyes. But he didn't speak a single word or so much as glance in my direction, prowling around instead like a tawny panther from his friend to the hatch, then back to his friend where he'd sit and watch like a cat at a mouse hole before jumping up to prowl again.

I gradually relaxed as he continued to ignore me and eventually set to work on that awful wound. There was no way I was going to use that water, but I squeezed out the whole tube of antibiotic cream on the bullet wound and surroundings and covered it with a loose bandage. Fishing out the Twinkie wrapper and most of the crumbs, I dipped another bandage into the bucket and used it to sponge down Mick's hot face. Whether it did any good, I couldn't tell as Mick didn't stir even with the pain I must have caused him replacing that bandage. But it made me feel better and gave me something to do.

Time crawled so slowly I found myself checking my watch every two to three minutes, sure that at least half an hour had passed. And yet I remember that when the knock finally came on the hatch, I was surprised, because if Maria had already made it to the Center and back, she'd been moving faster than I'd have thought possible. Rodrigo stopped prowling and reached for the hatch with a muttered phrase as relieved as it was inappropriate.

And that's when it all happened!

Rodrigo was still lifting the hatch when it slammed back, sending him sprawling to the floor. But it wasn't Maria who burst through or anyone else I knew. It was a man, big and muscular and older than any of the other gang members I'd seen. Maybe even in his twenties. He was dark—almost a chocolate brown and of clear African descent. But his hair had been straightened and bleached blonde and cut straight up in a brush. He wore a gold ring in his nose and a dozen chains around his neck, and there was something so cold and vicious in his face, he made Rodrigo look like a church youth group president. In one hand he carried the flashlight with which he'd made his way through the drainage system, but he dropped that as soon as he was through the hatch to pull out a handgun that was tucked into the front of his jeans.

"Icepick!" Rodrigo exploded, scrambling back to his feet. Then his eyes fell on the gun, and he froze.

And now someone else was hauling himself up through the hatch. Someone I recognized the instant I saw that shaved head. It was Luis, the lowlife Maria saved me from at the Werewolf hideout. He too had a gun in one hand, and in the other suddenly appeared a long knife that looked to be the same one he'd pulled on me Friday.

Of course, I'm describing it all from memory. But right then, it was all happening so fast, I hardly had a chance to get a good look at them. The crawlspace seemed suddenly bursting with people, and with the pipes and the lowness of the ceiling, they were all bumping their heads and having to stoop over and crouch down. The air was filled with foul language, and the lightbulb was swinging crazily on its long wire, the wildly shifting shadows this made adding to the confusion. All I could do was cower down beside my patient and hope frantically and stupidly that no one would notice me.

Which worked just as well as might be expected!

Within an eternity that was actually no more than seconds, the commotion had settled down, leaving Rodrigo backed up against the far wall with Icepick's huge frame crouched down on the balls of his feet in front of him and his gun centered somewhere in the middle of the right flap of Rodrigo's gang jacket. The smaller Luis was short enough to walk with only a bending of his head. Sliding his knife back into a sheath, the gun still balanced easily in his grip, he crossed over to the mattress, that skin-crawling grin of his spreading from ear to ear as he looked down. He was still grinning when he picked up the half-empty bucket of water and threw it over Mick.

If I could have killed Luis myself right then, I really think I might have. Mick was so deeply unconscious he couldn't even keep that cold stream from running into his mouth and nose. Grabbing the roll of bandages, I threw myself at him to wipe away the water. I was afraid he'd drowned until he gave a choking sneeze and cough and water started running out his nose.

But, of course, that brought me to Luis's attention. Dropping the bucket with a clatter, he grabbed my hair and yanked my head back. "Well, if it ain't the Jesus freak!" he sneered so close to my face I could smell the stale liquor and food on his breath. "Came back for the party, eh?"

Letting go of my hair, he ran his hand down my face and shoulder. My skin crawled, and I had to swallow to keep down the sandwich I'd eaten before the meeting, but that gun in his other hand tempered just how much revulsion I dared allow to show on my face. Then Icepick growled, "We don't got time for that, man!"

Like I said, I should have been more afraid right then. I was wondering where Maria was and questioning how they could possibly have found us and wishing desperately for my dad and praying hard all at the same time. But there was none of that horrible stomach-squeezing terror of the tunnel. It was more like one of those nightmares I used to have as a little girl where you've been scared for so long, there's nothing left. I just felt numb and lightheaded and not even particularly angry after those first minutes. I don't remember everything they said. But I do remember Rodrigo swearing at Luis.

"So it was you!" he snarled. "You set us up. I knew it!" He looked dangerous and angry, and I saw his muscles tense to make a dive at his Werewolf buddy—or ex-buddy. But even over the angry voices, I could hear the click as Icepick cocked his gun. Rodrigo settled back against the wall, his hands spread out and empty.

Luis was looking insufferably pleased with himself. "Hey, I knew if I followed the chick long enough, I'd find you. She thought she had me fooled, all that coming on to me as if I didn't know she hates my guts. There's only two people she'd put on a show like that for, so it weren't hard to figure out what she had to be hiding. She's good too—lost me every time. Till tonight when she got careless with her little friend here."

That's when I remembered that scuffling of feet and quick breathing I'd heard in the dark and the careless way Maria and I'd been talking and not watching, and I realized it was all my fault Maria had led these goons here. At the end, we'd been far enough ahead of them that they hadn't seen us duck into the alley. But they'd followed us far enough. They'd been prowling around the entrance to that alley, trying to pick up our trail, when Maria crawled back out of the tunnel. If it had been too dark to see her, they'd heard the same metallic clink I had as she lowered the grate. When Maria emerged from the alley, running too fast for them to catch, they'd decided instead to inspect where she'd just been. The loosened metal storm grate had told them just how Rodrigo and Mick had managed to elude them all this time. After that, it was just a matter of giving Maria time to be long gone before following our passage up the tunnel.

The most bizarre part was how the second-in-command of the Devil's Angels and one of his worst enemies, a Werewolf, had ever gotten together to plan the whole thing. It turned out, in all the yelling and swearing, that Icepick and Luis had known each other clear back in the days when they were both attending the same inner-city grade school—before they got caught up in rival gangs. They'd ended up in the same detention cell a few months back on minor charges that had them both out on the street again within days. With a guard there to keep them from killing each other, they'd talked instead. This is what had come out of it.

"Why'd you do it, man?" Rodrigo demanded. "Why'd you set us up? We never did nothing to you!"

Luis shrugged. "Hey, it was nothing personal. You were in my way. With you gone, I gotta shot at the Wolf himself."

"It was a deal. We both got what we wanted," Icepick said. It's the only time I remember him talking, and his voice was flat and cold, uninterested in Luis and Rodrigo's bickering. "I got the Angels.

A couple more months, with you two out of the way—boom!" He aimed the gun at Rodrigo's head. "Another hit, and Luis here's the Wolf."

"You know, this is perfect, man!" Luis was looking around the crawlspace. "Yeah, it's almost better this way. No lawyers, no cops. They just disappear. And when the chick gets back, she joins her pals. There ain't no one going to come looking for her here."

I didn't at first catch what he meant. I was sneaking a peek at my watch, figuring out how long it had been since Maria left and how much more time until she might be back with help. Then Rodrigo's voice intruded on my calculations, urgent, almost begging. "Just let the girl go! She ain't got no part in this. Just let her go, and I won't make no trouble."

"And have her squealing to the cops? Don't be stupid, man!" Luis sneered. Sauntering over to where I huddled beside the mattress, he stood over me, looking down with that nasty grin on his face. "Still, maybe we'll keep her for a while. There's time enough to party first."

His tongue came out of his mouth and licked his lips, slowly, leaving them wet and glistening in the sixty-watt bulb so that, for all my efforts not to breathe, I shuddered. And it was right then that it sunk into naive, suburban, *stupid* Jana Thompson's numbed brain exactly what he was saying. And I realized my dreams of rescue were foolish because there was only one way in here—that hatch—and Icepick and Luis could do anything they wanted with me and Rodrigo and Mick long before anyone could crawl through that tunnel and pound open that metal trapdoor. And though I told myself that at least they wouldn't get away with it because someone *did* know where we were and Maria was even now bringing help, there was no comfort in it.

Then that terrible grin had shifted from me to Mick, who was moaning just a little as though that cold water had gotten through to wherever his mind had gone. Luis touched his tongue to his lips again in a look of utmost pleasure and anticipation. Then he lifted his gun and said, "I'll take care of this one first. I've always hated his guts!"

He leveled the gun down on that unconscious face, and I saw then what Dad's seen a dozen times—the face of a murderer. I was so ice-cold inside I couldn't lift a finger. Then came an explosion and a scream that I later found out was mine. I didn't realize I'd thrown myself at his legs until Luis kicked me viciously away. A hole in the mattress still smoked not six inches from Mick's head. A puff of feathers floated out and scattered across my fresh bandage.

And then Luis was leveling that gun on me, his face so twisted with hate and anger he looked like the werewolf he claimed to be, and I *knew* that in the next second I'd be in heaven. But instead of seeing my whole life flash before me, I just felt horribly sleepy. It was so quiet I could hear a noise like a rat on the other side of the wall behind me and the cocking of that trigger, and I closed my eyes, wishing I could wake up when it was all over.

But when the blast came, I was still alive. I opened my eyes to see that it wasn't a gun, but the service door beside me, blown right off the hinges through those rotten boards, and suddenly and incredibly Dad was there, kicking Luis across the floor. Rodrigo was off the wall, going for Icepick's right hand, and strangely enough, Brian was there too, scooping Luis' gun up from the floor where it'd gone flying.

Then Luis and Icepick were both down, and Rodrigo had the other gun, and I found I was crying for the first time in all that nightmare, as if I wasn't now safe and sound. And Dad was looking angry, and I knew it was because he had two bad guys at the end of a gun and couldn't do anything. And then Brian was there and holding me tight against his chest while I bawled my heart out.

*Part Eight*

So that's how it all ended.

As soon as I recovered myself enough to be embarrassed, I peeled myself off Brian to find that the place was suddenly bursting with people—Maria and Mr. B and Karen, too, along with everyone else who'd shown up so far. Then Dad was calling for backup on his Motorola, and Karen was bent over Mick, peeling back my makeshift bandage. Within minutes, the place was swarming with police officers and paramedics. Karen supervised Mick's transfer to a stretcher. The police had Luis and Icepick and Rodrigo too, unfortunately, spread-eagled and handcuffed and were reading them their rights.

Maria went into hysterics when she saw Rodrigo rounded up with the others, but Dad managed to calm her down. I'd never seen Dad at work, and it surprised me just how gentle and yet firm he could be. At last he managed to convince her that Rodrigo wasn't under arrest but just being held for questioning and that he himself would guarantee that the police knew the truth about what happened and didn't charge Rodrigo unfairly.

With all that commotion, it wasn't until the police had hauled away their three suspects and an ambulance had carried Mick and Karen off to the hospital that I was able to find out how Dad and Brian managed to burst in just in time to save my life—and Mick and Rodrigo's, too. By then the whole thing was beginning to seem more like a nightmare than the horribly terrifying experience it really was.

The police still needed a statement from Maria and me, not to mention Dad, Mr. B, Karen, and Brian. But Dad used his influence to get permission for us to all stop at the hospital first to see how Mick was doing. On the way, we filled each other in as to just what had happened. Here is their side of the story.

It had never occurred to me that anyone might have noticed me leaving. But Consuelo, still up on the platform doing that last special number with the band, had seen Maria dive out the front door and me right behind her. When I didn't come back, she began to get worried. By that time Mr. B had started preaching, but she found Brian who, of course, knew about Maria and my run-in with the Werewolves on Friday. When Consuelo told him I'd gone after a girl in a Werewolves jacket, I guess he went ballistic! He certainly chewed *me* out as soon as he got me alone afterwards. It wasn't until I asked him, very meekly, what else I could have done in the situation that he calmed down enough to admit he'd have done the same in my place. But, he informed me severely, that didn't excuse me for scaring him out of a year's life expectancy.

At any rate, Consuelo and Brian checked around for me outside and finally found a couple of loiterers who admitted they'd seen me arguing with and then chasing a girl with a backpack. That was when Brian decided he'd better call Dad. I'd hate to suggest that Dad would speed off duty, but by the time Maria arrived at the Center, he was already there with Brian, trying to decide how best to track me down. Mr. B had finished preaching by that time, so when Maria explained just what had happened and where I was, he turned the rest of the meeting over to the director of the Center, old Mr. Jefferson, while Karen put together some medical supplies. Then the whole group, minus Consuelo who was singing again at the end of the meeting, crowded into Dad's car. On the way over, Karen used Dad's cell phone to make arrangements for an ambulance while Dad, seeing that both Rodrigo and Mick were wanted felons, called the situation in to the police, which explains how both groups showed up so fast.

But it wasn't because they thought we were in any trouble that they'd come through to that service door. Once Maria had explained the setup, Karen had judged it too dangerous to try to move an unconscious patient through that tunnel. Maria knew just where to find the other side of the service door—in the middle of a tangle of pipes down in the basement of an old utilities substation. The substation wasn't a manned one, and the only reason anyone ever had for going down there was to check on the drainage pipes through which we'd crawled, which in that abandoned area was never.

Maria had found the crawlspace when she was fresh on the streets. The hot-wired lighting had already been there and the mattress and other meager furnishings. Obviously long abandoned, she'd immediately claimed the place for her own. It hadn't taken her long to find the other exit to her hideout. She'd quickly learned enough about the dangers of the streets to be wary of anyone trailing her to that empty building, so she'd piled up old crates and boxes on the basement side of the service hatch and nailed those old boards across the inside and never used that entrance again. When I think that she was no more than eleven years old at the time, I am reminded again of just how gutsy—and frightened— that little girl must have been.

Of course, once she joined the Werewolves and had food and shelter with them, she had no need for the place anymore. It wasn't until Rodrigo and Mick needed a safe house that she remembered her old home. It had proved the perfect hiding place. With the crates and boxes still piled high outside the service door, not to mention the layers of dust that hadn't been disturbed since she'd moved out, not even another gang member wandering through the building would ever guess someone was hiding on the other side of that wall.

Now though, with Mick's life at stake and since their hideout was going to be blown anyway, Maria had agreed to show Dad and company the easier way in. The idea was that she'd give their special tap on the door. Then Rodrigo could pull the boards down from the inside so they could get Mick out. But they were just starting to shift the crates—which must have been all those rat-like scratching sounds I heard—when they heard the gunshot and my scream.

So Dad kicked the door in.

## Tuesday, December 31st

That's all been weeks ago now. The first couple of weeks were full of the police and Maria and Rodrigo and Mick. And school too, of course. It was my first experience at being interrogated in a police station, and I must say it's a highly overrated experience. On top of everything else, between the excitement and going out without my coat, I managed to catch a miserable cold. So it wasn't until Christmas break that I've been able to get around to writing everything I could remember in my journal.

Mick almost lost his arm, and Karen told us that he probably wouldn't have lasted another night if we hadn't gotten him to the hospital. The bullet was still in his shoulder, one reason the wound festered so badly. But antibiotics will do wonders, and he's finally back on his feet.

Icepick and Luis are, of course, both in jail. They might still have somehow lied their way out of Abdul's shooting, but not the attempted murder of a policeman's daughter witnessed by the officer himself. Besides, the bullet the surgeon pulled out of Mick turned out to be a perfect match for the one that killed Abdul, making it pretty clear just who had to be holding that gun when it was fired. That the gun had originally been stolen by the Werewolves, one of the strongest points against Mick and Rodrigo, was easily explained once Luis' connection to the whole thing came out into the open. And I turned out to have been right about Icepick slipping another bullet in for that second shot he'd fired. *And* about him swallowing the two remaining bullets he'd had on him.

So they ended up pleading guilty, which at least kept Maria and me from going to court. And since both Luis and Icepick are over eighteen, the Werewolves and Devil's Angels are going to be waiting a long time before they see either of those two again. Which is probably just as well for them, as the last word on the streets is that both sides have sworn revenge on the two of them for their little homicidal plot. Jail is probably the safest place for them right now.

As for Rodrigo and Mick, they aren't running with the Werewolves anymore. Once Mick got out of the hospital, the two of them were moved to a youth facility on the other side of San Diego. Mr. B wanted to have them at the Center, but Dad felt it was safer for them to make a clean break from Werewolves territory—especially as Icepick and Luis may still have a few friends out there eager to settle some scores. Rodrigo and Mick will be in the youth facility or foster care until they are eighteen, which is less than a year for both of them. I've been praying every day that things work out for them. I just can't imagine those two settling down to a life of homework schedules and English Lit.

But at least they weren't charged with any crime. I was really glad for that. I know they must have done their share of whatever Werewolves do, but I can't forget Rodrigo trying to make those creeps let me go. Maybe he was just thinking, like me, that if I could just get out of there I could warn Maria. But it showed something in him that was a whole lot different than Icepick or Luis or the rest of the juvenile delinquents that make up the Werewolves. Besides, whatever else they've done, they were kind to a lost little girl, and that means a lot.

I wish I could say that we found Maria's mom and discovered she'd gotten her life straightened out and was looking for the little girl she'd lost so long ago. But that's not what happened. We traced her down all right, and Maria hadn't been so far off. Her mom died less than a year after she left. It wasn't AIDS or alcohol; it was a knife wound from her latest boyfriend.

So Maria is in a foster home. I wanted to have her here, but Mom had a mouthful to say about that. And I guess I can't totally blame her. She doesn't have the bond with Maria that I do. Besides, Maria's foster parents are really nice. In fact, they are one of the families who help out in the Center now and then. I've visited her at home a couple of times and seen her at the Center too. With Luis and Icepick making a full confession, Maria never did have to testify about what she saw that day at the warehouse, so Dad isn't too worried that the Angels *or* the Werewolves will go after her for all of this.

We've talked a bit about God, and if she hasn't made a decision of her own to let God into that hole in her life, at least she's listening. The Paynes belong to a good church and have been taking her with them, and even if she's found the kids there as alien as I found the Center kids, she says she likes it okay. The Paynes don't have any kids of their own, and they want to keep Maria. On my last visit, Mrs. Payne whispered to me that they were getting her a puppy for Christmas. Somehow, I have a feeling Maria's got some happiness in store for her.

Dad told me he was proud of the way I'd handled things with Maria and that he really enjoyed working on this case with me. I'm proud of him, too. I never realized before just what a tough job he has. I told him I was sorry I'd never gotten around to telling him about Rodrigo and Mick until all this blew up.

"I wanted to," I said, "but it was never the right time. And Maria seemed so scared of the police. I didn't want to get her in trouble."

I asked him if it would have made any difference if I'd told him earlier. Not really, he said. The little she'd told me before that last weekend wouldn't have helped the police any, and Maria was right that they wouldn't have taken her word about Rodrigo and Mick's innocence without some serious evidence. But next time he hoped I'd come right to him when something was bothering me.

I feel like I've found my dad all over again these last few weeks. He's always been so quiet (compared to Mom and us girls, anyway) and gone a lot, and I never thought he cared about me that much—at least not since I was a cute, curly haired little girl and he used to give me hugs and throw me up in his arms. But the look on his face when he found me at the wrong end of a gun told me how wrong I was. I'll never forget it.

And things are going better with Mom. It isn't that she's changed so much. But I've been working hard to put some respect in my voice when I talk to her and to do my own share of chores and baby-sitting without complaining or having a bad attitude. Strangely enough, Mom doesn't seem to demand nearly as much from me when I'm a little more cooperative. I guess that shows how much of our battles was my own fault.

Julie came home for Christmas, and it was the best time our family has had together for years. No one was expecting her. The last time she came home was the beginning of summer vacation, and she and Mom fought so much Julie left three days early for her summer job as a junior clerk in a law office near her university. Before she left, she told me that she wasn't coming home for Christmas—or ever, if she could help it.

So when she called up a couple days before Christmas and said she'd be flying in the next day, I couldn't believe it. Danny was through the roof with excitement, and we were all happy to have her home—even Mom, I think. It felt so good to have her back in the room that's been mine since she left, I didn't even mind her dirty clothes all over the floor and makeup clogging the dresser, the cause of plenty of fights when she was still home. We spent a lot of midnight hours talking. She, like me, has had some growing experiences and seen enough in her law studies to realize that our home could be a lot worse, even if it isn't perfect. So I think she'll be coming home more often in the future.

And Christmas Day was wonderful! Even more so because I didn't expect it to be. To tell the truth, Christmas hasn't been much at our house for years. When I was a little girl in Montana, it was great. Grandma's house with all the cousins and aunts and uncles. Sneaking downstairs to see the Christmas tree all lit up and all the presents underneath. A big family dinner. Sledding and ice skating on the reservoir with all the younger generation and some of the not so young.

But when we moved to San Diego, there wasn't any snow. And after Julie and I griped a couple times about getting something we didn't want, pretty soon we were making out lists for each other. There wasn't much surprise anymore, and we didn't seem to have much to talk about either when we got together. I don't know how it all happened, but Christmas just wasn't special anymore.

So even though things have been going a lot better at home, I was feeling a little depressed as Christmas drew closer and definitely *not* looking forward to a repeat of Thanksgiving. Then Mr. B asked for volunteers to serve Christmas dinner at the Center. I mentioned it to my family, but without any expectations of participating. Dad's big about being together as a family on holidays, and while he's been really good about the Center, I knew he'd never let me go off on my own on Christmas.

But to my surprise, Dad thought it was a great idea. He was impressed with what he saw at the Center that night he was there and with Mr. B and Karen too, and before I knew it, he was tossing around the idea of the whole family volunteering. As for Danny, he's been wanting to meet Maria and Consuelo and Armal and the others ever since I started telling him stories about the Center. He twisted his arms around my neck and said he didn't care if he got any turkey or not, he just wanted to go and help.

Mom, of course, put up a squawk and said that if these people didn't spend so much money on drink and drugs, they'd have plenty for their own Christmas dinner, and why should she spend her Christmas encouraging a bunch of lazy street bums to expect one more handout. But Julie, when she got home, immediately said, "Sure, let's go for it!" And Dad, gentle but as firm as I've ever heard him, told Mom, "Looks like you're outvoted, honey."

So that's how we ended up spending Christmas Day serving turkey dinner to several hundred people instead of at home, trying to make conversation around our own overloaded table. The strange thing was, Mom seemed to enjoy herself more than any of us. When we arrived at the Center, things were in an uproar in the kitchen with volunteers from half-a-dozen churches going six different directions. Mom took one look at the chaos and waded in, snapping out "suggestions" right and left. And I'll say this for her: In ten minutes, that place was running like an assembly line.

The whole Center downstairs had been filled with tables, not just the gym but all the side rooms, and they were all full. The sound system was bellowing out Christmas carols, and just for once, every one of those street kids and people from those awful apartment projects looked happy. Brian and Patty and his mom had gone to spend Christmas with his maternal grandparents. But Sandy was there with her parents and younger brothers—and so were Annette and Sally. I know they've felt a little left out at times, even though our lives outside of school have been mostly separate anyway. But when Sandy and I told them what we were doing for Christmas, I couldn't believe they actually talked their own families into joining!

Maria was there with her foster parents. She was wearing a dress she'd gotten for Christmas and only the smallest amount of makeup, and without that hard, desperate expression, she looked fourteen again. While we served up plates, she told me all about the puppy and her new family and the classes she was taking to catch up with her grade at school and a friend she'd made at the Payne's church, and I knew everything was going to be all right with her.

Danny stood right beside me, handing me plates while I dished up stuffing—until Armal came by. Danny's eyes rounded into saucers when he saw the cornrows and gold teeth and those bulging biceps, and he ducked behind me. But when I introduced him and Armal gave that huge grin of his, Danny grinned back. Pretty soon he was trailing off after Armal and his younger brother to help carry food out from the kitchen.

It was late in the afternoon by the time everyone had gone through the line, and there wasn't much left but scraps. But we were all having so much fun, joking and laughing and singing carols while we worked, that we hardly noticed how hungry we were until suddenly we realized that the place had emptied out and one of the church ladies, bless her soul, was pulling out a whole turkey she'd set aside. There were a ton of dishes to wash afterwards, and it was dark by the time we got home. Mom got out a tray of Christmas goodies, and Julie and I whipped up hot chocolate and eggnog, and suddenly Christmas was special again—like we were a real family who loved each other very much. It was the best Christmas I ever remember!

## Monday, January 20th

Now it's back to my last semester of high school. It's taken all of Christmas break to catch up on my journal, bit by bit as I've remembered it and had time. The nightmares were pretty bad the first couple weeks, and I'd wake up gasping with Luis' cold eyes glaring at me down the barrel of that gun. But writing all this down has helped, and Karen says the bad dreams will eventually fade away.

Of course life at SCA hasn't stood still while all this was going on. Sections two and three of the yearbook made it off to the publisher on schedule, and we're halfway through section four. I helped Joel Blumhurst get out a special Christmas edition of the newspaper and passed semester exams well enough to bring my second quarter report card back up to where it should be. On the social front, Amos Lowalsky and Sandy Larson are now officially a couple. Annette has been accepted to Stanford. Sally started Weight Watchers and has actually lost ten pounds. She's made up her mind to skip college and get some on-the-job training with the catering company she worked for last summer—as a chef.

As for me, I forgot to mention that I'd heard back from a couple more colleges. But I've decided to take that scholarship from the university here in San Diego. Somehow, I'm not in such a hurry to get away from home anymore. And I'll still be able to help in the Center while I'm studying.

Brian is staying in San Diego next year too—though I can honestly say that wasn't my sole deciding factor. He's planning to switch all those science courses over to a major in Counseling and Social Services, maybe even go on for a Psychology degree. He'd like to work with troubled youth in the inner city someday. Why am I not surprised? He invited me to the Valentine Banquet the day he got back from his grandparents. Said he wanted to make sure no one got in ahead of him. It seems funny now that I was so worried about that. I wouldn't say we're exactly going together—not yet, anyway— but we've become real friends as I never thought I could be with a guy, and maybe that even counts for more. And maybe someday . . .

Mr. B and Karen's romance is flourishing too. Karen found a diamond ring in her Christmas stocking, and the discovery of that sparkle on the fourth finger of her left hand was one of the more exciting moments of Christmas Day at the Center. They're getting married in June, just as soon as she finishes her residency.

Consuelo was gone for a week or so just before Christmas, sitting for entrance exams to the pre-med course at Stanford. She just got *her* results—a scholarship that will make her own dream of being a surgeon come true some day. I wonder what the other students will make of her. A breath of fresh air, maybe.

As for Rodrigo and Mick, Maria told me the last time she was at the Center that they've had a couple of visits from an Army recruiter. Now why didn't I think of that? I can just see them in the SEALS or Special Forces.

With all the excitement and my cold and Julie being home for vacation, I missed most of the youth groups at church this last month. But last night I was there, and when Mr. Schneider asked if anyone wanted to share, I didn't wait for the usual embarrassed silence. I stood right up and told about Maria and how she has touched my life. It wasn't that big of a deal or very long, but Mr. Schneider was wiping his eyes when I finished, and he came over afterward to thank me for sharing. So that's okay now!

Oh, I forgot something else. I ran into Ms. Langdon in the hall at school today. Literally, as I was late for yearbook and hurrying. It seems she's finished her psychology classes and is back to spend a few days at SCA. To check up on the kids she interviewed for her thesis is my guess.

"Jana," she exclaimed, as bubbly and kind as ever and sounding absolutely delighted to see me. "How are you doing?"

Lowering her voice below the range of all the other students rushing by, she went on in a rush of sympathy, "Really, Jana, how *are* you doing? Have you been taking my advice? Has your self-esteem improved? Are you feeling good about yourself? I can fit you in for another session, if you'd like to talk about it."

The funny thing is I had to stop a minute to remember what she was talking about. All that seems so long ago—like it happened to another girl. "Sure, maybe," I told her, not wanting to hurt her feelings. "I'll have to check my schedule."

So, how *am* I feeling about myself? Do I have that healthy self-esteem she talked about? Am I self-fulfilled and all the rest? I'm still not even sure exactly what it all means. But I don't have time to think about it right now. I have a Spanish test tomorrow—on the second day back, if you can believe it!—and I promised Sally I'd study with her over the phone. So, maybe some other day. Somehow, it just doesn't seem so important anymore.

*Start Your
Own Journal*